# DEATH REPLACED

## A TWISTED TALE OF MISFORTUNE

MATTHEW SLEADD

EDITED BY
MARCIE MCGUIRE

Matthew Sleadd
A Small press family

*For my Family,*
*without whose support,*
*none of this would be possible;*
*thank you.*

Outside of a dog, a book is man's best friend. Inside of a dog it's too dark to read.

— GROUCHO MARX

# CHAPTER I
# FERRIS WHEEL

Death perched on the Ferris wheel and regarded the sea of humanity as the masses scurried below. No one observed him as he leaned precariously over the ride's ledge.

It was the second night of a somewhat annual winter festival near the unremarkable town of Rural Retreat. People traveled from across the county to attend these festivities and enjoy the rustic atmosphere. But as is so often the case at places of overindulgence, those in attendance did not understand how close they were to the Angel of Death.

Azrael preferred when people used the name from his mortal years rather than the immortal title of Death. He spoke casually to what appeared to be an oversized brown owl that clung to the ride's car beside him.

"Why is it they will eat fried cookies and ice cream tonight, but only salad for the next two weeks?"

Owls do not roll their eyes. However, the rotation of Strix's head gave much the same impression. Strix had endured this line of question from Azrael hundreds of times over thousands of years. "She's

1

trying to be healthy. The salad makes her feel better about herself and believe she is taking care of her body."

"Right, yes, but then the fried cookies?"

"None of them will live forever. Mortals want to enjoy themselves while they can." Strix did her best to mollify the immortal being who had lost touch with his humanity in ages past antiquity. "Let them be. They'll all come due in their own time."

This answer garnered only a grumble from Azrael as Strix tried the same argument she repeatedly used over thousands of years. Humanity changed every day, yet time passed like a river, one drop of water at a time but in an immeasurably swift current. How was Azrael ever expected to keep up with humanity? Perhaps he came to places like the fair for that very purpose.

At these gatherings, humans enjoyed themselves with reckless abandon. Other places existed where he also observed this, of course. Airports were an excellent place to watch people as they neglected everything but their travel. Their voyages created a beautiful ballet for leaving and reuniting with others. He also watched individuals while they were alone, but this seemed too much like spying, so he did it infrequently.

Azrael preferred pockets of celebration and separation from the everyday struggle of the routine. Here, people ignored tomorrow and forgot about yesterday. All that mattered was tonight and an attempt to pull enjoyment from a single moment.

As Azrael contemplated the mysteries of humanity and their struggle to enjoy the gift of life, the crowd shifted. At first, it was subtle, with a family on one side stopping and pointing at the Ferris wheel. But then others turned to one another and murmured as the focus from the carnival turned in Death's direction. "Strix, are you seeing anything?"

"Patience, nothing is happening yet," the older and more patient of the two advised.

People pointed up to the ride's top, and a woman screamed while dozens of men yelled. Spectators pulled cell phones from pockets and purses. Everyone recorded what they witnessed, but none of them called emergency services.

The oversized wheel ground to a halt, and passengers glanced around in confusion. Most of the riders focused their attention down while the crowd looked up towards the top and began yelling while pointing. Azrael glanced at the people who stared in his direction then down to the owl beside him. Strix appeared unconcerned with phones, people, or screaming. Instead, she followed something in the car below them.

"You don't suppose they can see us?" Azrael asked, his voice showing concern. Most people chose not to pay attention to Death. They understood he existed and, although not invisible, no one wanted to acknowledge his existence. If a crowd suddenly came to terms with their mortality, then something fundamentally shifted.

"Pay attention, old man. Look down," Strix said. Azrael cast his gaze to the next car and spied what attracted everyone's concern.

The safety bar had failed to hold a ten-year-old boy in his seat. It swung wide, releasing the child. The boy named William screamed. If not for his belt catching the ride's edge, he would have fallen to the ground below. Dozens of people with differing opinions yelled guidance on what William should do, though most advised against moving. He did his best to keep the ride from swaying, though he continued to scream.

Azrael cocked his head to the side and regarded the boy as he hung over a metal platform some thirty feet below. "That's curious. Do you know of any deaths scheduled for tonight? Here, I mean. I know someone is dying somewhere."

Strix ignored Death's question and considered the situation. Unscheduled deaths occurred worldwide, and it should surprise neither of the two when it happened. But the boy appeared to cling to his life. Strix turned her attention to the people on the ground. No one seemed ready to ascend and help the child. "No... but people have survived falling from tall buildings before. Perhaps the fall will only severely injure him."

In the car just below William, Riley Brewer also rode the Ferris wheel. He had attended the fair by himself and expected the night to pass without incident. He hoped the night would provide an escape from life and a way to help him remember a time before everything became complicated. Perhaps next time, he'd come here with a special someone, although he was unsure if that would make it less complicated.

After hearing William's bar break free, Riley's first instinct was to cover his head to protect himself from anything which dropped from above. If William fell, Riley's arms would provide little cover. Once he was sure there was no immediate risk of something hitting his head, he glanced up and saw the young man hanging above him. A panicked glance at the people below showed a crowd that had no interest in helping beyond documenting the disaster.

The first thing to note with a swarm of humans is that the fear of death does not prompt a civic-minded calling of emergency services. Instead, every person in the crowd who possessed a phone pulled it from their pocket to record the events. A ladder truck from the fire department wouldn't arrive until a half-hour after everyone was on the ground.

Riley was not that type of person. He left Rural Retreat the day he turned eighteen and drove four hours to Richmond, where he started school, first as an undergraduate in chemistry before attending pharmacy school. That was a long nine years, though he would have preferred keeping it down to eight. The extra year was unplanned but necessary after failing ethics for a second time.

Unfortunately, passing grades did not prepare him to rescue a child hanging from a carnival ride thirty feet above the ground. A lack of qualified training left Riley ill-prepared but fate made him the only person willing to act. He debated the risk to his own life and what might happen after a fall from such a height but abandoned caution and released his safety bar.

The ride's designers had constructed the Ferris wheel of thin steel and coated it with cheap paint, which resulted in rusted metal covered with flaking paint. Riley's stiff fingers had little to grip on, and as his bare skin grabbed the frame, his digits ached and trembled against the frozen metal.

"This is stupid. What the hell are you doing?" he asked no one.

William screamed, and Riley regained focus. He placed a foot on the back of the car he'd exited. It rocked precariously under his weight. After a change, Riley found a space to stand without falling and pushed himself higher on the wheel. He reached up and grasped the next connecting beam with the added height and wedged his fingers into a junction formed by the sharp metal.

The frozen steel bit into Riley's hands as he pulled himself up, and his feet came under him. He was within grasping distance of William's car. "Can you hear me? Just try to stay calm. I'll be right there."

Riley didn't give William time to respond but fired instructions out quickly and in a steady voice. He hoped this would relax the child enough not to swing his car further. The plan nearly failed as William twisted to see who called to him and slid down the length of his belt. It caught once more while everyone below gasped.

"Stop moving!" Riley yelled while failing to keep his voice calm. He laid flat on the support arm and undid his belt, pulling the thick leather through each loop. Once the belt was clear of his pants, he held one end in his right hand and reached with the left to pull it through William's thinner mass-production belt.

Riley tugged the end of his belt back to the metal support and clipped the ends together. He prayed and said, "Please, god of pants and underwear, let his stitching hold."

With the makeshift harnesses in place, Riley leaned over. "Reach up and slowly grab my hand. I've got you. We're just going to hang on until they can lower us down."

William reached a hand to grasp Riley's extended arm, but his belt slid off the ride, and he fell three inches. His total weight caught against both straps, and the voyeurs below screamed in unison. There was no possibility of reaching the young boy after he slid, and Riley hoped against all things that the belts would hold.

Riley straightened back up and spotted the ride's operator filming the event. With anger in his heart, Riley yelled, "You! Hey! With the red Hawaiian! Lower this down!"

It took two more tries and throwing spare change from his pocket to get the man's attention over the sound of everyone screaming and yelling. The operator eventually brought them down as smoothly as the ride allowed. The instant William's feet touched the ride's platform, its brakes slammed shut and threw Riley off his perch. No amount of effort could make the ungraceful landing appear intentional.

Dozens of people who wanted to play the hero's part but not take personal risk rushed the small boy. Each of them forced Riley to the side while he regained his feet and consoled William, checked him for injuries, then whisked him off for more care and compassion. Riley was sorry for how many people would comfort William over something the kid would probably rather pretend never happened.

As for Riley, the crowd relegated him to the back row as more people pushed forward to congratulate the boy on his bravery. William was the one who hung on after falling from the car. They also thanked the ride operator for his careful operation as he lowered the boy down. None of them considered this operator responsible for the ride's shoddy condition that led to the accident.

Their lack of attention all suited Riley just fine. He had no interest in becoming the hero of whatever daytime miniseries this would become. He was just as happy knowing he did the right thing and could now slip out the back door. There was, however, one older man who'd been watching the exchange and blocked his path.

"You did a brave thing today, saving that youngster."

"I don't know about that. I couldn't live with myself if the boy fell. Someone had to do it."

The man considered this, then waved off the idea. "Perhaps, but you can't take on the world's problems by yourself. Or you could try, but it would crush your soul."

"I'll keep that in mind next time I'm trying to save a kid from falling off a carnival ride. But if it's all the same to you, I'm going to sneak out before anyone remembers I was on the ride with him."

"Do what you think best, but I doubt I was the only one who noticed."

Riley shrugged and sidestepped the man, then made his way out of the crowd and to the gate. No one attempted to stop him from leaving. None of them cared if this twenty-six–year-old stayed or left. He was only a face in the background. The thought occurred to Riley that perhaps someone had recorded him as he saved the kid, but who would search for him? Likely, these people were only interested in the story they wanted to tell about the brave boy.

Any videos of someone helping the boy to safety only displayed how brave the child was. People pay no attention to the lifesavers, only those whose lives they saved. It was the same with firefighters and police officers. They were in the photographs, but no one remembered them, only the victims.

One figure none of the observers photographed was Azrael. This was partially because any pictures of Death would come out too blurry to be of use. People frequently discarded them without a second thought. The ride continued to rotate and bring riders to the ground, and after finishing one complete turn, Death and Strix were once again at the top. Azrael leaned over to his companion and asked, "How do you suppose he did that?"

The sudden question confused Strix, and she twisted her head to consider the angel beside her. "What exactly did he do?"

"The Fates went to a lot of trouble to arrange for that boy to fall out of his seat. It's difficult to set a young mortal up for an untimely end, but there he was, and here we were. I take none of it for granted or coincidence."

Strix rolled her head, then turned to look back at the departing

Riley. "You're reading too far into this. You always get sentimental when you think life and death have some greater meaning."

"Someday, I'll prove you wrong," Azrael said as he put a nail back into an argument they had hundreds of times before. "But no, I think he may be the one."

"The one what?" Strix was becoming tired of the exchange, and they had much work to do that night. Time did not exist in its same linear form for the two celestial beings, but it was still not a resource to be squandered. For as long as they remained at one location, time would progress where they stood. But they could equally be at any other place during the same passage of time.

Azrael appeared unconcerned and continued to follow Riley as his shadow became smaller. "I think it's time I took a vacation. Yes, I deserve a few days off. He should do nicely as a replacement. Maybe if things work out, he can even take over the job long-term."

The ordinarily unflappable Strix bristled her feathers and stared back at the angel. It was hard to judge how much time passed before she formed a coherent sentence. "This is a joke? You're attempting humor again. Death does not take a holiday."

For a moment, Azrael considered these words and nodded. "You're right. It would make little sense to take a vacation. If I'm to do this, we need to find someone to become Death on a more permanent basis." Riley was only a speck in the distance as Azrael viewed him from his perch. "How do you suppose we interview for this job?"

"We don't. You leave the kid alone, let him live his life, and we go back to doing our job. This talk is complete nonsense," Strix said as she attempted to place reason into her companion. But the longer the conversation continued, the more apparent it became that he would not drop the idea.

Something caught Strix's eye, and her head swiveled until she focused on an older man at the edge of the crowd. "Wasn't that the man he was talking with before leaving?"

Azrael's thoughts had him entranced and lost to the world around him by that point. It required the sharp bite of Strix's beak to bring him back to the task at hand, and the owl repeated her question. "That man, was he the one your boy talked to before he went out the gates?"

Azrael focused his attention on the man and nodded, "Yes, I think that's him." He was ready to dismiss the entire question until he, too, saw what stood apart from everyone else. "Well, now that's something, isn't it?"

Human life creates a glow about the people who possess it. Younger, more vibrant, healthier people shine a radiant aura of fantastic colors, while the sick and infirm appear pale and flickering. A recently deceased body will often have a haze about it as its previous occupant continues to hold on to its former life.

Some were ready to meet Death and greeted the end as one does the final curtain of a beautiful play. They know their time upon the stage is short but have experienced every moment to its fullest, and as the curtain closes, take a final bow and wait for the applause to end. These souls discarded their bodies and awaited what came next.

If Azrael chose which souls to work with, he preferred to guide these performers to the Elysian Fields and no one else. The man standing near the gate was not ill. He was not healthy. He had departed and, as curious as it seemed, had passed some time before the night's excitement began. "Are you sure that's the same man he spoke with?"

Strix searched around the back of the crowd for anyone else it could have been. No other people came close to the same description. Everyone else focused on the child Riley had saved. After saving William, the only person who talked with him was that one man, and the glow of life was no longer around him.

"It's rare, but it can happen. The boy nearly fell and was close to death. Perhaps he had one toe across himself," Strix tried to explain, though she did not sound convinced of her idea.

"Perhaps," Azrael repeated. "In either event, we have work to do."

The Angel of Death stepped off the Ferris wheel and fell lightly to the ground while he walked towards the man at the gate.

"Good evening sir, do you know what has happened?" Azrael asked in a gentle voice.

"It appears I had one last adventure on the only night no one would take notice," Andrew, for that was his name, answered matter-of-factly.

"So it seems. I'm sure someone will find you come closing, or if not, then perhaps in the morning." Not that Azrael lacked compassion for the remains of the departed; he simply viewed the body as discarded baggage that no longer served any purpose. The sooner he separated the soul from feelings of attachment, the better it was for everyone.

Andrew chuckled as he thought, "That or it will create quite a stink. But not my circus, not my monkey. Now I don't know your name, but I know who you are. Have we reached that point in my life?"

"I'm afraid so, but you're going home, and it is a place of peace." Azrael always reassured people before they passed on, which struck him odd. It made little difference. Either way, they would reach their final destination. Occasionally someone would attempt to run, but it was rare, and Death always found them.

No, Azrael tried to guide them gently because he wanted the progression to be smooth and quick. Creatures that would hunt the dead existed in the space between life and death, in the penumbra. His responsibility was to guide wayward souls to Elysium before those monsters found them. But he'd not tell them that part of the story. He'd learned their passing was trauma enough.

# CHAPTER 2

# RETURN TO WORK

S taying out late at the carnival was not his best plan, but Riley had made many mistakes in his years at pharmacy school. Now that he had graduated, he had no standing rule that required him to act responsibly. No, instead, after staying out past 10:00 PM the night before, he stared at the flashing 8:00 AM and attempted to block out the blaring siren of his bedside alarm.

He first attempted to regain peaceful sleep by pulling a pillow tightly over his head to try to smother the racket, but the noise continued. The alarm clock had one task during the day, and it only buzzed louder as Riley tried to ignore it. The cacophony ended when Riley tossed the offending clock across the room.

"Why did I ever buy that god-awful thing? Damn." He said in a clear voice, "Hey Max! What's on the calendar for today?"

He lived alone in the one-bedroom apartment, so no one heard him talking to himself. He had never lived with someone named Max, but from the other side of the room came a computerized voice, "Morning, Riley. Today work starts at 10:00 AM, and Glen will pick you up at 9:00 AM for breakfast. Would you like to add anything else?"

"When did my life become this dull?" That was a rhetorical question. Riley's life was never exciting. He drank with his friends for a short while during undergraduate school, but that ended once the coursework accumulated into insurmountable stacks. Then he began his doctorate in pharmacy and had no time for anything except school. "High school. I should just go back in time to enjoy myself again. Forget this mindless work/sleep cycle."

He had friends and a boyfriend; they hung out together. Things were good in those precious years before entering the real world. All of them hung out together. "Why did I go and ruin everything by moving so far away? Though I suppose there is no point worrying about that now."

Who knows, Glen was coming to pick Riley up for breakfast his first week back in town. That had to be a good sign that things might have a chance of returning to something resembling normal. Maybe. This was the closest Riley would allow himself to come to optimism this early in the morning.

They could debate those issues later. First, Riley needed to clean himself up after last night's excitement at the carnival. Had he climbed on a Ferris wheel to save some kid? If Riley had a TV, the news would show events from last night. Instead, he owned the computer from his first year in the doctorate program. He made friends with his neighbors for their internet, and they were letting him use their Wi-Fi, at least for the moment.

The only utilities Riley paid for were his electricity and a cell phone. Everything else was either unnecessary or part of the rent, which was an astronomical six-twenty a month. Perhaps the rent was not unfair. He had paid more for a smaller dorm room. But it took a sizable bite out of the monthly check when he only made fourteen dollars an hour.

The crushing weight of this hourly rate remained a fresh wound as he reviewed the last eight years of his life. He invested all that time accumulating a sixty-seven-thousand-dollar education. And while the school promised fantastic jobs post-graduation, the market showed a reality where even the educated barely earned a living wage. Even with a doctorate, the only job he could find after graduation was an hourly job at his hometown pharmacy.

Any way Riley considered things he was in the mire with his loans. There was no way to repay those banks that invested in his future. Or were they trying to do something more sinister? Either way, he tried not to think about their motives. He could defer the loans and pay only interest, but that plus rent still left him with barely enough money to survive.

There had to be a way to make more money than he pulled in at the pharmacy. Riley didn't know the answer to this problem, but there had to be one. With thousands of successful people, many of whom were half as bright as him, what were they doing right, and he was missing?

Riley remained dressed as he climbed into the shower took a combination bath while washing clothes to forget the march of numbers that tormented his thoughts. Once finished, he hung the shirt and jeans up to dry and changed into his work uniform. He took pristine care of these clothes and made sure they always appeared professional. If there was a way out of this mess, it required hard work, or so the adage continued to tell him.

Riley opened the computer in the living room and sifted through junk mail until he left nothing in his inbox. The next thing was to find the morning news. One town over had a daily, and their head-line featured a brave child who survived a harrowing escape from death.

Nothing in the article talked about who rescued the child or who might have been negligent and put the kid at risk. The only thing the paper cared about was a headline, and the news printed in today's headline in bold red, "Child Cheats Death."

Riley rolled his eyes. "Somewhat presumptuous. I didn't see Death sitting on the ride with a pennant rooting for gravity to win."

No one answered. The silence continued in the room, accented only by the hum of the refrigerator. At least that still worked.

When fifteen minutes to nine arrived, Riley searched the internet for an affordable used car. He had little chance of finding anything within his price range, but while the dream was fleeting, it was still alluring. The problem wasn't his job. He could walk there without issue. Instead, the problem was having a way to escape this town. Rural Retreat's number-five hotspot of things to do that year was the highway Safety Rest Area.

As a stickler for time and punctuality, Riley was dressed and ready for work as the digital clock adorning his living room wall switched to 9:00 AM. It was important to him that every clock displayed the same time. Only this way was he sure that he knew his time to be correct within a second. If anyone, or any other clock, told him a different time, they were simply wrong.

This meant Glen was now late picking him up for breakfast. It didn't surprise Riley that the boy he'd dated in high school hadn't arrived on time. Glen never maintained punctuality, and there was always a factor of some fifteen minutes allotted to any schedule to account for his sense of 'on-time.'

An altered sense of time left Riley with nothing to do in the intervening space as he waited for his friend to arrive. Was that the right word to use? Glen and Riley were now friends? It would not be easy to think of him in those terms, but it had been eight years since the two of them last dated. Many things could have changed in those years, and they had not stayed in contact.

Not that he intentionally broke contact with Glen. That's just how things happened when he moved. The two were only kids, and their grand idea of a long-distance relationship lasted less than two months before the calls became less frequent. These turned into messages on social media, and then those dried up and stopped. It was little more than wishing one another a happy birthday towards the end.

Another good question, when was Glen's birthday? Riley tried to remember and knew it was in the fall but pulled out his phone to double-check the date: November sixteenth. OK, good. Not good in the sense that he remembered to send Glen a card, but that he had almost ten months to plan for next year.

Riley continued to mull over the minute details of a dried-up relationship when a knock came at the door. He put his phone back into his pocket and stood, went to the peephole, and glanced out to confirm it was Glen standing on the faded welcome mat.

"Hey man, been too long. How are things?" Riley asked in a stream of consciousness as he opened the door and assaulted the young man in a light-weight brown coat with a warm embrace.

Glen held back that fraction of an inch to make the hug uncomfortable but put his arms around and gave Riley's back a friendly pat. "How's it been going. buddy?"

Riley would like to have crawled into a hole and buried himself in soft peat at that moment. The embarrassment and pain of that awkward greeting lasted a heartbeat too long and hung in the air while he attempted to regain his footing. "Oh, um, yea. No, things have been good. Graduated from school and everything."

The two of them twisted in the wind before Riley asked, "You want to go grab something to eat?"

That was the original purpose of Glen picking him up, but the question functioned as a segue to avoid standing in the hall staring at one another any longer. The two of them nodded and agreed to an idea they had decided on days before.

There were far fewer spaces outside in the parking lot than most would suspect. As things turned out, the apartment complex was more a collection of split-level townhouses, which the original designers determined only needed one car per occupying family. The current owner had divided these to make single-bedroom apartments, leaving fewer parking spaces than expected cars. Likely, this was why Glen parked his five-year-old hatchback on the walkway rather than in a marked area.

Both piled into the compact car, and Riley pushed the floor trash aside with his foot. Glen pulled out onto the street. The original plan was to drive to the nearest Pancake House and have a quick breakfast before returning in time for work at Marvin's Pharmacy. Everything about this plan rested on an issue of timing. As Riley looked at his watch, he saw this would be a problem.

They were leaving the apartment at thirteen after. The restaurant was no less than twenty minutes away and then twenty minutes back. It was improbable that the two of them could finish eating and pay for their meal in seven minutes. This left the diner down the street as a less than desirable option.

"Hey Glen, we will not make it," Riley said after checking his watch.

"Nah, we're good. I'll have you back in plenty of time."

"No, seriously, let's go to the Kitchen. That's not my first pick either, but I'm not looking to get fired my first week at a new job."

It looked as if he pulled the air from Glen's tires. But he conducted a thirty-seven-point turn on the narrow road and drove back in the direction they'd come. "Fine. I suppose breakfast is the same everywhere."

How often had Glen used that tone of voice with the word fine? It was the end of the conversation. Using the single word was his way of saying Riley upset him, but rather than arguing, he would acknowledge Riley was wrong and leave it there.

The Kitchen served decent enough food, and with it being late morning, the crowd had thinned out. Locals considered anything after eight as the middle of the day. Food was also plentiful and cheap at the Kitchen. As Glen said, there was rarely much difference between breakfast at one place than another. Though it was not the preferred way to start back a relationship Riley had hoped to rekindle.

"So, what's been happening since I left?" Riley asked.

"Since what? Eight, nine, ten years ago? When was it? What's been happening since then?" Glen's quick response informed Riley of the level of irritation he was up against. "You have to be kidding, man."

"I didn't mean it like that. I have just been out of the loop. Are any of the old guard still kicking around? Any chance we could meet at the BootStrap. We're old enough for a drink now."

"That place closed down, what, five years ago now. And a few of the same guys are around. A lot of the 'old guard' have moved on to the big city looking for work." Glen tried to soften his approach and smiled for the first time since seeing Riley. "I'm sorry. It's just been hard being the one abandoned while everyone goes off to have adventures. But yea, we can go out somewhere."

Riley's face lit up with the prospect. "That would be great."

"Here, I'll pick you up after work. We can go grab something to eat and maybe a drink."

Breakfast continued without incident, and the two finished their assortment of eggs and hash browns. When the check came, Glen put a hand out to swipe the slip of paper. "It's OK. I'll take care of this one. I'm sure I owe you back for something."

He paid for their meals at the register, and they squeezed back into Glen's car to make the short drive to Riley's work. By design, Riley chose an apartment within walking distance of his job, and the town was small enough that he could reach everything on foot in less than thirty minutes.

"I appreciate the ride, even if it is only ten feet," Riley said while leaning down at the driver's window. "You know you can come over for lunch if you get free."

His heart kicked a beat faster while he waited for an answer but cracked down the middle when Glen shook his head. "Na, that's OK. I've got some things to deal with. I'll pick you up tonight."

Riley took a deep breath and focused his attention back on the task at hand. He walked the fifteen steps to the front door and pulled it open to the sound of an electronic tone. "Welcome to Marvin's. I'll be right with you," came a man's voice from somewhere in the back.

"Just me, Dr. Green," Riley called out from the front and maneuvered his way to the employee lounge.

Last week when Dr. Green showed him the repurposed broom closet with a reclining chair and coat hook, Riley wondered how the closet came to be named a lounge. He imagined some employees from years past hid in the four-by-six room to avoid work or perhaps took naps there during their break time. Month after month, things escalated with a stool or a cushion and then the recliner. Either way, it became a permanent feature to the shop.

Riley hung his jacket and tucked in his shirt before returning to the store, searching for his supervisor. When he found him, the sixty-something-year-old man was doing his best to match a printed inventory sheet with numbers on the shelf. He called Riley over, "Dr. Brewer, come here a moment and help me with this."

The young man winced as he'd not become accustomed to the honorific. And to use it while he was earning less than fifteen an hour seemed like a joke. "It's Riley, sir, and sure, what you got going on?"

"Then call me Mr. Green or Billy. That 'doctor' stuff makes me think I should do tonsillectomies at the cash register." He was in a good mood, which would make work easier to endure. "It's this god-forsaken biennial inventory of the scheduled medication. I think they make the reporting forms deliberately confusing."

Riley chuckled under his breath, as it would not have done to laugh openly at his boss. "Here, let me look at it," he offered and held out a hand.

They exchanged the computer printout, and Riley glanced over the numbers and names on the various pages. "This looks like you're supposed to be using a tablet with a scanner. All these pages are telling me is that we haven't done the inventory yet and still need to check everything."

Whatever Green grumbled under his voice was not English or fit for polite conversation, and he snatched the page back from Riley. "Well, isn't that just great? They try to make everything better by making it all just so god-damned complicated." He turned and walked back to his office while continuing to talk. "Couldn't just keep a simple checklist? No. They had to add something with lasers and buttons."

He had no way of telling how long Dr. Green would continue to work at the pharmacy, but no one else in the town would be qualified to take his position. Once the pharmacist retired, Riley could step in and inherit the shop. If it wasn't for the potential of running his own store, Riley never would have returned home. All that was required of him was to play his cards right and not laugh while the man threatened to "melt the demon box."

"I've got this, sir. It seems like whoever set up your system used one we played with in school. I should be able to figure it out pretty quick." This was mostly true, as Riley took a one-semester class covering general inventory systems. How different was one from the other? He was also confident that a help file would be somewhere if he got stuck.

Riley spent the rest of the day learning a new computer system. Things were more complicated than he'd expected. Dr. Green purchased an upgraded inventory program, and while the doctor did not know how to use the system, he wanted to be confident that he had the best. This left more features than they would ever use in the small shop, and it required Riley to go through them and find the ones they needed.

More importantly, he was now responsible for finding the controlled-substance inventory. In theory, there would be a stock record from two years ago. A quick check of the system showed the shop installed this new system a year ago, and Riley was left to search for whatever hard copy of the report existed beforehand.

Doctors lost their licenses every year over missing medication, and some went to jail if accused of theft. The only saving grace was with some creative bookkeeping Riley could hide anything that appeared out of place, and given the state of affairs in the pharmacy, he likely would need to adjust some numbers again.

Riley suspected that with things as confusing as they appeared at first glance, this report was going to need some creative accounting of its own. What was the worst that would happen? He suspected the federal government did not give two flips about some dime store in a town that doesn't show until you zoom on the map.

He would figure out a solution later. Saturday was devoted to learning how to use the system and hunting for dusty boxes of receipts. He approached Dr. Green before leaving. "That's about it for me. I think we've got everything ready to start the inventory on Monday. It took a bit to find your old records, and I don't know if we have all the sales data, so that may slow us down too."

None of this brought a smile to Green's face, and he grunted. "Fine." There's that word again. Why do people use it when they want to yell things at others? "Just get it done. If we get shut down, many people will have to find a ride to the next city for their medication. You know as well as I do that not everyone here owns a car."

He hit home with that comment, and Riley nodded. "Yea, I got you. I'll make it work. Don't worry about it."

# CHAPTER 3

# PANCEA

One good thing about the pharmacy was that Riley still had most of his weekends free. Nearly every shop and store in town closed on Sunday, and Marvin's was no exception. And on Saturday, he only stayed at the shop until noon. However, the schedule created an additional problem. He had nothing to do.

Rural Retreat did not have its own movie theater, but there was one in Wytheville, the next town over. This meant that to see a film, he needed to find the money for a movie and the cab ride. All of which added up quickly. Riley pulled out his phone to check the movie schedule and considered his options. The new *Specters of Death* blockbuster showed at 2:00 PM, so he had plenty of time. But did he have the money?

"So what, eight dollars for a ticket, thirty for the cab, and that's assuming I don't eat. That's today's paycheck out the window." Riley added the numbers together in his head. Then he finished putting the problem together and winced.

He wanted to scream, but no one would listen, and if they heard, who would have understood the frustration of working eight hours to earn just enough money for a ninety-minute movie. Riley picked up a stone from the road and chucked it as far as his tired arms allowed. It came two feet short of the stop sign at which he aimed. "Oh, come on!"

"Bad day?" A woman asked.

The sudden voice from an empty street startled Riley. In his frustration, he had overlooked the thirty-something-year-old with matted blond hair. She was dirty, not filthy, but she looked like one who lacked regular access to soap. Her face still wore a smile, and she shifted a military green canvas bag from one shoulder to the other.

"Sorry, I don't have any money on me," Riley said reflexively upon seeing the woman in her condition.

This elicited a tired laugh as she waved off the notion. "No worries, you're new. Most people about these parts have already met me and my little one."

"Oh, sorry, I meant nothing by it, only that..." he trailed off, unsure what he intended when he first started the conversation by implying she was a beggar.

"It's ok," she said and tried to reassure the new man in town. "Maybe you weren't wrong." She dug at the ground with the toe of her worn-out combat boot.

The woman didn't appear old enough to be a Vietnam veteran, or were the new wars creating younger veterans now? The boots showed wear, and she had rubbed holes along the edge. Rural Retreat's rock-strewn streets tore through the best footwear, and her boots had traveled many miles.

She asked, "You work at the pharmacy, right? The one around the corner?"

No other pharmacies were in town. Specifying which one caught Riley's attention. He cocked his head to the side and waited for her to continue with the explanation. She added nothing immediately, so he said, "Yes, I work at Marvin's. Not sure there is anything else local. Can I help you with something?"

"Yes, well, my little girl is sick, and we don't have the money for medicine."

He'd not prepared himself for this type of encounter, so she caught him off guard, and it took time before he responded. "I'm sorry. There's nothing I can do to help. I'm not familiar with your little girl or what she may need. Even if I gave her any medication off the shelf, there'd be no way to choose the right one without a doctor's prescription."

Again she shifted, digging her boot further into the dirt and gravel. "We can't afford to visit a doctor either. She needs your help. The other people in town are nice, but none will stick their necks out for someone like me. I've lived here a long time and know their charity ends at the Sunday donation plate."

This seemed like a reasonable policy to Riley, who was not sure he wanted to risk his new job or license for someone he didn't know. But it was harder to ignore someone's suffering when you faced it than when you read about it in a book. did he have the heart to tell her he wouldn't help her little girl?

"OK, here. I'll look at your girl, but I'm not that kind of doctor. I'm a pharmacist." This was close to the truth. Riley possessed the correct certifications to prescribe medicine, but the process was more complicated than writing scripts for random children. The number of things that could go wrong was extensive.

Before he could convince himself that it was a wrong idea, Riley allowed the woman to lead him to a small shack she described as her home. There she opened the broken screen door to lead him inside to find the place clean but untidy, with only a space heater for warmth. She bent down beside the girl, who appeared not yet thirteen, and whispered until she woke, "Angel? There's someone here to see you. Can you wake up for a few minutes?"

With her mother's help, Haley moved to a sitting position and propped herself with a set of pillows. Her mattress lay on the floor, which forced Riley to squat while he spoke. "Hello, I'm Dr. Brewer. Can you tell me how you're feeling?"

She hesitated and glanced at her mom, then back to Riley. When she spoke, her voice was quiet and with a rasp, "My throat hurts."

Riley would have hoped for more information when diagnosing a patient, but he took what he had. Too often, small children lack the experience to express how their bodies are feeling and can only provide the vaguest of descriptions. "Can you open your mouth for me?" he asked and pulled out his cell phone, then turned on the built-in flashlight.

Haley dutifully followed instructions, and Riley inspected her throat. To his relief, she had the classic discoloration of streptococcus. Most mothers in the country have seen these same red tonsils with white patches. They told their doctor what was wrong with their child before running any tests. With confidence, he turned to her mother. "It's strep. She'll be fine. All she needs is an antibiotic, and it will clear right up."

The woman waited, and Riley hesitated but realized the issue. She expected him to provide this medication to her daughter. "I don't carry that kind of thing with me. You'll need to come to the pharmacy and talk to Dr. Green."

"We can't pay," she said.

Riley stood back on his feet and thought. He looked between the girl and the woman, then back to her mother. "Does she have any allergies?"

"I don't think she has any. She's very healthy. Please, you have to do something."

"What I mean is, are there any medications she is allergic to?" The risks were astronomical to the young girl, and he ran through possibilities in his mind.

Her mother shrugged. This was less than reassuring. "We've never had the money for doctors or medicine, so I don't know. Probably not. She doesn't have any other kinds of allergies."

"I'll see what I can do."

He walked to the door, with Haley's mother following him out. She said, "You're a lifesaver. We won't forget what you've done for us. You can bring it any time; we'll be here. She's always here, and I rarely leave."

Riley left the small shack and checked his watch. It was still early afternoon, and the chances of running into Dr. Green were too high to head directly to the pharmacy. Instead, he needed to kill a couple of hours.

As Riley thought over his options, he realized his only option for a distraction was to eat, which meant The Kitchen, and this required money. Seeing as he lacked the funds for such an outlandish outing, he chose instead to return home. There his food options were more limited and after a brief search of the cabinets, he found a half-empty jar of peanut butter and declared it lunch.

"Am I doing the right thing?" he asked himself once inside with the door closed. "Strep is not normally fatal." Thinking further on the issue, he debated the problem. The little girl would not be comfortable, but she would live without him jumping in and dispensing medication. Why was he willing to risk eight years of pharmacy school and toss out everything to help someone he'd only just met?

Riley pulled down the half-empty jar and found his only clean spoon. That was the moment he took inventory of his life. An ex-boyfriend bought him breakfast. He worked all morning for minimal wages and now faced lunch comprising a couple of spoonsful of peanut butter. Helping this family could put everything at risk, but what he had at this point did not make it a high-stakes game.

Reflecting further, he realized that was the reason he saved the kid the night before. What did the article say his name was, William? He didn't stick around long enough to learn the name of someone whose life he saved. But he didn't save William's life out of some form of altruism. He did it because he believed someone else's life mattered more than his.

That little girl, Haley, had all the potential to grow up to become someone of worth and value to the world, something Riley believed escaped his reach during the years of school. He finished lunch and put the jar away, rinsed the spoon, and set his mind to the task. "Now, how am I supposed to do this?"

There were cameras in the store, though Riley didn't know if they worked or if Dr. Green ever reviewed the footage. Likely, they were a deterrent or something to check after they learned someone stole something. Either way, no one would examine the video looking for theft or simple misconduct.

The clock on the wall showed 3:43 PM. Was that late enough? Riley considered what he knew of his new employer. The pharmacy closed at noon, and he knew Dr. Green would stay behind to close the shop, but how long would he stay? The doctor had a wife and a son. No, he wouldn't stay at the office more than an hour or two past closing time.

Riley still wore his work clothes, and after reviewing the options, he decided this was not the best choice. How would he explain not changing clothes for four hours? This prompted him to change shirts and toss on a dark gray hoodie. He checked his pocket for keys, wallet, and phone, then turned off the lights and locked the door. "God help me. Tell me I'm doing the right thing."

Clouds began coming in from the west, but they did not threaten rain, so Riley squared his shoulders and continued his task. But with the temperatures dropping the last few nights, the possibility of snow loomed. He walked the five minutes to Marvin's Pharmacy and loitered on the far edge of the parking lot. No cars were near the building, and the doctor's red sedan was not in his common space.

Not that Dr. Green had a reserved space, but the pharmacy possessed one handicapped sign, and the doctor arrived early enough always to occupy this space. Did it defeat the point of having a reserved handicapped space if the owner always parked in the spot? No one in town questioned the longstanding member of the community, but it was a question Riley thought about each time he walked past the car.

No one was visible, and the shop appeared closed. Riley took a deep breath and strolled across the parking lot to the doors with as much confidence as he possessed. Upon reaching the front entrance, he used his newly gained keys and twisted the lock. They gave a dutiful click, and he pulled them open to a welcoming electronic tone.

Riley debated turning on the lights but decided not to attract any more attention than was necessary. He already established that if questioned, he'd claim he was at work to do inventory before the store opened on Monday. It was almost true. Well, no, it was an absolute lie, but it would cover for the truth.

Streptococcal was a simple enough condition to treat, and Riley knew which medication the young child needed. He hopped behind the counter and ran his fingers down the labels of antibiotics until he found the amoxicillin. It took little time to prepare what he believed to be the correct dosage based on what he thought was her size and weight. He gave himself room for error, but he was confident with the results when finished.

Adjusting the medication inventory was a different issue. Riley paused as he considered the computer system and what to do about the now missing drugs. "Would Dr. Green even take note if something went missing? Shit, half the store could disappear, and he'd only think about how much more to order."

This didn't fix the problem, but antibiotics were not on the controlled inventory list, so no one would come behind him to double-check his work. He only needed to mark a quantity on hand when placing a new order. Dr. Green wouldn't question him. He'd helped at the pharmacy when he was younger, before leaving for school. In the interview, he clearly stated that he wanted someone to run the place without supervision.

Riley cleaned up his workstation and double-checked to ensure he had left nothing out of place. That was something the doctor's keen eyes would catch. If any of the stations behind the counter were disorderly, he'd ask Riley about it first thing Monday morning. The man ran a tight ship, and everything had its proper place.

Confident that even the trash cans contained no incriminating evidence, Riley left the way he arrived and pushed the door, then locked it behind him. Crossing the parking lot, he stopped at the far edge and looked back at the shop to check if anyone watched him. It was a crazy thought to believe someone would have been paying any attention to what Riley was doing on a Saturday afternoon. He worked in the pharmacy; he had every right to be inside.

While he saw no people and only the occasional passing truck, an owl perched on a streetlamp, she stared down at him. Riley knew little about birds and where they lived, but the avian didn't belong here, and ice gripped his heart. That thing was looking at him, judging everything he did.

"OK, that's creeping me out," Riley said before he turned and walked back towards the woman's shack.

Riley kept an eye behind him and walked the distance to Haley's mother's house. Had he ever asked for her name? Was it odd to do all this without asking for something as simple as a name? At least he knew the name of her daughter.

As he continued to think about it, Riley realized she had not described the little girl as her child, only "my little girl." Now that he thought about it, she could be a stepchild, cousin, sister, or anything. "Come on, Riley, what are you doing? You're asking to get hemmed up. People like that are nothing but trouble."

No sooner had those words left his mouth than he wanted to kick himself for saying them. Humanity was everyone's responsibility. Even if he didn't know the woman or the child she was looking after, he had a duty to care for the sick. This wasn't a doctor thing. This was how someone functioned as a decent human being, and there were a scant few of those these days.

Riley glanced over his shoulder to ensure no one followed him. He feared that someone saw him steal the medication, but more than anything, he wanted to make sure the owl left. Did owls live in that part of the country?

If Riley had paid more attention to his surroundings while growing up, he'd have known a family of screech owls nested in the barn not a mile from his home. Now that he had moved back from college, that same owl family had new members but still lived in the barn near his apartment. Someone who was more attentive might also have noticed that the owl watching him in the parking lot was not one of these birds.

Strix continued to follow the child, which was how she thought of Riley, meandering his way back to the shack where Haley and her mother, lived. Azrael was interested in this boy, but Strix would lead him off into the dark woods if she had her way. The bird flew ahead of the shuffle-footed Riley and waited outside the shack. Strix had an appointment, and she was there for business that had little to do with this boy.

Riley stepped up to the porch and knocked on the warped aluminum screen door. "Ma'am, it's Dr. Brewer from the pharmacy. I've come back to talk with you and," he decided it best not to assume their relationship. "Is anyone home?"

Silence followed the sharp metal rap of the door, and Riley shifted from one foot to the other. Again, he glanced over his shoulders for anyone who might have followed him. He was doing the right thing; they had to understand that. Why would anyone punish someone for trying to do what was right?

Across the street stood a tree that did everything to hold its leaves well past fall. In the branches of this tree sat the owl that followed Riley from the pharmacy. He locked eyes with the animal, and he shivered. Something was wrong.

Riley knocked again on the door before he twisted the knob and eased it open. "Haley, ma'am, anyone here?"

Silence answered before the woman's voice came from the bedroom, "We're in here. Grab some water!"

Riley rushed to the kitchen and drew water from the tap without knowing what happened while he'd been gone. He was horrified to see cloudy brown water flow from the faucet. After waiting for it to warm, he gave up and brought a pan of cold water. "It's the best I could do," he apologized.

Her mother wet a strip of cloth and held it to Haley's forehead. "Her fever just started. Poor girl. I know she doesn't feel good."

"Were you able to find the medicine? Is it going to help her?"

Riley pulled the small bottle from his pocket and hesitated as he considered Haley. Other issues could cause the same symptoms, but what were the risks in treating the most apparent source? He debated the question until she sat up with a cough, and he poured out a measure of pink liquid to hand the mother. "Here, this won't help right away, but should over time."

Her mother gave Haley the medicine and eased her back to the bed. "Ok, girl, you try to rest. I'll be in the other room if you need anything."

She stood and ushered Riley out the door, then shut it behind them. "Thank you, doctor. I don't know what we would have done without your help."

"Is there no one in town who will help with something like this?"

"Closest is the next town over, and we can't afford to drive," she said.

Riley understood this predicament as he recalled his difficulty planning a trip to the movies that day. It hadn't occurred to him how hard it would be to find something as simple as dental or health care. Moving back home was looking more expensive every day.

"There are other people in town who can't go that far either." She hesitated to ask her next question, and Riley had a guess what it was.

Instead, he asked, "And you wondered if I would help them too?"

Though unable to voice her question, she nodded. "You could save lives. You told us you're a doctor but not that kind of doctor. How much difference is there that you couldn't do this to help people?"

"It's a big difference. I didn't go to school for that kind of medicine." The wheels turned in his mind as he debated if it was possible somehow to transfer one type of medical certification to another. What would be involved in such a thing?

Riley said, "Let's keep the dispensing medicine to someone

30

who's not a patient between us for now. I could lose what license I have for doing this."

Haley's mother nodded her understanding and shifted from one foot to the other. When the silence became overwhelming, she stood and walked Riley to the door. "I'm never going to forget what you did for us."

This warmed Riley in a way he'd been missing for years. Had it been that long since he helped anyone, other than William? But somehow he wasn't counting the Ferris wheel. Riley contemplated finding some public works projects and helping on the weekends. He discarded this idea once he realized it would probably require a car.

"It was my pleasure..." again he paused, "I didn't catch your name."

"Miranda."

"Thank you for letting me help, Miranda. Sometimes it feels good to know you made a difference in the world."

Riley stepped out the door and strolled back to his apartment with a self-satisfied accomplishment in a job well done. As he left, Strix slipped past him and into the shack. She took exceptional care for Riley not to see her. The others in the home would ignore her the same as everyone always had, but, there was something different about this human. Perhaps the fates conspired to bring him closer to Death.

Riley glanced at his watch, and it stared back at him, showing the time of 5:07 PM. Glen would arrive at the apartment in a few minutes to pick him up. If this were an ideal world, they could then go together to catch a bite to eat. It would not be at the one restaurant in town, but they'd succeed where this morning they'd failed to drive to Wytheville.

This all depended on Glen holding to anything resembling a regular schedule, the thought of which brought a chuckle to Riley's lips. No, he had at least two hours before dinner. This was plenty of time to get ready. Riley walked the short distance back to his apartment without looking once over his shoulder for the mysterious bird.

Strix was not following Riley, so he would not have seen her even if he had looked for the bird. Instead, she finished her business in the house and pushed open the screen door before lighting on the lone tree in the yard. Behind her followed the spectral silhouette of Haley.

The girl's door did not open, but she left the house without regard to the barred passage. Her form passed through the door as if it were air, and she stood under the tree, looking up at Strix. "Why is mommy crying?"

The bird had seen thousands of mothers, fathers, lovers weeping and had not developed a satisfying answer why they cried at the passing of life. She suspected it had something to do with missed opportunities. Those left behind sobbed as they thought of all those things they did not have the chance to accomplish with the departed.

Whatever their reason, the two would reunite in such a short period that the immortal had difficulty thinking of it as requiring any measure of patience. Their lives were so quick, and those who were closest to death cried the most, but they would soon join their loved ones. It was all a strange concept to Strix.

She still needed to answer the young soul standing below her, and she considered the options before she said, "Your mother is crying because she is sad." This did not fully answer the question, so she continued, "she must now wait a long time before she can see you again."

Haley thought over the answer and weighed its meanings. "I should tell her I'll be OK. Can I let her know I'll wait for her?"

The owl rotated her beak back and forth in what she'd best developed as shaking her head. "No, my child. She must be patient."

In the distance, a tortured dog howled through pain and fire. Strix straightened and turned her head to face the direction of the sound. Nothing seemed to move as the old owl listened to the rustle of dead leaves as they clung to their branches.

"It's time to leave. Can you follow me?" Strix asked, her voice quick, with a sense of urgency.

Children are not stupid. They understand the body language of adults, and while this adult was an owl, she saw Strix's fear. Without a sound, she closed her mouth and nodded.

"Good, stay close," she said and took to the air, then flew towards a sunrise only she and Haley could see.

None of these events were seen by Riley, but one sound did reach him. He was most of the way home and unconcerned with the young girl he left or the medication to which she had an allergic reaction. Something echoed in the night, something similar to the howl of a wolf or the scraping of metal, a rusted train car crying to the moon. "Nothing living should be allowed to sound like that."

The howl echoed off the trees and disappeared into the wind as Riley tried to know from where it came. He wanted to run. The sound terrified his very soul, and whatever creature called out in such a tortured way was to be feared above all others. But the sound planted Riley's feet to the earth.

Only as it died and faded into the distance was he able to move again. Riley made a mad run for his apartment and slammed the door behind him.

# CHAPTER 4
# THE IRON HORSE

"After work" turned out to be 7:20 PM. The clock on the wall showed the time as a knock sounded at the door. An hour prior, Riley debated eating dinner without Glen but waited for his "friend." That word still felt wrong when he said it. He could never think of Glen as a friend and nothing more.

It didn't matter now. Tonight, they would try to forget the intervening time and, at the very least, discover what the other had done with their life. With a smile firmly on his face, Riley opened the door and stepped aside so Glen could enter the apartment.

"Hey Glen, good to see you. You want to come in for a minute while I get my stuff together?" He had nothing he needed to ready for the night but wanted to force Glen to wait for that fraction of a moment. This was Riley's way of letting him understand he was late.

"Yea, OK," Glen said, then, after stepping into the small room, placed himself on the side of the door and waited. A burglar arriving at a bat mitzvah would appear more comfortable than Glen. He shifted from one foot to the other, and his eyes darted about the room. Riley thought back to their time together. They separated before either of them had their own place, and Riley thought perhaps he should not have made Glen wait on him.

To ready himself, Riley only required shoes. There was a plan to take more time, but with Glen wringing his hands and attempting to avoid direct eye contact, Riley decided against this. "Let's get out of here," he said and grabbed his phone and keys off the table.

"I didn't need to come in for that. Were you just trying to show off the palace you moved into?" Glen asked. Riley attempted to decide if he said this in jest but couldn't.

Given the option between starting a fight or opening with a joke, Riley chose the latter and said, "I know, right. Open floor plan with inclusive kitchen and en-suite bathroom."

Glen snorted a laugh before responding, "OK, yeah. Not that bad. You had to have stayed in worse places in the big city. I've seen shows on the TV with those rat-sized apartments costing two months' pay."

"That's what roommates are for," Riley said and squeezed into the passenger seat. He'd had his share of roommates while at school. It was the only way to afford to stay anywhere near campus. Things were strangely quiet now that he had the entire place to himself. Perhaps he'd buy himself one of those white-noise machines or a fan. Probably a fan. It would be cheaper.

Riley asked, "So where are we going, or is this a surprise?"

The indifferent shrug did nothing to inspire confidence as the car pulled onto the highway, which ran next to his apartment. This was another selling feature when looking for the cheapest place to live in a town. It also came with the added benefit that you could reach the interstate and leave that much faster if you gained a car someday.

"The Iron Horse," Glen answered and realized he needed to provide more information before Riley knew what this was. "It's a newer bar, or well, the bar's not new. It used to be the Snake Pit, but they're out of business."

With supreme effort, Riley held back from making an audible groan. Somehow, when Glen offered to meet for dinner, Riley had imagined a quiet restaurant. They didn't need to go anywhere fancy; the Pasta Garden would have been fine. Nowhere in his conception of the evening was there a run-down biker bar off the side of an interstate.

"That sounds..." he attempted to find the right words.

Riley took too long to say something, so Glen broke in with, "Don't worry about it, you'll love it. The place is perfect. There's solid music; sometimes it's even live. Drinks are cheap, and food is passable. They put in a full kitchen so you can order burgers, pizza, or really anything."

The list of food that made up a full menu was missing many of the critical items Riley expected to find at a pleasant restaurant. But they would chat and catch up on old times. Breakfast went by too fast, with them being up against the work clock. At least at a bar, they could stay as long as someone was buying drinks. Maybe this wouldn't be as bad as he first thought. "That is terrific; who knows, maybe I'll like it."

"That's the spirit," Glen encouraged as Riley opened up to the idea. "You'll love seeing the guys again. They are first-rate people to know, now that you're back in town. You can meet Clay."

Riley's thoughts stopped short. Did Glen turn a quiet evening for two at a nice Italian restaurant into hanging at a filthy bar with some of his drunkard friends? Riley's mouth hung open as he tried to process the information into something deserving a response other than stepping out of a moving car.

Glen saw none of the expressions on Riley's face as the man's eyes stayed fixed on the road, so he continued to talk. "Clay and I started dating about a year ago. He began hanging out with everyone about that same time. Nothing serious, just well... you know."

There were so many things that this could be that Riley's mind sorted them into piles of terrible and disgusting. But he was unwilling to let this destroy his first evening back with Glen. No, as bad as things seemed, they could not ruin a homecoming. "Great, looking forward to meeting him and seeing everyone else again."

Riley could think of nothing else to say and twisted in his seat to face out the window. The lights of distant farms and homes flashed past in the darkness. Was it right for him to return home after being gone so long? Things changed while he was at school. This should not have been a surprise. What was the adage they keep telling him, "you can never go home." As every moment passed, the phrase made more sense.

True enough, The Iron Horse was where he remembered the Snake Pit had been. Nothing about the place other than the sign looked any different. Riley recognized the same row of polished chrome motorcycles to the left of the door and battered trucks in the gravel parking lot. The massive front window was a combination of a heavy tent and reinforced thick plywood, accented with neon signs.

They used to come here in high school because the bartender's idea of carding someone involved a credit card. But now that everyone was old enough to go to any bar they chose, there were so many better establishments. Why would anyone voluntarily come back here?

Riley squared his shoulders, followed Glen past the no-smoking sign into the smoke-filled bar, and let his eyes adjust to the haze. "I'd almost forgotten that this place smelled of dog urine and beer; how things bring you back to your youth. So do you see any of the guys here yet?"

Glen scanned the room, though he guided them purposefully to the side lounge, where a cluster of young adults circled about a pool table. "That's them," he said and led Riley the ten yards from the entrance to pool corner.

"Hey everyone, you remember Riley, the guy who abandoned us for bigger and better things. Well, guess what? He's back." Glen's introduction brought a sour bubble up from Riley's stomach, but he did his best to smile and wave. "OK, so Sara and Jacob are from the old crowd at school. The only update is they're married now, and Sara's still trying to convince him to have a baby."

"That is not true!" the only woman in the group protested as she moved around to line up on the cue ball. "We're just waiting for the right time. No sense rushing into things if you don't have to, and places like this don't like it when you bring toddlers."

Jacob stepped over and clasped Riley's hand, giving it a commanding shake. "Good to see you again, man. So what was the big city like? Everything you hoped for, full of all the opportunities it promised? That why you came back home at the first chance you got?"

It wasn't clear if Jacob was joking or trying to make a dig at being one of the abandoned pack. Either way, Riley winced. Or perhaps it was the pain as Jacob's handshake threatened to break the smaller bones in his hand. "Something like that," Riley said while sidestepping the issue. His eyes then fell on the one face he did not recognize from school.

"Oh, right, you two haven't met yet," Glen pointed out as he caught the blank stare from Riley. "This is Clay. Clay, this is Riley; he's the one I told you about from high school."

All different manner of questions ran through Riley's mind about what Glen might have told Clay or why they talked about him. Who was this man? While all these questions screamed through his mind, the only one that he voiced was, "How did you two meet?"

The mysterious stranger continued to avoid joining the conversation as Glen fielded the question, "We knew each other in school." He then clarified, "We were both on the football team together."

Riley never talked about it with Glen, but he always felt that the camaraderie between the players was the one thing that drove a wedge between the two of them. While Riley played the trumpet in the band and Glen ran tight end, the two would attend home games. But when the team traveled for away games, they left Riley in Rural Retreat.

They never discussed this subtle difference in friends, but as soon as Riley left town, the first person Glen turned to was from the one group of friends Riley never knew. Jacob was also on the team, though it was odd that he played the tuba and was a linebacker. Few were in both camps.

This made the cluster of people at the bar a group of ex-football players and their significant others. Then Riley paused. Was he reading too much into this? Riley extended his hand to the well-built blond with the military-style haircut. "Good meeting you. I hope he didn't tell you too much about me. I like to have some secrets."

Clay drew his eyes from Riley's shoes to his crown and appraised the worth of the other man. His face showed a calculation as he attempted to sum the value of adding a new person to the group. Riley shifted his feet as he debated running for the door, but Clay placed a firm hand on his shoulder. "Nah, you're good. I think he said just enough. Come, let's get you a drink. You can join in on the next game."

It was impossible to relax as Clay's predatory stare followed Riley. Every attempt Riley made to speak with Glen in private was fruitless as Clay followed the pair relentlessly. It wasn't until Clay left for the bathroom that Riley was able to ask, "So what's up with him?"

"With whom, Clay?"

"Yea, are you two a thing, or is he just alpha male with everyone? I want to hit him with a stick to keep him away from us." Riley shifted uncomfortably as the words left his lips.

Glen raised an eyebrow as his friend squirmed in the booth. "You and I are not an 'us.' Not since you left. People can have lives that exist without you, and what happens while you're gone doesn't need your permission."

The words hurt more because they were accurate than unexpected. Riley knew everyone moved on with their lives, but to have it laid out in front of him was more than he was ready to handle. "So you are with him, then?"

"You don't listen well, do you? And what if we are? Are you going to wish me luck with my relationship or scream at me for backstabbing you?"

Riley didn't have a suitable answer and instead focused on finishing his beer. He was not a heavy drinker, but there was good reason to numb the experience of nights like this. With several more ounces of courage in his system, he strengthened himself enough to say, "I hope the two of you are happy together. Or well, I hope you are happy, and it doesn't matter what it takes for that to happen, even if it is with him."

Glen's expression softened, and he reached over to put a hand on Riley's. "It will be OK; you'll meet more people. The town's gotten bigger since you left, or rather, we've gotten closer to Wytheville. So there are all kinds of chances to get out and meet people."

"A fat lot of good that will do me without a car."

"You'll figure it out. You were always resourceful."

Their moment alone ended as Clay slid into the booth and placed another pitcher on the table. "So, guys, Riley, I hear you're in the pharmaceutical game. What's that all about?"

The shift in conversation had the same effect as attempting a U-turn at thirty miles an hour, and Riley did what he could to keep all his wheels on the pavement. "The what? Oh, yes, well, I guess it's like any other retail job. You go in, do inventory, sell things, talk with customers, leave tired and poor. Not much to talk about."

"Nah, that can't be everything," Clay waved off the answer. "There have to be fringe benefits to working at a place like that. I remember when I worked at the Burger Shack, we used to get lunches for free." He leaned in and poured a fresh beer for Riley. "I mean, do you get any kind of employee type discount on writing your own prescriptions?"

The question caught Riley off guard, and he stared back, waiting for more of an explanation. When nothing was forthcoming, and Clay continued to stare back, he asked, "Are you asking about getting drugs illegally?"

Clay backed away from the table while putting his hands in the air. "No one said anything about that. I know I didn't. I was just asking about how things were at your new job."

Riley gave a sideways glance at Glen, but the other man was no help and did everything he could to avoid making eye contact with either person in the booth. Clay ignored the awkward nature of the last question, even while he was the one who asked it, and spoke again, "You need to learn to relax a bit more."

"I think we're all pretty relaxed. But thank you." Riley glanced at Sara and Jacob, but both of them were involved in a game at the pool table that had little to do with billiards. "You know what? It's getting pretty late. We should probably head back." It wasn't late, but he was ready to leave.

Glen cocked his head to the side before pointing out, "It's Saturday; you don't have work. Are you planning on going to church suddenly because I don't remember you being all that devout of a kid?"

This was getting out of hand, and Riley bit his teeth together hard enough he feared breaking a crown. "No, I have not," he said. It was like trying to explain something to a child who had not caught on to the unsaid part of a conversation. "It's just late, and we should be leaving."

It had not yet passed midnight, so by most accounts, it was still early. The married couple at the pool table heard the escalation and turned their attention to see where things went. That was when Glen put his hand on Clay's and interlocked fingers with the other man. His next words drove nails through Riley's chest. "You can leave. We're staying here. Everyone else is enjoying themselves."

Riley stared at the clasped hands and then back to his own as they clutched the glass of beer. Hours seemed to pass as everyone waited for someone else to say something. Riley was the one who spoke first. "I'm going to call a cab."

There was no fanfare or other words as he slid from the booth, turned, and walked out back into the official smoking section. Contrary to belief, many patrons smoked outside on the back patio. While most of the bar smelled of cigarettes and a general gray haze hung in the air, only two or three regulars ignored the signs and lit up inside.

The night was frigid since the sun went down, but the wooden fence endured the buffeting wind enough to keep everyone from freezing. It didn't hurt that they also had propane heaters set on full force. Riley pulled a phone from his pocket and opened the RuralCab app. It quickly located him and the bar. He then selected his destination as the $35.75 shown on the "estimate with tip" screen declared how much his fight with Glen had cost him.

Riley cursed loud enough to be heard by everyone on the back deck, which was not as quiet as he intended. No one paid him any mind. People yelled at inanimate objects all the time, more so when drunk. After hitting the "accept and pay" button, Riley stuffed the phone back into his pocket and debated going back inside.

There were advantages to going into the bar. For the first thing, it was warm. Alternatively, he would be forced to deal with the other as they judged him and stared at him. What did they think about him and the choices he'd made in life? Did it matter? It took ten minutes for the warmth to win and Riley to go inside.

The other four were engrossed in a new game of pool, and none of them reacted to Riley's return. That was probably for the best. Riley made a sharp right turn and sidled up to a barstool without drawing attention to himself. The bartender glanced at him, which was the equivalent of an age check at the place, and asked, "What you want, son?"

Riley couldn't remember the last time someone called him "son" but figured arguing with a woman who had enough tattoos that he thought she wore long sleeves was not the best idea. "I'm just waiting for a ride."

"That's great; I'm glad. Now order something or find somewhere else to sit."

There were no menus to judge price, and he panicked at potentially outrageous prices. Riley had not frequented bars enough to be prepared for times like this. Ordering at a bar was one of those things he should have learned in college but was too busy studying for classes. "Just a bottle of domestic."

The tender offered a gruff "four dollars" and dropped the bottle in front of Riley. Fishing into his pocket, Riley found a five and handed it over. Whatever change he was expecting never materialized, and he didn't dare to ask.

Seated next to Riley was a lanky man of Mediterranean descent dressed in black from head to toe. It was hard to judge his age; he moved like he was old but looked young. He watched Riley and the exchange for the beer without saying a word. When the bartender left, he asked, "If you don't mind me saying, you look like you're having a rough night."

Small talk with strangers was not high on Riley's list of ways to pass the time, but he had little else to do and gave a shrug before pulling at the bottle. "Things are not going according to plan."

The man in black turned and observed the cluster in the pool corner. "Young people often make plans that will never succeed. Their plans are far too optimistic. Sometimes they need to include failure in planning. Then things will work out according to plan."

Riley raised an eyebrow. "So what, plan to fail? That sounds like terrific advice. Just doom yourself from the beginning."

"Not exactly. More, to know that someone else is sitting across from you while you try to play the game of life. You can plan to be with the person you love forever, but it won't be forever. At some point, two people, no matter how in love, need to prepare for one of them to leave one another."

"Hate to break it to you, but some people stay together for the long haul," Riley countered back confidently.

"And then what? Eventually, one of them will die and leave the other."

Riley thought about it for a moment, then shrugged. "Maybe, but who's to say they don't get back together again on the other side? I'm no expert on the afterlife, and I don't expect anyone else has the answer either."

The corners of the man's lips curled into a smile, showing two rows of perfectly white teeth. He nodded his agreement, "exactly."

Riley's phone buzzed, letting him know the cab had arrived, so he left his mostly empty bottle and the strange conversation at the bar, then headed for the door. Before he slipped from the room, Clay called, "Hey buddy; you take care. I'll try to stop by some time, and you can show me around that workplace of yours."

Riley waved and ducked out the door without saying a word. The cab's impending arrival became fifteen minutes of standing in the cold, and when the driver pulled into the parking lot, he rolled down the window to ask the one man standing in the empty parking lot, "Were you looking for a cab?"

There were many things Riley wanted to yell back, but he chose "yes" and climbed into the back. The ride was uneventful, though whatever arctic country built the car did not have heaters. Twelve minutes later Riley exited the cab and walked to his apartment to unlock the door with frozen fingers.

# CHAPTER 5
# SHOPPING LIST

By the time Wednesday morning crested the horizon, Riley had all but forgotten the adventures of Saturday, and he tossed his alarm clock across the room. Thankfully, nothing broke. He was confident the infernal machine would work again come Thursday, but for now, he was awake. In a clear voice, he asked, "Hey Max! What's on the calendar for today?"

A digitized voice answered, "Morning, Riley. Today work starts at 08:00 AM. Would you like to add anything else?"

"Well, that was short and to the point," Riley observed and began dressing for work. Not every day was going to be full of adventure, and it looked as if Wednesday was going to pass without incident. There wasn't time for a shower, so he applied an extra layer of deodorant, shaved, and put on a clean undershirt before donning a discount button-down without a tie.

Breakfast consisted of cereal, a modern staple of the bachelor's diet. He had no milk, so this became a dry sugar-crusted trail mix rather than a balanced breakfast. But it was enough to pull him through until lunch. Riley made a mental note to pick up more peanut butter when he was near the grocery store. He then checked the headlines of the local paper on his computer.

Can people still call it a paper if it's online? The digital paper had posted an article on Monday about a little girl who'd died of an allergic reaction to a medication. Her mother refused to say where they acquired the medicine, but Riley knew. Each morning, he checked if the newspaper showed his name as an accused murderer of children.

Even without the headline saying he killed the kid, it weighed his soul down with the responsibility of what happened. He had no business issuing medication when he didn't have a patient's medical history.

The people who lived in Rural Retreat had their patterns of behavior and few things changed. The regulars woke early and parked outside The Kitchen, and the same three spaces stood empty in the apartment parking lot. However, one thing stood out that morning. A heavy-set big-block car with dark red paint and tinted windows idled in the handicapped space.

This was not the type of car Riley thought wise to stare at, but he continued to glance back as he turned to walk the short distance to work. That was when Clay's voice called out from the behemoth, "Hey killer, need a ride?"

Those words sent a shock down Riley's spine. It had to be a coincidence, just some idiom that the other man used with everyone. Maybe something he'd picked up from the city where he and the car belonged. However, this didn't answer why Clay was standing with his door open, offering to drive him the tenth of a mile to work.

Riley took a deep breath to calm his nerves, then turned and yelled back, "Clay, hey, man. How are things? Didn't expect you down here."

"Exactly. I don't like to be predictable. It keeps people guessing." His smile spread from ear to ear and was more predatory than cordial. "So, get in the car," he ordered. The tone of his voice offered no alternative.

Instinct from years of playing things safe told Riley to turn and run, but those instincts fought with society, demanding him to remain civil. Beyond societal norms, if this man knew where he lived and worked, there was no place Riley could run where Clay wouldn't find him. Politeness won out, and his feet dragged him to climb into the car as it rumbled in idle. "Um, OK, yea, why not?"

"See, knew you'd see it my way," Clay said and dropped into the driver's seat before closing his door and locking both of them inside. "Thought we'd chat about a couple of things."

Riley searched the vehicle's interior with his eyes. They were alone, and the car was immaculately clean. Nothing was out of place. There were no food containers, no trash. Clay's car looked as if he detailed it every night before going to bed. He left nothing forgotten inside the vehicle, and if anyone left something behind, he'd find it.

"So, what did you want to chat about?" Riley asked while noticing Clay had turned in the opposite direction from the pharmacy. He didn't mention this, as it was unlikely that anyone ever drove the wrong way by accident when the sign for the pharmacy was visible from the intersection.

"Oh, you know, this and that," he pointed the car towards the interstate. "So you and Glen were a thing in high school. That's interesting. I'm not one to hold a grudge about old friends or whatnot. What's past is past." He made particular emphasis on the relationship being no longer current or relevant.

Riley shifted in the seat and, for a second time in a week, wondered if jumping from a moving car was as bad as people described. "Yea, something like that, but then I left for school."

Clay nodded his head as he put pieces together, building towards the point he wanted to make. "And you went to school for pharmacy; that's pretty cool. You graduate and now work for that senile Mr. Green."

"Dr. Green," Riley corrected, though he didn't raise his voice over a whisper.

"Whatever. So I was just wondering..." Clay paused and turned to look at Riley as the car sped down the road. "Was it you or Green who gave the little girl the medicine that killed her?"

The effect would not have been more pronounced if Clay had hit a passing car. Riley's brain smashed a solid object at a hundred miles an hour, and he did his best to recover while only gibberish came out. "I what? What do you mean? Which little girl?"

"Oh, you know. Haley. It turns out I'm friends with her mom. She and I were talking, and she told me this story of how someone tried to help her but ended up murdering her daughter." Clay said this was such calm that Riley questioned whether those were the words he heard. "It was you, wasn't it? You killed her little girl."

Riley wanted to pull his feet up close to his chest and huddle into a ball. No words came as Clay turned the car around and drove back to town. When he parked the car outside Marvin's Pharmacy, Clay shifted from the friendly guy at the bar to a dangerous man whose words threatened everything Riley had worked for.

"You see, I know it was you, and she can point at a lineup and say that's the guy. Now no one's saying anything, but that could change real quick. You follow what I'm saying?" Clay waited for Riley to nod his head. "Good. So here's all you have to do to help make things right."

Riley interrupted and asked, "What can I possibly do to make this right?"

"I'm fixing to tell you if you'll shut your trap and listen. Just go back into your little store there and return with the right medicine. I have some friends who will pay good money for the kinds of things I'm talking about. Just nod if you understand what they're looking for."

Riley had a shopping list of the controlled medications Clay was talking about. There was a reason the DEA required the inventories. It was to prevent people like Clay from getting their hands on it. Riley nodded his head.

"Good boy. I knew you were smart. We'll be great friends. Now you get into work. Don't want you being late and getting fired. You need to keep this job."

Riley shut the door behind him and strode to the pharmacy entrance. He didn't look back when Clay's engine thundered out of the parking lot, and he refused to check if anyone saw him exit the man's car. Nothing had gone right to this point, and if he could put the entire thing behind him, he would.

The door opened to the sound of an electronic tone. Dr. Green called out from the back room, "Welcome to Marvin's; I'll be right with you."

This was going to become a morning routine, and Riley rolled his eyes as he yelled back his practiced answer, "It's just me, Dr. Green."

"Oh, good. How far are you on the inventory? Any chance you can finish today?"

Instead of shouting back and forth across the store, Riley crossed the distance and stepped behind the counter to talk in a conversational tone. "Probably not. I still need to find signature cards for half the sales. Though we may be out of luck on a lot of them. Is that going to be a big hit?"

Green frowned as he set a pill sorter on the counter to consider the situation. "As I think about it, I may have some of that stuff in a box back at the house. We cleared our space last year and moved a couple of boxes to free up the office."

A doctor would not store private medical information at their house in an ideal world, but Riley suspected few would raise a fuss in the small town. "OK, yea, is there any chance you could pick those up today? It would be better if we had a handle on how much paperwork we were missing."

Dr. Green grumbled several choice words under his breath as he picked up the pill sorter again. "I'll check after the lunch rush. If you ask me, they make too much of an issue with these pills. Not only do we keep up with the medication, but now they want me to be a librarian."

Riley opened his mouth to explain the underground drug market but thought better of himself and shrugged in agreement. "You're right. They make a big fuss over nothing, but what are you going to do? They're the government."

Again the unintelligible cursing from the doctor before he said, "I'd make more than a few changes with that government if I had my way." He took a deep breath and steadied himself, then said, "But I don't get my way. I keep working and pay my taxes just like everyone else. I'm not rich enough to get out of either."

"Don't worry about it; we'll sort it out," Riley said to mollify his boss as the man continued to work himself into a fit. "Why don't you head out now to check on those boxes? We're slow in the morning. I can take care of things until you come back."

Green glanced at the clock and the empty store. "You sure you can handle it until I'm back?"

No one was in the store. If the trend from the past three days held, they could expect it to remain empty until people left for lunch around 11:30 AM. Riley answered with as little condescension in his voice as possible, "I'm sure I'll be fine, and if it's too much, most of our regulars will understand if they need to return when you come back."

This worked for Green, and he nodded his agreement. "Fine, but I'll have my phone with me if anything comes up."

He finished counting out the prescription in front of him and sorted it on the shelf before hanging his coat and putting on a jacket. "I'll be back in at most an hour."

Riley gave a reassuring smile and dropped the keys to the medicine cabinet into his pocket. "I've got this."

Green walked out the front door, and after entering his vehicle, drove off around the corner. Riley followed Green's car with his eyes and checked the clock. Five minutes passed and then ten minutes. That had to be enough time for the doctor to be gone. He wouldn't be back for at least another fifteen minutes, maybe more, if he had trouble finding the missing box.

Next, Riley went to the controlled medication cabinet, and once there, he hesitated. The control sheet sat to one side of the free-standing locker. He had accounted for every pill over the last three days but could just as quickly change one number to another during the inventory. If he kept the quantity low, he could take whatever he wanted, and no one would notice it was even missing.

This was when Riley reconsidered his plan and moved to the computer. Opening the prescription and patient list, he created a new patient, Laura Willis. Riley selected chronic pain and chose the controlled opioid painkiller with dosage. At that point, it only became an issue of dispensing the medication. Then he paused. "Dr. Green shouldn't notice one new patient; would he? It's not like he knows how to search the computer; does he? Either way, how does this woman pay for it?"

Every option he considered came back to the same answer; he had to pay for the medication, or they would flag it as missing. Either the drugs would be missing, or they were short of money. In the world of computers, the system was binary with no alternative. Riley checked his wallet for how much cash he had on hand, thirty dollars.

An ATM stood in the far corner of the pharmacy, and its imposing red and white sign offered itself as a beacon to solve Riley's problems. He stepped up to the machine and, after hesitating, pushed his card into the slot and withdrew a week's paycheck to pay for the one-month prescription. Riley returned to the counter and finished his transaction with the ephemeral customer.

An hour after Riley made his purchase, Green returned with a shoebox. "Found it. Somehow left the thing in my closet with the clothes. I guess I thought it was actual shoes in there. But you should have everything you're looking for in here."

Riley took the box and opened the lid to find a collection of receipts held together in stacks with binder clips. "Thank you, sir. This should do it. I'll get started on this after lunch," he said, then slipped the opioid signature card into the box before closing the lid and placing it under the counter.

With a glance at the clock, Riley saw it was 10:14 AM, and he had an hour before the lunch rush started and two before it ended. He glanced about for anything to distract him from the bottle of pills in his pocket. "I'm going to go vacuum the rug," he declared and headed out into the main area without waiting for Green to answer.

Time ticked by on the slowest clock Riley had ever known. He spent days watching three hours pass until it reached 1:00 PM. The second the display showed double zeroes, he yelled across the shop, back to where Green continued to work, "I'm heading to lunch."

The rest of the day passed without incident, and when 6:00 PM arrived, Riley grabbed his jacket from the break room and walked to the door. "I'm out of here, Dr. Green. I'll see you in the morning."

He received a noncommittal cluster of words from behind a medication shelf and took that to be as good as permission to leave. But then what? Riley stood in the parking lot with hands stuffed into his jacket pockets, fingers wrapped around the squat bottle of pills. Clay didn't give good instructions on what to do once he acquired the drugs.

Riley pulled his phone from the other pocket and texted Glen, "Do you have Clay's number?"

It was a ridiculous question. If the two of them were now a couple, he would, of course, have the other man's number. But how else was he supposed to word it? This brought up another question. How much did Glen know about Clay's side business? Riley decided not to assume anything at this point.

No answer arrived, so Riley stuffed the phone back into his pocket and walked to the apartment. Halfway there, his jacket buzzed as his phone received a message. On its screen was not a message from his ex, but from a number he didn't recognize. "Hey, killer, this is my number. Meet me at the bar. It will just be the two of us."

That appeared to answer the question of how involved Glen was in everything. If Clay wanted the other man to know what was happening, then all three of them would meet at the bar. This also brought up an extra complication. How was he supposed to reach the bar if he couldn't call Glen for a ride? It didn't sound as if Clay was interested in picking him up.

"In for a penny," Riley said in a huff and pulled up the taxi app for the second time in a week. "At this rate, I'll be the first person in history to lose money selling drugs."

It was a new cab, with a different driver, at the same cost, and still without a working heater. Riley arrived at the bar at 7:02 PM. He'd not been to the bar during the week. It was odd to see so few trucks or bikes in the parking lot. He hoped the place was closed, and he could turn around and head home until the sight of Clay's car crushed his hopes.

Pulling open the door, Riley stepped into the familiar setting of the same bar he'd seen dozens of times before. Clay looked up from the booth where the two of them had sat that weekend and waved Riley to join him. "Hey killer, glad you could make it. I would hate to think you would skip out on me or anything." His tone was friendly, but under the smile remained an unspoken threat.

No one in the bar, meaning the five other people, not including the bartender, paid any attention to the two of them. This didn't help Riley relax as he slid into the booth with his back to the door. He hesitated against making the first move and said, "I got what you asked for."

"See, I knew you were resourceful," Clay smiled back and poured a beer from a pitcher at the table. "We're going to have a good little thing going on here. Two smart, resourceful people. No one doing anything to make the other one nervous."

Riley's eyes darted back and forth between his hands and the beer, trying to understand the unspoken words. "I thought this was a one-time thing."

"Oh, no, no, my friend, we're going to be making some good money together. Now go ahead and show me what you brought."

Riley hesitated, but fear won out, and he produced the bottle. Clay inspected the label and didn't bother asking whom he'd prescribed the pills. He slid a small roll of bills over to Riley. "And here's your cut. Keep it up, and we'll see about fixing some of those annoying minimum-wage issues you've been having."

"You did the right thing, killer. I'll let you know when I need you to go shopping for me again." Clay slipped from the booth and stood beside Riley, putting a firm hand on his shoulder. He then waved to the bartender and left without another word to anyone, leaving Riley alone.

# CHAPTER 6

# THE INTERVIEW

Riley sat alone in the booth with a pitcher and two half glasses of beer. How did he get to this point in his life? Did he not do everything asked of him? He wanted to scream and throw things across the room, but he controlled himself. Part of him pouted at his cowardice at not giving the world his middle finger. Instead, he sat staring at a scratch on the table.

Perhaps this lack of attention is how he failed to notice the new arrival in the booth. Riley looked up and saw the same lanky man he'd spoken with the other night. Before Riley asked why, the other man thought it appropriate to sit uninvited. He said, "It appears tonight is not how you expected."

This forced Riley to pull his beer closer for added comfort. "You could say that. But I don't know that I'm ready to drop my life story on a stranger in a bar. Who are you again?"

"Of course. Where are my manners? I'm Azrael," the Angel of Death said and extended his hand across the table.

Riley wasn't sure what was so unsettling about the man's offered hand, as if the distance between the fingers and his shoulder was an inch too long. Should he make a run for the door? Every primal instinct told him to flee from this man, but he gripped the offered hand, and they shook. "I'm Riley."

"A pleasure to meet you, Riley." His voice, though pleasant, carried a hint of unspoken danger that screamed at the back of Riley's primitive mind. "I believe we spoke before. The other night we talked about developing a more rounded plan for life."

Riley's spine tingled as Azrael said the word "life." An icy finger ran down the length of his back, warning him again that he should leave the table and end the conversation.

Without waiting for a response, Azrael said, "did you per-chance find answers to your questions?"

Disregarding the warnings in his mind and body, Riley answered, "I don't know that I figured out what the questions are, let alone found an answer. Things keep getting more complicated." He paused and thought about whether he should have said as much before deciding to sideline the conversation, "Would you like a drink?"

Azrael pushed Clay's abandoned glass away from him to the far edge of the table. "That's quite all right. I'm not interested in following in that man's footsteps."

"He can't be all that bad," Riley defended the man who'd black-mailed him into stealing drugs. This caused him to stop and reevaluate his approach in the conversation.

Death raised an eyebrow, and Riley explained, "Everyone has some redeeming value. You can't just toss people out the door because they have a few problems. We've all got our issues."

This brought a smile to the gaunt man's face as he peeled his lips back to reveal two straight rows of identically white teeth. "You have an interesting view of the world. So, should we save every soul?"

Again, as with the word life, when Azrael mentioned "soul," a chill grasped the base of Riley's spine, as something tried to warn him for a second time. Things were not right with this man or their conversation, but he didn't listen to either of these feelings. Instead, he did what most people do when faced with a life-threatening situation. He ignored the danger.

"Save every soul from what? They're not going to recognize me at Sunday service. There's not enough time to work and go to church during the week. Figure I work six days a week and supplicate to God on the seventh. All that just to push the rock up the hill again come Monday."

Azrael took a sip of Cabernet and set it down. Riley paused as he shot his eyes back at the table. Two glasses of beer, a pitcher, and now wine were at the booth. Was there always a glass of wine? He must not have seen it earlier, or so he attempted to convince himself. Did they serve wine at the Iron Horse?

"Perhaps I worded the question wrong, but I didn't want to know if you believed souls should go to heaven. I don't particularly care whether God forgives them for their past transgressions. If a soul is in mortal danger, for lack of a better word, should we save it?" Azrael asked. He scrutinized Riley as he waited for a response.

The conversation became more uncomfortable with each passing moment, and Riley's best course of action was to finish his first glass of beer and pour another from the pitcher. This bought him time as well as helped lubricate potential answers. "People should save others when they can," he answered with definitive conviction.

Riley added, "People can do so many things wrong in their lives, but that doesn't mean they shouldn't help when people are in trouble. Like Miranda's daughter, she needed help. Someone needed to be there for her."

He'd said too much, and tears strained to flood past his eyes. Determination alone kept streaks from appearing along his cheeks. Azrael watched the display of emotion on Riley's face and listened to his explanation. "So you tried to save her."

Riley slumped forward until his forehead impacted the table with a dull thud that shook the glasses, but Death waited patiently. Riley said, "I did my best. I thought I was doing my best. I didn't mean for her to die."

Silence hung over the booth, and Azrael let Riley have his moment alone with his thoughts. Only after he pulled his head back off the table and steadied himself with another swig from the beer did Azrael say anything. "When I was younger, which was longer ago than I feel comfortable telling people, a man lay on the side of the road. A cart had turned over, and the wheel pinned him to the dirt."

Riley sniffled and wiped his nose with the back of a sleeve but listened to the story. "I thought I'd help him by pulling off the cart. This was a poor decision. We knew so little about medicine, but the weight against his stomach was what kept him alive. I moved the wheel, and he bled out. He died."

"If he were hurt that bad, then he would have died either way," Riley said after considering his knowledge of trauma medicine.

Azrael waited for the point of his story to sink in with his drinking partner. Something clicked. Riley said, "You killed him but could not have stopped him from dying."

"The same is true for you and Haley. Some people have an appointment that they will not miss, and nothing will change the time. The only thing that anyone can do is change how and where."

Riley's mind worked to wrap itself around the moral of the story, considering any complication that he may have missed. Was it even strep? Did he misdiagnose the condition, but if he could do nothing, was he responsible for her death? Either way, the medical board would never see it like that. They would blame him every time.

Then another question occurred to Riley. "How do you know Haley's name?" Riley asked, his voice raised as panic crept into the conversation.

Azrael sat, saying nothing, and waited for Riley to continue. "I never told you that name. Are you following me? That's why you saw me the other night and tonight. You're spying on me, aren't you?" Riley accused the man sitting across from him.

None of his outbursts phased Azrael, who had the same expression a parent wears when waiting for their child to finish a tantrum in the candy aisle. Azrael asked, "Are there more questions? Or will those cover everything?"

As much as Riley's voice raised in panic, it didn't carry far. None of the other patrons in the bar looked up from their drinks to pay the two any attention. He had already finished his beer and reached for Clay's abandoned half-empty glass. "What do you want from me? Are you with Clay? Is this more blackmail?"

Azrael again waited to see if there were any further questions, but when nothing presented itself, he addressed the pertinent issue. "I'm not with the other gentlemen with whom you were speaking, though I use the term loosely. His choice to hold you ransom for an attempted good deed is in poor taste but is still his business."

"So what then? What do you want from me?"

The interruption caused Azrael to pause and take a sip from his glass. This was not a conversation he would allow Riley to rush him into, and the more Riley pushed, the slower he answered. He sat the glass on the table, then continued, "I have been following you, though not for more than a few nights. So that's up to you to decide if that's spying."

Riley recoiled from the answer. "Of course it counts. Even one day is still stalking. Why are you following me? What do you want from me? You're not a cop, are you?"

Again, Death took his time waiting for Riley to finish before he responded. "This may go more smoothly if you wait for an answer after each question. I may not answer them all, but it would allow me to answer the ones I'm willing."

Both glasses were empty, the pitcher was barren, and Riley was feeling a little off-balance. He tried his best to focus on the hazy image of a man in front of him. Rather than form words, he nodded and went silent. Azrael smiled, showing all his white teeth. "Excellent. No, I'm not a cop or with Clay, though I don't know that I'm ready to explain much more, and you appear overwhelmed at the moment."

"I'm fine," Riley lied and slurred.

"Of course you are. But tonight is more about you than me. You contend that every person deserves to be saved, so I ask you a different question, saved from what?"

The room rotated around the table as Riley held on to the booth to steady himself. "From well, from dying. You can't just let people die, not if you can do anything about it."

After he said this, Riley thought more about it and realized he never actually saved anyone from death. He wasn't that type of doctor. Maybe those who studied emergency trauma could hold back quietus, but Riley only eased the suffering of life. Was that as noble a cause?

"Has anyone saved someone from death?" Azrael asked. His expression was curious, with a Cheshire smile. "No, I don't believe so. The most someone can do is politely ask Death to wait and come back later"

Was that true? Everyone eventually died. A patient cured of terminal cancer would still die, though they might die years later and of something different. Riley thought about this. "I guess, but you have to try. What kind of monster sits back and allows people to die?"

"Would that person be a monster? What about hospice nurses? They care for the elderly and the dying and do everything in their power to make their patients' lives comfortable but do nothing about their impending death."

Riley thought about, or tried to think about, it. His mind was having a hard time focusing on any one thing at any singular moment. "Well, they can't do anything. Their patients are already dying. There's nothing they can do but make them more comfortable."

"Is any other doctor different? Are they not trying to make their patients' limited time more comfortable? Should that not be what we try to do for one another?" Azrael led the intoxicated man to a question, while trying not to give him the answer.

The curious thing about drunk people is that they lack general common sense yet hold profound wisdom. Not that people should follow the advice of drunks, but they shouldn't discount it. Their lack of rational thought often gives them insight that most block from their minds. Riley was in such a condition when he said, "Well, maybe just because they're dead doesn't mean they're not going to die again."

No one at the bar overheard this nonsense of an answer except Death, and only he understood the truth behind the words. Azrael nodded and then extricated himself from the booth. "Exactly. Someone has to care for the dead. Everyone looks after the living and tries to see that their finite lives are as comfortable as possible, but who cares for these souls?"

"I don't know; I guess someone is doing it. Otherwise, there'd be a lot of, I don't know; it just seems like someone should be responsible." Riley thought about the idea. "How would you even interview for a job like that?"

Death placed a firm hand on Riley's shoulder. "I'm sure it would not be as complicated as you might imagine. They would only need to find the right type of person. It would be the searching for the applicant that could take unfathomable time."

Riley wanted to say something profound in response to the man's words, but the most he could manage was, "One way!"

He pushed past the specter of death and rushed to the toilet. Once behind the closed door of a stall, he relieved himself of a considerable portion of the imbibed beer. "Mental note, don't do that again."

He washed his face and did what he could to clean himself up before looking in the mirror and deciding to return to public. Riley observed the empty booth as the barback collected the glasses and pitcher. As for Azrael, he was standing by a woman who'd fallen asleep in a different booth.

Azrael gently helped the woman to her feet and guided her to the door. The two of them left, and a glow of what must have been headlights lit the door frame. "What a strange man," Riley thought to himself and then noticed the woman Azrael led out from the bar was still sleeping in her booth.

Riley ran outside to an empty parking lot without knowing what else to do. Though they had only just left, neither the woman nor Azrael was in sight, but Riley heard the same distant baleful howl from nights before, a sound that drove him back inside.

Riley placed himself back at the bar and ordered the cheapest domestic beer available. The watery beverage had little value other than buying him a seat. But where to go from there? He'd spent more money than he wanted in an attempt to purchase freedom from Clay's blackmail, and yet it seemed he was as trapped as ever. How was he supposed to get home? Would Glen be willing to give him a ride home?

Riley reached into his pocket and pulled out a phone, then texted the only person he knew who wasn't trying to blackmail him. "Hey Glen, you doing anything? Want to meet at the bar?"

No answer came for over ten minutes, and Riley gave up on receiving a response minutes before the phone buzzed. He glanced at the screen and saw Glen's message. "Can't do anything tonight. Clay just showed up, and we were going to spend the evening together."

If cell phones were not so expensive, he would hurl the offending device across the bar. Instead, he calmly hit delete on the message and set the phone face down on the counter. He then dropped his head to the somewhat clean wooden surface. Riley contemplated leaving his body there and giving up on life, but the sound of a shot glass dropped beside him broke his thoughts.

When he looked up, the tender shrugged. She left a shot of something brown where his head and phone had been, a simple kindness from a stranger. It didn't matter at this point what it was. Riley appreciated the burning liquid as he tossed it down his throat. He grimaced; how do people enjoy that kind of thing?

Riley's newfound courage helped him first request a cab to pick him up at the bar. As much as he'd prefer not to spend money on a ride, his only other option was Glen, who was doing God knows what with the person who started this mess. He summoned his resolution, finished the watered-down beer, and pushed back the bottle.

When Riley turned on the stool and put one foot toward the

door, everything stopped. The lights in the bar dimmed, and sounds became less distinct. Riley glanced from person to person, and none of them paid any attention to this change. So what was it? Did the tender drug him? He was ready to confront the woman when the sound of claws scraped across the wood and the slow deep breath of an animal caused him to hesitate.

Turning slowly, he locked eyes on a creature he'd never seen nor heard described. It was a canine, in the most general sense, with powerful front shoulders and a short stub of a tail. At the shoulders, the dog, for there was no other word to describe it, stood the height of a man, and its eyes stared Riley in the face. But the terror of this creature came from two features it did not share with any animal.

It possessed no flesh. The thick twisted cables that formed its muscles glistened with viscera in the dim light. Also, when it entered the room, its body passed without resistance through the solid form of the door. People like to think of themselves as brave and play through their minds what they would do in the worst-case scenarios. There was no room for bravery in the face of this creature. If it came for Riley, he prepared himself to run.

With what courage he possessed, Riley disregarded logic and asked the thing, "What do you want?"

The dog stalked across the room until it stared into Riley's face. His plans to run failed him, and he quivered in fear while clinging to the bar for support. It sniffed, taking in his scent and considering what to do with the only man who showed any fear. Opening its maw, it screamed fire and pain, something Riley had first heard only a few nights before.

The dog turned away from Riley as a second similar, though somewhat smaller, creature passed through the door. The two barked a sound of rusted metal in train yards, then advanced on the woman sleeping at the booth. Riley then did the only brave thing he could. He yelled at them, "Stay away from her!"

Both of them turned as Riley made strange noises with his mouth. Perhaps they were words. The creatures disregarded them as unimportant. Instead, they sniffed and examined the woman's body, who showed no reaction to their inspection. The larger of the two growled and bit at the smaller, who whined and backed away before the two ran out of the bar.

Everything resumed its typical grungy atmosphere with the dogs gone, and Riley clung to a stool with his back against the counter. The tender observed this for a minute before asking, "You OK, son? Can I call you a cab?"

Unable to answer immediately, Riley waved vaguely, but this did nothing to reassure anyone involved. He took a deep breath and straightened himself. "Yes, thank you. I mean, no, I have a cab coming, but yes, I'm doing OK. Is that woman OK?" Riley asked, indicating the woman who had not awoken from the booth.

No one paid the sleeping woman any attention until Riley pointed her out, but once he did, the bartender's eyebrows knit together, and she set down her rag. Approaching carefully, she called out, "Ma'am, you OK?"

There was no response, and the tender shook the woman's shoulder. Again, no answer, and she checked her outstretched hand before recoiling. In a clear voice, she announced to everyone present, "Bar's closed, folks. If you need a ride, call a cab."

Riley was unsure what he'd just witnessed and stayed near the counter as the tender returned. She said, "I'm going to call an ambulance for her. You may want to leave with everyone else."

This wasn't enough information for Riley, so he asked, "What's wrong with her? Is she going to be OK?"

The look of compassion from the tender betrayed her body of tattoos and scars. "I'm sorry, son, but she's dead. Now, unless you want to play the drunk version of twenty questions with the police, you'd best catch your cab and be gone before they show up."

Riley felt numb as he walked out the door, tapping his foot on the frame to reassure himself that it was solid. The rest of the bar cleared out, with the regulars driving their cars home after a night of drinking. The ambulance arrived before his cab, to his bad luck.

Thankfully, the cab was next, and Riley left the scene before seeing law enforcement. Riley had no desire to explain why he thought something was wrong with the woman. He also didn't want to mention demon dogs or why he didn't check a pulse.

Once inside the cab, Riley texted Glen, "Had a terrible night. Can you call?"

There was no call, Glen did not text, and when Riley checked messages in the morning, there was nothing on his voicemail. Taking the phone back, he tapped the screen harder than necessary. "Don't bother. Someone died. Your boyfriend is a drug dealer, and you know what? You can keep him." He then threw his phone across the room, where the screen cracked on impact.

## CHAPTER 7
# RENT IS DUE

Nothing of interest occurred at work the following day, and Riley continued to process the inventory sheet. Dozens of signature cards that belonged in the shoebox were missing. Once he and Dr. Green finished the count, there were going to be discrepancies that the shop needed to explain. Even without Riley having illegally obtained a month's worth of pills, there were still too many instances of controlled medications disappearing. And the federal government did not let these numbers slide, even in a small pharmacy like theirs.

"Dr. Green, you understand what all this is going to turn into, right? This is either theft or loss, and either way, we need to report the discrepancy to the Drug Enforcement Agency. I'll keep doing what I can to find everything, but inventories should have been done daily, weekly, something. Waiting two years isn't going to work." Riley tried to remain calm as he explained the situation to the senior pharmacist.

There was resignation on Dr. Green's face, and he nodded his agreement. "I understand, but we'll deal with what we have. There's no sense in trying to go back in time to change what's happened. But now that you're here, maybe things will be smooth from this point forward."

How was Riley supposed to argue with someone who agreed with what he said? He gave up, retrieved his jacket from the break room, and dropped off his lab coat before ducking out the front door. An electronic note chimed to let Dr. Green know he'd left.

The weather remained brisk but clear, with only the slightest threat of snow in the far distance. This suited Riley just fine, as he did not find it fun to walk home in a blizzard. Riley had no reason to rush home, so the ten-minute walk gave him time to think. He stuffed his hands into the jacket's pockets and trekked to his apartment. The streets were empty as most people left work at five or sundown depending on their vocation. The pharmacy stayed open later to ensure everyone could pick up their prescriptions before heading home.

Riley didn't mind staying late at work; it only meant more money in his pocket. It wasn't a lot of money, but every dollar helped. His fingers ached from the cold as he fumbled with the keys and unbolted the door to his apartment. As the door opened, the lights turned on, and he stepped over a small pile of envelopes, which the postman had pushed through the mail slot.

"Welcome home, Riley. Hi, how did your day go? Oh, just great; how about you? I can't complain." Riley said to the empty apartment while he picked up the stack of letters and walked them to the kitchen table. "So, what's for dinner?" The apartment didn't answer.

From the freezer, Riley retrieved a Starving Man dinner. "Oh, great, meatloaf, my favorite." He tore off the cardboard container and stabbed holes in the plastic film that covered frostbit food-colored objects. He tossed the plastic container of what claimed to be an edible meal into the microwave, set the timer, and hit start without reading the box's instructions.

With dinner prepared, Riley dropped the cardboard into a blue recycle bin and walked to the table, where he picked up the first envelope from the stack. This one stood out in a hot pink envelope with no stamp. Riley tore the top open with his finger and retrieved the typed letter inside.

The letter's contents were direct and expressed the apartment manager's discontent with Riley's failure to pay rent. The language spoke about eviction, fees, and at one point said something about shutting off utilities. In general terms, Riley believed he had a good relationship with the manager, but that relationship only extended as far as the check traveled before it bounced.

Riley reached into his pocket to pull out a phone and check the bank to see what money remained in his account. Then he remembered he no longer had a phone. It exploded the night before when he tossed the offending device against the back wall. Pieces of glass and plastic still littered the kitchen counter, and no amount of staring would force them to function. Clearly, it was the broken phone's fault it stopped working.

As an alternative, he retrieved his computer, opened the bank's web page, and checked his account. There was a thousand dollars remaining, more than he expected, which brought good news; he could pay rent. The problem would be if he had money for anything else? What other bills were there? Did it matter? He had to pay the rent first. If he had the money for food but didn't have a place to cook and eat a meal, he was still out of luck.

The telephone number for the apartment manager was on the letter, and again Riley glared at his broken cell phone. In a desperate attempt, he pulled up a phone dialer on his computer and placed a call. When it connected, the sound was choppy and distorted. He had difficulty understanding the voice at the other end.

"Yea, what is it?" answered the person he assumed to be the apartment manager. It was the manager or a wrong number. The background sounded noisy as Riley heard either a television or a room full of children fighting. He was not interested in inquiring about details.

"It's Riley in apartment B. Can we work something out with the rent check? I don't get paid until next week." Riley expressed in his most clear voice, using focused enunciation on each syllable.

"You moved where?" came the response, and Riley rolled his eyes while grateful it wasn't a video call.

"I'm in apartment B. Can I pay you on the fifteenth?"

No response came from the computer, and Riley checked to see if he'd lost connection. It was possible he hung up on the woman with his neighbor's limited Wi-Fi. But the screen showed a ticking clock that implied an active connection.

After a minute of nothing, she said, "If the money's not here by next Friday, I'm bringing Bobby, and we're tossing your stuff in the parking lot."

Richard Wallace, or Bobby, as the manager liked to call her bowling partner, was the local sheriff. The town continued to elect him because everyone went to high school with him. He made friends with over fifty-one percent of the people who lived in Rural Retreat. "That's fine. You'll get your money. I'll make sure you do."

"Wonderful, nice chat," she said, and hung up the phone without another word.

As much as Riley wanted to save the money for other things, he needed to pay rent. He could use any that remained to buy food or perhaps a new cell phone. Life in a small town without a car or a phone was almost as bad as being homeless. He opened the bank browser once more and selected the bill-pay option before issuing a check to the apartment manager for this month's rent.

At that moment, the microwave dinged, and Riley closed the lid of his computer to retrieve the gourmet dinner. One option with the burning plastic and questionable food was to put it on a ceramic plate. That would only make more dishes to clean later. So instead, he used a folded towel to keep from burning himself and found a fork before returning to the table and a dinner for one.

Riley turned to the next letter and found it was from the university bursar's office. "Not enough that I give the loan people all my money. Now the school sends me separate letters asking for cash. This is going to be perfect."

With the letter slit opened, he reviewed its contents and saw it described a graduation debt not covered by loans. They were going to withhold official transcripts from the university until the matter was resolved or turned over to collections if it extended past three months. "Well, isn't that just terrific? Let's put that in the blood-sucking vampire pile."

Riley set the bursar's letter in the now-empty corner of the table before turning to the last letter. This one was from the student loan collections department, and without opening the thing, he set it in the vampire pile. "Like when you throw meat into a pit of dogs. Everyone dives in looking to rip off a piece."

Riley turned over the envelopes and saw they were from the electric company, rental insurance, and cell phone. "Oh perfect, I'm now paying a phone bill on a broken phone. That seems to sum things up just about now. I need a drink."

It was an idle speech to talk about alcohol. Riley didn't have money for food, let alone beer. So he finished his Starving Man dinner and dropped the refuse in the bin, and returned to his stack of bills. "Ok, let's see what we can do," he said before opening them all and jotting down the amounts due on one of the discarded envelopes.

He kept a running total with the amount he had in the bank and what he expected to earn when his next check arrived. No matter how he tried to balance the numbers, someone would not receive the money they wanted. The problem then became a question of who would cause the least stink for him if they didn't get paid. Utilities would be problematic, as having the power cut off would put a crimp in his plans of not freezing to death in the middle of the night.

On the same line of thinking, paying rent was something he needed to prioritize. He should also set aside something for food. As often as Riley attempted to go without eating, the plan didn't work the way he wanted, and he always reverted to the habit of ingesting sustenance. What about insurance? The expense wasn't a lot each month, but what was he insuring?

Riley surveyed the apartment and checked the things he owned. If someone broke in to the place and took everything, he would not be much worse off than he was already. "OK, so can probably drop the insurance." He drew a long line across the page, then tossed it to the side. "Just have to call them and cancel officially."

"Phone? There's another one. That one's broken, so it's not going to work until I buy a new one, and that is going to cost me a few hundred dollars. So drop the cell phone." That was another page he crossed off and set aside.

The subsequent letters were the school loans and the bursar's office. What good had they done him in finding a job? If anything, it was the school's fault he couldn't pay them back. If they had done their job correctly, he would make a lot more money and paid them off by now. No, they would wait on their money until he had that job they promised.

Riley regarded the much-reduced pile of bills and added up the amounts again. "See, that's manageable. I can swing that. Just have to cut out doing anything other than work and sleep." As he said this, a frown creased his lips, and the hopeless nature of his existence struck him. "I should jump off a bridge. Not that any bridges are within walking distance, and I still don't own a car."

Riley closed the computer lid with a heavy smack and picked up the bills, which he dumped into the recycle bin. He left the ones he agreed to pay on the table. "What the hell have I gotten myself into? I should have just stayed home and gotten a job working at the Burger Shack. Probably would have been promoted to manager and be making more than I am now stocking shelves." Riley dropped himself on the couch and stuffed his hands into the pockets of his jacket.

Inside his right pocket, his fingers gripped a small roll of bills, held tight together by a rubber band. Riley pulled out the roll and considered it. He'd not thought about this money since the other night when Clay handed it to him.

Riley glanced over his shoulder at the empty apartment to ensure that no one had materialized behind him. Being in a first-floor apartment, Riley did not enjoy the idea of others being able to look in his living room. However, he confirmed that the place was empty, and he kept the curtains closed at all times.

He rolled the bills over in his fingers before stretching the rubber band away from their cotton surface. The roll was so small. How much potential money was it? Riley pulled out five twenties and a hundred-dollar bill, then stared at the currency in his hands. "Well, damn, that beats retail."

Hundreds of things ran through Riley's mind, and he sat there staring at the wall and the money. "OK... That's enough to keep the phone turned on and buy a cheap replacement. I don't care, right or wrong. I need the money," he justified to himself. And it's not like I can give this back to anyone. The cash is mine now, no matter what I do."

Once he finished rationalizing why he would keep the money and use it to better himself, Riley put the money into his wallet. "Now why can't I make that kind of money working at the pharmacy?

Climbing to his feet, Riley secured his coat and said, "Hey Max, I'm leaving." The apartment was silent, but lights turned off, and a blue glow flashed in the far corner. Riley left through the front door and locked it behind him. The temperature of the night's air had dropped, and Riley huddled in his jacket as he leaned into the wind, walking towards the town's gas station.

The place stood abandoned at this time of night. Whoever needed gas or snacks had already passed through and headed home. The station only remained open to catch the occasional interstate traveler, and it was unclear how that was enough to maintain business. None of this was Riley's concern as he entered the room of brightly lit shelves. Instead, he focused on a rack near the register where inexpensive unlocked and no-contract phones waited to be purchased.

Riley found the one he looked for, a hundred-dollar smartphone. He purchased the phone, a month's worth of service, and forty ounces of cheap beer, using his recently acquired cash, then walked back to the apartment. He had some planning to do.

Once inside the apartment, Riley attempted to crack open the plastic shell that held his new phone. This simple task turned into a half-hour of frustration and required a screwdriver and a kitchen knife. Grateful that the phone came through the ordeal with only minor scrapes, Riley turned it on and set the device for new service.

All the numbers that lived in the old phone were lost, so he only transferred numbers he knew from memory or had stored on the computer. This worked well, though he knew few people, which caused him to question whether the purchase of a phone was necessary. "I can't keep living like this. Something's going to snap," he mumbled while punching in the last number.

"Glen can lend a hand. He's been there for me before." As those words left him, he realized that Glen was no longer someone upon which he could rely. Riley was on his own. All the friends he'd known in school were gone. His boyfriend was gone. It all disappeared in a vain attempt to educate himself past the level of a fry cook. "See where that got you."

"So who can I call? Not like Green will give me a raise after less than a month." He continued to think about the problem. Then, slowly, the thought formed at the edge of rationalization. It was too crazy to consider at first. But the more he thought about it, the deeper it wormed its way into his mind. "What if I called Clay?"

Sure this was the same guy who was blackmailing him with prison time for killing a small child. But maybe this could work out. All he'd have to do was shoot him a text and ask if he needed Riley to pick anything up from the store. Clay would know what he was asking about. It might be just that easy, and he'd have another two hundred in his pocket. There was only one slight problem.

Riley didn't have a way to reach Clay. Before his phone broke, he'd talked to the other man by texting him, but he never memorized the man's number, just assumed the phone would always store it electronically. "Good move, genius. So now what?"

Thinking about the list of who might know Clay, Riley only came up with Glen's name. Did he want to call his ex to ask him for his current boyfriend's number? Something was wrong with the exchange. Ok, nothing about the conversation felt right. But what about Jacob? He and Riley were never the closest friends, but they knew one another well enough from high school. It would be OK if he asked Glen for Jacob's number.

Deciding against further debate, Riley texted Glen, "Hey man, it's Riley. This is a new phone. Do you have Jacob's number?"

After hitting send, Riley sat back on the couch. A wave of realization hit him. Waiting for Glen to reach out had started this whole mess. Was he being a fool to think his friend was going to talk to him now? Ten minutes passed, and nothing appeared on the phone, so Riley gave up and flipped through the internet's news site.

The same night he had been at the fair, someone had died. Everyone was so caught up in William's story of surviving the Ferris wheel that the papers buried the death of Andrew McGuire. The article described a kind elderly gentleman who had lived in Rural Retreat his entire life. He did jobs from factory worker to farmhand and was liked but forgotten by everyone. None of this was surprising. Many people go through life without being remembered, but Riley remembered one thing about the man. He'd talked to him the night he died.

Even when enlarged on the screen, the photo was small and unclear enough to be definitive, but that was him. "I had no idea," Riley said to himself as he looked over the man's obituary. "To think I might have been the last one to talk to him before he died. I should reach out to his family or something." But the more he thought about this option, the less appealing it became.

"Then again, what would I tell them? I saw your grandfather the night he died. He seemed like a nice guy. Sorry, I didn't think to call an ambulance; I got distracted? No, let's leave this alone."

When Riley's phone dinged, his heart leaped into his throat. He took two slow breaths and checked the screen. Again, it was from a number he didn't recognize. It said, "Heard you wanted to reach me, Jacob."

"So he's not willing to text me directly, but at least he passed on the message. I guess that's something."

Riley sent back, "I've been trying to reach Clay and lost his number. I didn't want to ask Glen for the number. Can you reach him?" He looked at the short novel he wrote on the screen and frowned. He hit send, deciding it was easier to send a lot of garbage than edit the message to something shorter.

Jacob's response came quickly. "I'll let him know."

Nothing followed those four words, and Riley set the phone down. "Well, that's something. Do I want to be getting myself mixed up into this?"

Riley pulled up more news articles and began researching people who'd received punitive sentences for selling prescription medication. Several served long stretches in prison, but the punishments appeared arbitrary, and the difference from a slap on the wrist and ten years could be anyone's guess. "I guess it just becomes a game of how lucky I feel." He considered the situation further. "Of course, I've done it. I killed that little girl, so no matter what, I'm going to jail if things go bad. May as well make money on the way."

Clay's text came an hour later with the simple, "You rang? Clay?"

Riley turned the phone over in his hands while he debated the next part of the plan. He then typed out his message, "I'm going to the store later; anything you need me to pick up?"

Nothing happened for the longest five minutes. Then came Clay's response, "Oh, you know. Just the usual."

That was it. No other texts came, and Riley was left with the brief message and knowledge that he had agreed to steal medication from his employer again. Was this becoming a regular thing? How many more times was he going to do this before he had enough money that he could quit? Would he ever have enough? Would Clay ever let him stop?

These questions tumbled over in Riley's mind as he attempted to focus back on the various news stories, but none of them held his attention. Eventually, he gave up and pulled up a movie site and began watching a ten-year-old film about a father whose son was imprisoned after being set up in a drug deal. It seemed fitting enough.

"How bad could prison be? Hell, I bet they don't send you eviction letters when you're in there. No rent, utility bills, food paid for... shit, the more I think about it, it doesn't sound that bad. I may try to get caught on purpose."

## CHAPTER 8

# FIVE STAR HOTEL

Friday 8:00 AM marked the time of death for Riley's alarm clock as it impacted the wall opposite his bed. The velocity was sufficient that the plastic box disintegrated before hitting the floor. "For fuck's sake," Riley groaned upon seeing the pieces fall to the laminate floor. "That is one more thing added to the list of things I can't afford to replace."

He crawled his way from the bed. "Hey, Max! What's on the calendar for today?"

In its monotone voice, the digital assistant said, "Morning Riley, today work starts at 10:00 AM. Would you like to add anything else?"

"Why do I keep asking for a schedule when I do the same thing every day?"

Max responded with, "Please restate your question."

At times, Riley considered throwing Max at the wall, but he kept his opinion to himself. After Riley swept the broken pieces of a shattered alarm clock into the waste bin, the morning progressed without incident. But when Riley left the apartment and encountered a stranger waiting for him on the front walk, he took a step back.

"Dammit, what the heck?" It wasn't the most articulate question, but it was the best he could manage before composing himself. After planting both feet under him, Riley tried again. "I'm sorry. Who are you? Did you want something?"

The man on the walk was taller than Riley, with hippie-length black hair and dark skin. He wore a beaten military surplus jacket. Was it just a trend that poor people in town wore old military clothing? Or was it something else? Riley didn't answer the question and didn't care enough to inquire further. The man said, "sorry about that. Are you the doc who helped Miranda's little girl?"

"Helped" was a relative term, and Riley's eyes darted around to see if they were alone or if anyone else was circling to turn this into an ambush. Once satisfied it was only him and the man, he nodded, "If you want to call it helping. Yea, you can blame me for that. You here for your pound of flesh?"

Silence held in the cold air while the man's eyes lingered on Riley's face. After a moment, he answered, "I need your help. Thought maybe you'd be willing to do for me what you did for them."

"What, murder one of your children?" Something in Riley wanted the man to yell at him. Why had no one punished him for the atrocity he caused with the little girl?

"No, and she doesn't blame you. You see, I'm diabetic. I know what I need. I've used it before, as often as possible, but things keep getting more expensive, and I just can't afford insulin anymore."

"OK, no, that is not right. You can't keep someone from receiving insulin. They are putting your life in danger by doing that. Who's your doctor?"

The man shrugged while showing both his palms. "Can't afford one of them either. The veteran's hospital two towns over said they'd help, but I don't have a way to get to the VA. So I was hoping you would be able to..." he paused before continuing.

Riley filled in the rest of the man's statement, "to help out with unscripted medication."

He nodded.

"I can't. You know what happened the last time. I can't risk anything like that happening again. I am not sure I can risk saving people's lives. You need a real doctor."

The wind cut past the two as the man considered this. "My name's Marcus. Would you mind if I walked with you?"

Nothing appeared to be wrong with walking beside the man. They were only talking. It was only a crime if Riley did what the man asked him to do. "Yea, sure, that's fine. But it's a real short walk."

The two turned on the sidewalk and began the ten-minute stroll to the pharmacy. It was Marcus who spoke first. "You ever consider that a person is responsible for the things they don't do?"

"I don't follow. If you don't do something, how can you be responsible for not doing it? That doesn't make any sense. You can only get in trouble for the things you do."

Marcus shook his head and explained, "Not quite. If you don't pay your taxes, you're held responsible. If you don't stop at a red light, you'll receive a ticket."

"OK, yea. So some laws tell you to do things, but that is not the same thing."

Silence lingered as they walked, then Marcus asked, "What about a little boy on a Ferris wheel?"

This stopped Riley, who dug his feet into the gravel and snapped his eyes to the older man. "How do you know about him?"

"Come now, Riley. You were in the newspaper photographs too. Miranda recognized you, and I do, too, now that we've met." He gave Riley a moment to let the realization sink in. He did not rescue the child in secret. The crowd's ignorance and their general desire to forget him were not the same as no one knowing he was there. "Would you be morally responsible if you hadn't tried to save him?"

Riley considered the situation again. He ran through the events of a night that haunted his dreams and knew the answer to the question. "Yes. If I did nothing, it would be my fault that he fell."

"I'm not a child, not anymore, but I'm proverbially too high above the ground to help myself. My situation is much the same. If you don't do something and find a way to bring me my medication, I don't know how far I'll fall."

It was an unfair comparison, but Riley didn't have it in him to argue, so he walked in silence. Once they reached the far edge of the parking lot, Riley turned and asked, "So why did none of you ask Dr. Green for his help? Why did everyone wait until the new guy showed up to beg for drugs?"

Marcus recoiled at the offending words and stared at Riley. "I don't like that tone or what you're implying. But Dr. Green has been in this town a long time, and we already know his answer if we ask him for help. He may be a nice man, but he will do nothing to put himself or that pharmacy in danger. That includes saving the occasional young girl from an untimely death."

Riley didn't know how to respond. This was just as well, with them being at the far edge of the parking lot, and Riley turned to Marcus. "I think it best if you don't follow any farther."

The stranger nodded and stopped before setting foot on the paved surface.

Riley then added, "I can't make a promise, but if there is something I can do, I'll figure it out. How do I get back in touch with you?"

"Oh, no worries about that. I have nowhere to go. I'll meet you after work."

This didn't bring confidence as Riley considered the implications of the possibly homeless man hanging around the pharmacy all day, but he let Marcus do his thing. Riley crossed the parking lot and slipped into the store. He called out before Dr. Green said anything, "It's just me."

The doctor stood by the controlled medication cabinet as he counted labels. Each bottle showed a series of numbers, which the doctor compared to Riley's notes on his clipboard, then made a pencil mark beside his printout. "Morning, Dr. Brewer. I was going over your numbers from the other day. Are you certain about the missing signature cards?"

This was the first time Riley had conducted a controlled substance inventory outside of an academic environment, so he shook his head. "Not a hundred percent, no. I can tell that we have the right number of pills compared to the paperwork. OK, we're missing some, but not enough to be a problem. But each time we fill a prescription, we're supposed to have a matching signature. We're just missing some of them."

"Not the good news I'd hoped to hear," Dr. Green said and hung the clipboard back on the locker before securing its doors. "Either way, I think we should be able to report that we're not missing any medication. No sense bringing the DEA into all this when it is only a paperwork issue."

The idea of a federal law enforcement agency crawling through every piece of paperwork made Riley nervous. He agreed this was less than desirable. "Yea, let's try to avoid that." He left off the detail about the medication he'd already stolen or what he planned to take before the end of the day.

"OK, today I want you to go back into the store and start rotating inventory. There are a few items in the bread and staples section we need to remove."

It was annoying to Riley that while he held a doctorate, he effectively did the job of a shop assistant. Most of his career involved cleaning floors, adjusting shelves, and customer checkout. He didn't argue, though, because no one else was going to do those jobs. It was only him and Dr. Green working in the pharmacy, and it would be unthinkable for the senior pharmacist to do those lesser jobs.

Riley moved slowly on his task. There was nothing better to do once he finished, so having something to occupy his time seemed more important than completing the task. This gave him time to think, and while removing the expired loaves of bread, he developed his plan for the insulin.

At 01:00 PM, Riley took his lunch and ate in the employee break room, sitting on the reclining chair. It was unfortunate that the chair could not lean back all the way, but there was not enough room in the broom closet. This prevented him from catching a few minutes' sleep. Once finished, he switched places with Dr. Green, who left for home. This gave Riley about an hour to execute his plan.

After retrieving his lab coat, Riley opened the medication fridge. He found the oldest batch of insulin in the pharmacy's inventory. He compared the manufacture dates with the labels and noted that some of the insulin would expire next month. Riley pulled these vials out and slipped them into his coat pocket. He then made a note claiming they had been "previously opened, past 28 days."

That was one item off his shopping list, but it was simple. Riley opened the controlled medicine cabinet and looked at the drugs inside. "I can't keep taking the same thing. He'll notice if we keep going short. What else can I sell Clay?"

While looking over the various bottles and ampules, Riley's eyes landed on a container of hydromorphone in the back. "I can't imagine that drug dealers are going to know what that is, but they know about morphine, so there has to be a market." Riley took out the bottle and checked the inventory sheet.

The log showed the pills in the correct quantity, which prevented him from simply stuffing them in his pocket. "Come on, Riley, what are the other options?" He glanced around the room. The option of replacing the medication with similar-looking tablets came to mind. But would Dr. Green see the distinct marks on the medications on the next count? "I'm making this harder than I need to."

Riley pulled out an extra card from the handwritten records. He put in the quantity twenty on this prescription issue card and the medication hydromorphone 2 mg. This card he stuffed back into the pile where it should have appeared chronologically and then picked up the inventory sheet. "And here we just need to correct the count showing those pills as issued last year."

With rapid movements of his pen, Riley moved the pills across paper and through time. He then took the bottle of pills, counted twenty, and slipped them into an unlabeled bottle. This, too, he placed into his pocket. Riley took both pilfered items to the employee lounge and tucked them into his winter coat.

Dr. Green didn't return from lunch until 2:45 PM, and by that time, Riley had completed all the work. He updated the doctor on everything at the shop that didn't involve the theft of medication. From there, he had little to do, so Riley spent the rest of the day trying to learn the features of his new phone.

As it turned out, the contract phone possessed only the most essential features. Its designer marketed it as "smart," though they failed to select anything but the most basic apps. "Looks like I'm stuck using the web browser for everything from this point forward. This is starting to feel like the dark ages." No one listened to Riley.

From the back of the shop, Dr. Green asked, "Riley, did you change the inventory while I was gone?"

Shouting back and forth across the building was not Riley's idea of a professional relationship, so he walked the distance to talk in a conversational volume. "Yes, sir. I found an old issue card while I was looking for signatures. It made me go back and recount a couple of the bottles, and one of them had to be changed. Everything should add up now."

Riley's heart thumped loudly, and he was sure the doctor heard the thundering in his chest. Dr. Green watched Riley, his eyes examining the young man's face, but he said nothing. Moments before Riley confessed to everything, Dr. Green said, "Very well, as long as the numbers add up. Let's just make sure there are no more changes from this point forward."

Dr. Green held Riley's eyes after he said these last words, and it was unclear whether he knew or was only implying that Riley deliberately changed something. Either way, Riley didn't want to take a chance on anything. "Yes, sir. We should be good. The inventory is almost complete except for the paperwork."

"That is good news. I hate having someone breathing over my shoulder while I'm trying to do my job."

"I can understand that one," Riley agreed. "Was there anything else you needed me to take care of today before I headed home?"

The store was clean, shelves were in order, they'd put inventory away. "It appears you've handled everything. Go ahead, grab your jacket. Just do me a favor."

Riley hesitated and turned to wait for Dr. Green's request. "Try to remember that bad habits are the hardest to quit. Many doctors have been where you are. You may want to take a box of syringes with you as well."

Riley's mind hit the brakes as Dr. Green recommended the needles. "What makes you think I would need any needles?" Riley said as he attempted to play off the event.

Dr. Green raised an eyebrow as he considered Riley. "They're on aisle four. Don't worry about ringing them up. I'll cross a box off the inventory. Now get out of here. We don't need to talk anymore about this."

With the vials of insulin in his pocket, Riley crossed the store to pick up a small box of needles and placed them into his jacket with everything else. He wanted to ask many questions, but from Dr. Green's tone, it didn't sound as if he would answer any of them. Instead, Riley slipped out the door to the sound of an electronic chime and crossed the parking lot.

The man he'd met that morning didn't say where to meet him after work. As Riley scanned the surrounding area, he saw no sign of life. As best he could tell, the veteran had wandered off during the day. "So, where did you get to?"

The wind whipped around his jacket and made the rigid plastic vials clink together like glass. His only option was to continue back to the apartment and hope to find the mysterious man somewhere along the way.

Bad weather had worked its way into the town and made the ten-minute walk twice as long. However, it didn't produce the missing Marcus or reveal where the man had gone. "I give up. If you can't bother to come get your medicine, I'm not hunting you down," Riley grumbled while forcing his key into the lock.

The apartment lights remained off after the door shut behind him, and his breath hung in the frosted air. "God damn, it's cold. What the hell? Hey Max, what's the temperature?"

No one and nothing responded to Riley's voice, so he reached over and toggled the light switch. Again, only darkness. "Wonderful. They're freaking quick to shut off power, aren't they?"

Riley left the apartment and went to the far end of the walkway to look back at the complex. What he saw was good news to a limited extent. There were no lights on in any of the other windows. "Guess everyone's out then. That's something, at least. Won't stop me from freezing to death while I sleep, but I'll have company."

The door slammed behind him as Riley returned to his arctic living conditions. He went to the kitchen to consider the options for dinner and laughed as he found his choices were all frozen dinners. "At least the food won't spoil. I can't cook anything, but it will stay cold."

Riley took out the vials of insulin and put them into the refrigerator. The fridge had the best chance of being the warmest place in the apartment if things progressed through the night. His next option was to finish what remained of the peanut butter. Next, he turned on his laptop to see if he could pay the power bill while it was fresh in his mind.

"Oh, right. Neighbors don't have power, so they don't have internet," he complained and closed the lid. His cell phone had a connection, but the small screen and poor web browser made accessing the bank difficult, so after three attempts, he gave up. "Could play twenty fingers and toes, counting them as they freeze and fall off," he said and tried to laugh at the situation.

The temperature in the apartment was hovering around thirty Fahrenheit, so as much as he complained, it could have been much worse. There were additional blankets and jackets that he could huddle about himself and, while not comfortable, were passable as warm. The real problem was that it was 07:00 PM on a Friday, and he had nothing to do until it was time to sleep.

Riley pulled his phone out and hid under the blanket while flipping through social media until a knock came at the door. The sound startled him, and he struggled to extricate himself from the blankets and walk to the door. Through the peephole, he saw the same veteran he'd met that morning. With a deep breath for calm, Riley opened the door. "Hey Marcus, didn't see you earlier."

"Yea, didn't want to cause you a problem at work."

"Don't worry about it. Do you want to come in? I don't have any heat, but at least it's out of the wind," Riley offered and stepped aside so the vagabond could enter.

Marcus stepped across the threshold and shook out the chill from his surplus jacket. "Thanks. It's starting to be a killer out there." He then hesitated before asking, "Were you able to find the insulin?"

"Right to business. Yeah, I got it. Here, give me a second." Riley moved to the refrigerator, retrieved the medication, and took the box of syringes from the counter. He returned to Marcus and said, "My boss caught me, so I don't know that I'll be able to do this again. Just make them count."

These items disappeared into a pocket of the veteran's jacket, and he nodded his understanding. "I gotcha, and yea, I normally don't eat enough for it to be a problem. Hate to impose, but could I crash here for the night? I have things set up for nights like this most of the time, but no one was home today."

Riley shifted uncomfortably and looked about at the meager belongings in his apartment. How much would Riley be out if the man took everything he owned? Would he suffer significantly if this man robbed him of all he was worth? He had nothing of value besides the computer and his phone, and neither was worth much. "Yea, that's fine. You can use the couch. I've got a couple of extra blankets, and who knows, maybe the heat will come back on."

"That would make this place a five-star hotel, but I'm happy just being out of the wind," Marcus said. Something forced Riley to hesitate, but his mind refused to acknowledge what it might have been. "Yea, I think that's the first time anyone has called my place five-star anything. But I can't offer you anything to eat, and assuming the pipes aren't frozen, then water's all I got to drink."

"That will all be just fine. I'll stay out of your way. You can do whatever it was you were doing before I interrupted your life. Although sitting alone in an apartment in the dark does not seem like a productive evening for a young man."

Riley sighed. "Well, I'm about one paycheck away from being your next-door neighbor in the gutter, so I don't have a lot of options in leisure activities."

"What about friends? Surely there are people you can call upon to spend time with. Friends don't always need to cost you money."

"I guess it depends on the types of friends you have. I'm starting to believe they're not interested in having me around at the moment."

Marcus shrugged and pulled his jacket closer about his shoulders while sitting on the couch. "That's their loss. There's a lot of potential in you I don't think they are seeing," he said with a grin that showed two rows of perfectly white teeth.

## CHAPTER 9

# DENIED IMPRIMATUR

Something about Marcus, especially his smile, brought back feelings in Riley as he tried to place where he'd seen this man before. Each time he attempted to reach back and gain a firm purchase of the memory, it slipped past his fingers. Riley continued to work at it. Eventually, he asked, "Do I recognize you from somewhere?"

The question only caused Marcus' smile to broaden and show more teeth. "We met once, not so long ago. I believe you and I discussed whether someone had the power to intervene in someone's death."

With those last words, the memory flooded back, and Riley recoiled from the image of the skinned hound and a terrifying night surrounding the deceased woman. Was this the same man with whom he'd had the conversation before those dogs arrived? "You!" he accused. "You did something to that woman in the booth."

Though he introduced himself as Marcus, his name was Azrael, and he did not appear insulted by the accusation. Azrael tilted his head to the side as the outburst came. "What do you think I did?"

"I saw you," and Riley attempted to put into words what he witnessed that night. Did he see anything? Riley took a seat at the kitchen table and sat facing Azrael. "You left the bar with her, but she didn't leave. Did you do something to my drink?"

"You went past several great leaps from me doing something to Rosa to me doing something to you. That was her name, as you didn't bother to ask." Azrael talked down to Riley and rebuked him for his behavior, both at the bar and then at the apartment.

This was all more than Riley signed up for when he agreed to steal medication, and things continued to spiral out of control with his life. "Were you responsible for those..." He stopped before describing the beasts to a stranger. There was always a risk that he had lost his mind or hallucinated. In retrospect, both options seemed plausible.

"No," Azrael answered, and Riley let out a breath he didn't know he was holding. Then Azrael continued, "I did nothing to your drink."

If a medical professional were monitoring Riley's vital signs, they would show concern about the hummingbird heart rate and balloon-bursting blood pressure. "And the dogs? What about them? Did you send those too?" Again, words failed him.

"You appear to be at a loss for words to describe what occurred. Perhaps you drank too much that night."

Riley waved his hand to swat away invisible gnats. "That's not it, and you know it. What did you do with that woman?"

"Rosa," Azrael reminded Riley, "Her name was Rosa Smith. She was seventy-eight years old and a Leo. It is important not to forget people who have passed from this world into the next."

"Whatever. What did you do?"

Azrael rose to his feet and towered over the seated Riley. His commanding voice filled the room. "Never disregard the dead! They are as important as the living. Everyone takes their chance at life and their rewards in death." After saying this, Azrael caught himself and regained his composure. "I'm sorry. It's a personal subject."

Although he attempted to lean back further in the chair, Riley had nowhere to go and cowered under the imposing figure of Death in a Vietnam surplus jacket. "Right, sorry. Rosa. I'm sure she was a wonderful woman, but the same question. Did you do something to her? What did you do to her? You left, but when I looked back, she was still sitting at the booth."

These words appeared to mollify Death, and he settled on the couch. "I, too, am sorry. I try not to let my emotions get the better of me. It's not healthy in my line of work to allow anger to control my actions."

Azrael again avoided the question. This appeared to be a recurring trend in conversations with the vagrant Riley invited into his home. "OK, what about a different question? If you could afford to be at the bar, are you really homeless?"

Again Riley posed a question Azrael did not prepare to answer. As he thought on it, his eyes drifted to the closed window blinds. "I suppose that is a matter of perspective. I don't own or rent an apartment or house, if that was your question."

Unsure what else he intended with the question, Riley shook his head in defeat. "Whatever, man. Talking to you is like trying to get answers out of a television tuned to the wrong station. How about this one?" he said before trying a different question. "Did you kill the woman? I'm sorry, Rosa. Is that what you're doing here? Honestly, at this point, I'm not sure that I care. Were you just going to rob the place?"

Azrael pulled back with his hand on his chest and a look of shock on his face. "I'm offended. I've never killed a person." How best to rephrase? "No one has ever died because of me."

"I'm not sure I liked that pause, but whatever. I'm sure some serial killers go through the same rationalization. What about me? Did you come here to rob the place?" Riley was fishing for any reason to distrust the man. Something did not sit right, but he couldn't put his finger on it.

"Do you have anything worth stealing?"

Riley considered his meager belongings for the second time that night and shook his head. "No, not really. I mean, you could take my phone, but it is not worth anything, and that computer might be scrap metal in a month or two."

Azrael followed the thought with, "And you have no money or other resources. You live here alone and struggle to get through life. Everything you do is only just enough to survive. You never accumulated enough things for someone to bother stealing from you."

"Are these guesses, observations, or insults?"

"A bit of the first two. I asked you for the insulin because I wanted to see your commitment. How willing are you to put the one thing of value you possess on the line for a stranger and risk being fired? Then when you came home, I asked you to go one step further and let me into your home, where you sleep. You put your life and all your possessions in my hands."

Riley had not thought about things in these terms but nodded his agreement. "Yea, I guess that is about the sum of it. So what's the point? I'm just some kind of world-class sucker."

Death squared himself on the couch and searched the empty room with his eyes to ensure they were still alone. "My point is, I am going to ask you to go one step further. You offered me nearly everything you thought was of value to your existence, but you were wrong. What I'm going to ask of you requires genuine commitment and danger beyond letting a potential serial killer sleep in your apartment."

Riley coughed as Azrael's assertion caught him off guard. "You're ridiculous. Look, I don't know what more you think I will do for you. But we're getting close to where I toss you into the cold and let nature take its course."

With a raised eyebrow, Azrael shook his head. "I don't believe you would. No. I'd be willing to wager you would have saved that woman at the bar the other night if given the ability.

"Yea, well, what could I have done? She was dead, and that is the end of her story."

"We'll get back to that," the man said without further elaboration. "What would you have done if the Ahemait arrived at the bar and you thought you could save the woman?"

The blank stare from Riley showed Azrael that he needed to explain further. "The Ahemait were those four-legged dog-like creatures that followed the smell of death. They were looking for Rosa and would have destroyed her if she were still there."

Nothing in Riley's mind appeared to be working quite right, and he spent most his mental energy blinking. Death waited for him to regain his senses and allowed Riley to speak next. "Those creatures were real?"

His house guest shrugged and considered the pattern of the herringbone couch. "I suppose that would depend on your definition of real, but yes."

"There's no way those things existed. They were monsters." Riley tried to describe a few of the finer points of the creatures. Instead, he found his tongue tied into knots, and his stomach lurched at the thought of the revolting thing. So he gave up. "But wait, you said 'if she was still at the bar.' I saw her. She never left." As he said this, the memory of Azrael walking out the door with Rosa recurred to his mind.

"So what was I seeing then?" Riley asked as he gave up on anything making sense while attempting to put the pieces together himself.

Azrael rose to his feet in the shifting shadows of the parking lot's street lamp and strolled to the kitchen. There he began rummaging through the cabinets while continuing the conversation. "What do you believe happens when you die?"

The shift in conversation caused Riley to adjust his chair and question why he never purchased a firearm. A weapon to defend his home against strange intruders seemed like a prudent investment at that point. Perhaps he would ask Clay about getting a gun when he next talked to the man. Clay would know where to buy a gun or at least gain one, even if no money was exchanged between them.

"When I die? I guess all my debt collectors get to fight over the twelve dollars left in my checking account," Riley said.

Azrael found the insulin inside the refrigerator and pocketed the vials in his jacket. "Not exactly what I meant. And thank you for this kindness. I'm asking instead what will happen to your soul after your body dies?"

Riley gave an indifferent shrug, though he continued to keep a close eye on the man sifting through the contents of his meager food supply. "I don't spend a lot of time thinking about it. Most of my day I spend trying to keep this body alive." He then hesitated before asking, "Why do you ask?"

"Everyone has a time of death. It may shift one way or the other as the Fates make their adjustments, but for the most part, it's immutable. There may be a chance to extend your life by a year or two, but generally, fate sets your time. Are you curious about how much time you have?"

Death closed the refrigerator and faced Riley. His eyes showed a glimmer of mischief in the offer of forbidden knowledge. Or was it something more? Azrael reached into his jacket and pulled out a book at least twice as large as should have fit in the coat. Cracked gray leather covered the book, and a clock with bronze hands was stamped on the front.

Under any other circumstance, Riley would have thrown the man out the door, but he was curious. What did the book hold? Something about the binding and glint of metal drew his eyes and would not release them. After such a long time that Riley swore the clock's hands had moved, he shook his head, "No. Who in their right mind would want to know that?"

Azrael put the book away. "Perhaps you're right. There is a gift in not knowing your future. I enjoy the occasional surprise myself, though they are hard to come by. Your rescue of young Master William was just such a remarkable event."

How many times would this man pull out information to shock

Riley? Was it his intent to push the young man's buttons? Riley recoiled and came to his feet. "OK, that's getting to be too much. I don't know how long you've been stalking me, but it's time you left."

"You'd throw a homeless man out in the cold? Someone who didn't secure shelter for the night will surely not survive with the temperature as it is." Again, Azrael tested the resolve of Riley and waited.

Riley stormed to the front door and unlocked the deadbolt, then opened the door. "I don't care. You can fend for yourself. It's not that much warmer in here, but you're seriously creeping me out. Everything is telling me you're going to stab me in the night."

Death strode through the room to stand in front of Riley and look down upon him. "You're quick to judge people, but answer me something."

He let the question hang in the air, which forced Riley to shift uncomfortably before asking. "What is it?"

"If I knew you would not die tonight, would you trade places with me? Would you go into the night to find somewhere warm? What if I told you that you would be safe, but I might perish?"

The first instinct was to yell at the man, but Riley thought better of himself and took a step back. Under the shadow of his house guest, he appeared tiny and unable to bring himself to raise his voice. "Show me."

Death brought the book from his jacket's pocket and opened it. As pages flipped in an unfelt wind, they settled on a chosen page and a hand-written ledger of names. Each name was on a single line, with a date of birth, death, and time. This would have been problematic enough, except the death times frequently changed as the ink erased itself and new numbers appeared.

Riley stared at the numbers and the dates. Then, as Death pointed his finger at Riley's name and traced over his date of birth, Riley woke up on the couch. The living room lights flickered on, and he heard the heater kick in. "Oh, what the hell?"

The clock on the wall showed 09:00 PM, and there was no sign that anyone else was in the apartment. Riley brought himself to his feet and scanned the room. He appeared to be alone, but this wasn't enough confirmation, so Riley moved deliberately through the apartment in search of the house guest with whom he had been talking. "OK, where did you go? What's going on here?"

No one was in the kitchen or bedroom, and the exterior door remained bolted, the windows locked. Whatever had occurred must have been a dream, though it left Riley's heart pounding in his chest. The situation was wrong. Something did not sit right. Riley checked the last place, the refrigerator, before deciding to call the search off.

Opening the door, he looked where the vials of insulin had sat, but they were gone. "OK, that's not funny," he said to the empty room. "Did he take them, or did I never steal them?" Riley next checked his jacket and found nothing in any coat pockets. Likewise, after he tore the place apart, looking for the small containers, he admitted that nothing was in his pants pockets, on the counter, or anywhere else in the apartment. The only thing he found was the box of syringes on the kitchen counter.

"Maybe I didn't take them. Was the whole day a dream? Did I even go to work today?"

It was too late at night to call Dr. Green and ask if he'd missed his shift. Riley checked his phone for any missed messages. He had not. So Riley figured it unlikely that he slept through the day. "I can't take much more of this."

Riley hesitated with the phone in his hand, but after waiting, he texted Glen, "Do you got a minute?"

There was no one else to ask, though Riley didn't know what he would ask his ex. Was there any way to confirm whether he was going crazy without flat-out asking people? "OK, let's inventory. Let's start with the dogs, or whatever they were. We also have the disappearing man who may not have been here, and now the missing medication I thought I stole from work. Did anyone else see any of this?"

The hounds were in a crowded bar with several other people, but Riley was the only one who appeared to notice their presence. So it was likely those either did not exist or no one saw them. What about insulin? Riley had the syringes, which Dr. Green recommended. Was there any other reason for the doctor to suggest he take home a box unless he knew Riley had stolen injectable medication? No, that didn't seem likely.

Given this information, he had the insulin at some point, and now it was gone, but not the syringes. What about the man who vanished? Perhaps he was in the apartment, and Riley was talking with him. Were they having a conversation and Riley blanked out the last bit of whatever they were discussing? "What were we talking about?"

Riley's phone buzzed before he could answer his question, and he looked at the screen. It was a text from Glen, which read, "Kinda busy at the moment. What's up?"

Riley said to himself, "Of course you're busy. I guess you're going to be busy every time I call for the next ten years, you backstabber." He felt his heart rate climb and took a minute to calm himself with a deep breath.

The text he sent back said, "...."

What was he supposed to send to Glen? "Should I tell him I had a bad dream and I need a hug? Something tells me he'll tell me to go 'F' myself." Riley considered his options. What if he told Glen that someone broke into his home? No, that would likely have the police at his place, and he didn't need that when he was stealing medication from work. That's when it occurred to him.

"Clay asked me to pick something up. Can you give me a ride to the bar?" Riley sat on the couch to wait for Glen's reply.

This plan seemed to be well rounded, except that Riley had not yet contacted Clay to see if the other man was interested in meeting for the exchange. Hell, he didn't even consider asking Clay if he would pick him up. That could have cut out an entire middleman. Whatever. He sent the text, and now Riley could only wait for a reply.

The clock marked the passage of time while Riley waited for his phone to vibrate. He almost gave up before Glen sent back a message. "Had to check with Clay, but yea, we can do that." Riley winced at Glen's mention of checking with Clay. "I'll be there in about an hour."

"Sounds great. I'll be here. Message me when you're outside."

No reply came after Riley's last message. He set the phone on the kitchen table after turning on the ringer to its loudest setting and plugging it in to charge. "So what do I wear to a drug deal?" he asked himself and walked upstairs to the closet.

There were many clothes to choose from, and Riley picked a pair of worn blue jeans and an old sports-team sweatshirt. He hung his work clothes in the bathroom and pulled out a couple of ratty running shoes. Riley glanced at himself in the mirror and said, "You're not winning any awards for best dressed. But who's judging?"

With an hour until Glen arrived, Riley used the rest of his time to cook a Starving Man dinner. The less-than-perfect meal of some reprocessed brown meat and potatoes checked the block of life-sustaining calories, but little else. His meal took a little less than thirty minutes. As he watched the clock tick past the hour mark, he thought, "And here is when we wait for Glen Time to catch up with reality."

Riley flipped through the online news headlines but found nothing of interest until the obituaries drew his attention once more. On a back page he read that Rosa Smith died at seventy-eight. "That has to be a coincidence," he said and read further. The article mentioned nothing about being found at a bar, but the date was correct. "Maybe I just read this, then dreamed about it."

It was a comfortable thought to believe he confused bits of reality with fantasy until he remembered the power had been out. He could not have read the news article before leaving for work, and after work, his computer had no internet. "OK, that is just getting creepy. But I've had enough strange shit for one week already. I don't know that I'm ready to scratch too much at the surface to see if there is more underneath."

Riley dropped the lid of his computer and set it aside before grabbing his phone and checking the time. His heart took a skip as the phone dinged just as he picked it up. A text from Glen showed on the screen with the simple message, "Out back."

# CHAPTER 10

# MORPHEUS

After locking the door behind him, Riley crossed the walk and slipped into Glen's passenger seat. "Thanks for the ride. I didn't want to have to find the money for another cab."

Glen put the compact into reverse before pulling out of the parking lot and onto the highway. The entire time, he paid more attention to the nonexistent traffic than Riley's statement and let the car's silence linger like the stale food smell that permeated the air. It wasn't until they were on the interstate that he said, "No, I got you. When you're looking to save a couple of dollars, it is easier to call a friend."

Riley winced at the bitter tone and attempted to read Glen's expression. Though Glen remained focused on the road and gave little away. "It wasn't like that."

"Oh? Please elaborate then. You were sitting at your apartment and thought, I would love a reason to call my good friend Glen, but instead, I'll use him to bum a ride." His words were ice, with a controlled tone. Glen wasn't yelling. He kept his emotions tight to his chest, but they showed through the cracks.

The mile markers drifted past Riley's window as he tried to think of what to say. "I had a bad dream." He had no other way to explain the situation.

Glen took his eyes off the road and focused on Riley, attempting to judge his friend's level of sincerity. "You're yanking me. You called because of a bad dream?"

With a shrug, Riley explained, "I met someone on the way to work. Well, I didn't meet in that type of way but bumped into. He asked if I would help him." Riley hesitated. "He needed medicine. So I helped him find what he needed."

Before the car drifted off the road, Glen returned his focus to the lines in front of him. He kept them there while continuing the conversation. "So you stole drugs to help some random guy you met on the street. Not a great idea, but whatever. I'm not your mother."

"Let me finish. I found him what he needed. Then he came back to the apartment, or at least I think he did. Everything got confusing at that point. He had a book of when everyone was supposed to die, and the medicine disappeared. I woke up on the couch, and now I'm not even sure if he came to the house."

Silence mixed with the sound of a small car engine and filled the vehicle as they rode down the interstate. Riley had nothing more to describe, and Glen did not respond to what Riley had said. Things continued this way for two miles before Riley pleaded, "Please say something."

"What should I say? Sounds like you had a bad dream, same as you said."

Riley bit his lip and tried to put his emotions into words. Nothing about the situation sat right with him. "Come on, Glen. You know me better than anyone else. That is not the kind of thing I dream about. Something's messed up."

"It's not the normal rainbows and fluffy clouds, no, but I'm not a therapist. I can't interpret your dreams. If I had to guess, I'd say that what you're doing for Clay is getting to you." Glen paused while he considered what to say beyond that point. "He hasn't told me everything, but I can piece things together. Are you sure you want to become involved with this type of thing?"

Riley shook his head as he expressed a desire to have nothing to do with the current situation, but life was not that simple. "Do I have a choice?"

"There's always a choice," Glen responded.

"It's just that he knew some things about me that if anyone found out, I would either lose my job or go to prison. Neither one sounds like a good option."

Glen shrugged and took a poorly lit exit towards the Iron Horse. "That is still a choice, even if you don't like the options. But I don't care."

Those last words struck Riley across the face and he turned towards Glen. "What do you mean, you don't care?"

"Just that. It's not my problem. Look, you had years to stay in touch and tell me about your bad dreams and how you were feeling. I'm not about ready to let you in because you moved closer. Phones work no matter how far away you are."

Arguing with Glen would be easier if he were wrong. Riley sat in his seat with his mouth agape as he tried to put together a compelling argument. "You're with Clay. I understand that. It doesn't mean we can't be close."

Glen's car pulled into the Iron Horse parking lot. As the gravel ground under Glen's tires, he put the car into park and turned to face Riley. "Yes, it does. Don't you understand? I can't be with two people. Life doesn't work like that. Sure, we can be friends but only friends with other people around. You can't have me showing up at your apartment in the middle of the night. It only worked this time because we were coming here to meet Clay."

While Riley didn't want to understand what Glen was talking about, it made sense, and Riley lowered his head. "I just want things to be different. It feels like everyone I've known is gone, and I'm left with a hometown where I don't know anyone anymore."

Glen reached over and squeezed Riley's hand. "I understand. I do. But life goes on, even when you're not there."

Riley looked at the hands of two former lovers before Glen pulled back and nodded his understanding. "Everything may work out OK."

"That's the spirit. It will turn around. Now, before we go in, check yourself in the mirror." Glen gave Riley a chance to remove any tear stains from his face and straighten out his clothes. He then asked, "Do you have what Clay asked you to bring?"

Riley thrust his hand into the pocket of his jacket and felt the plastic container. "Oh, thank God."

"Good. I don't know what you two have arranged, but Clay does not like people jerking him around. Terrific guy when he's in a good mood, but avoid him any other time." Glen then popped his door and stepped out into the chilly night air.

Out of the corner of his eye, Riley caught sight of movement. His head spun, and he saw the outline of a large dog standing at the far end of the parking lot. It had been watching the bar, or perhaps Glen's car. When the two exited, it turned and ran into the darkness.

Riley pointed to where the animal had been. "Did you see that?"

"What?" Glen asked while catching the hint of fear.

Nothing remained, and there was only emptiness for Riley to show Glen, so he shook his head and said, "Never mind. Let's go inside. I don't want to be out here any longer than we have to."

The two of them pushed past a row of polished motorcycles and entered the smoke-filled establishment. It was early on a Friday night, with only half the tables occupied. Riley expected it would be an hour or less before the place became standing room only. A scan of the room revealed Clay sitting in their usual booth, the one Riley had begun to think of as belonging to the other man.

He was alone with a pitcher of beer and three glasses, one of which was half full. It is possible it had initially been filled and now was half emptied. Riley didn't look for his friend with the perfect teeth. Instead, he turned in the table's direction once the pair crossed the bar's threshold. Together, they joined Clay and slipped into his booth.

Glen scooted onto the seat beside Clay and gave him a deliberate kiss on the lips before filling his glass. It took everything Riley had not to turn and walk back out of the bar as his former boyfriend engaged with another man. His instincts told him to scream something inappropriate and leave, but he endeavored to remain calm.

"Hey Clay, how are things?" Riley asked between clenched teeth.

Clay filled the third glass and pushed it over to Riley. "Things have been good. Business picked up last week, which makes everyone happy. Cold weather has a way of bringing out the shopping spirit in people. I guess that is their way of trying to escape the family."

The cheap beer filled Riley's glass but did little to settle his nerves. He attempted several additional swallows to check if volume would solve what quality did not. "I guess that is one way to escape the holidays."

"Exactly," Clay agreed and gave cheers with his glass, though none of them clinked together. "So, what have you and Glen here been chatting about? You could have called me for a ride if you wanted to talk business."

There was a measure of discomfort from Glen as he shifted in his seat, but he remained silent and focused on his drink. Riley said, "I guess nothing, really. Just trying to catch up on old times. I know you two met in high school, but I don't remember you ever hanging out with the rest of us."

Riley did not intend his tone to be as accusatory or challenging as it came out, but Clay's eyes narrowed, and he watched his opponent across the table. "Perhaps he didn't think your little group was something to advertise." The statement hung with the bar's noise while none of the three spoke.

After a minute of what passed for silence in the crowded room, Clay broke into a smile and laughed. "I'm just hanging you. No, since we were on the team together, I guess he got enough of me at practice, so we never thought about doing anything else until after the games stopped." Something about his smile was too broad and friendly to be reliable. "Then you left, and we started spending more time together."

"That makes sense, I guess. And then you two started dating after that." Riley attempted to push the question one step further.

Clay reached an arm around Glen and pulled the man in close. "That's right," he said, while staring at Riley. "You left. We didn't."

Glen said, "Was there some business you two wanted to discuss? Or was this all about memory lane?"

With a snap of his fingers, Clay pointed back at Riley. "That's right. You said you did some shopping for me earlier. Did you find anything interesting?"

This was only the second time in Riley's life that he had exchanged illegal drugs with someone, so his eyes darted around the room. Of course, when he gave the medicine to the little girl, that was also illegal. He only had a lesser chance of going to jail. And then there was the matter of the insulin. But those seemed different somehow than the exchanges with Clay. "Do we have to keep doing this stuff out in the open like this?"

The people in the bar had paid no attention to any of the men after entering. The regulars only cared that they did not occupy the only working pool table. With the three in an infrequently used booth, no one bothered with them. Clay motioned to the indifferent room. "What here? No one gives a flying leap. I bet someone could die in their beer, and no one would find out until closing time."

Riley' face blanched at this statement, and his eyes snapped around to the booth where Rosa had her last drink. "Yea, about that."

Clay followed Riley's eyes and put the pieces together before saying, "Oh snap, you were here when they found the body, weren't you? That's baller."

"It's not as perfect as you make it out to be, but yes, I was the one who noticed she was dead." Riley gave an involuntary shiver as he remembered not the body of the woman but the two skinned monsters who'd followed her into the building. And one of those creatures had been out front tonight when he and Glen arrived to meet with Clay. "Can we speed this up? I don't feel comfortable here."

Clay studied Riley for a lingering moment. "Do you know something you're not sharing with the rest of the class?"

Riley had shifted from socially uncomfortable to genuine fear, and he did not hear Clay's question. His mind drifted far away from the conversation. It wasn't until the other man knocked on the table and asked again that he answered, "No. I just remembered seeing someone outside that I don't necessarily want following me into the bar."

It was the truth, although he didn't try to explain that the someone was a six-foot demon hound without skin. Clay kept his eyes locked on Riley, even while he milled over the kernel of doubt. "Fine, keep your secrets. So let's get this over. What did you bring with you tonight?"

No longer concerned with who in the bar might report him to the authorities, Riley pulled the unlabeled pill bottle from his pocket and set it on the table. Clay reached for his beer, but his hand went too far and came back with the bottle instead. He pocketed the newly acquired pills. "So what are they?"

Riley provided the first answer that came to mind, which was the one from his school textbook, "hydromorphone two milligrams."

"That's great. Now, if you could put that in English, that would be outstanding," Clay requested while showing the beginnings of someone who was losing their patience.

"The drug is an opioid painkiller, moderate dose. It is intended to be used every four to six hours," Riley answered, and tried to think of anything he could add for clarity. "Kinda like an updated form of morphine."

This last description appeared to do the trick, and Clay cracked a smile. "Oh, yea, that will do nicely. I know just the right guys for that one. See, I knew you were a resourceful guy," he said and refilled Riley's glass. "Now on to the next order."

"What do you mean? I thought that was it. What more do you want me to do other than tell you when something becomes available?" Riley asked, looking back and forth between Clay and Glen.

Clay shook his head and answered, as if explaining things to a small child. "Oh, no, that is not how things work. You see, I have customers who need regular shipments, and I can't leave them hanging. You're going to have to help me find them what they want most for the holidays."

Everything was getting to be a bit much, and Riley's only option to delay the conversation was to drink more of the somewhat warm, poor-quality light beer. He tried to put his thoughts together and ask, "What exactly are they looking for?"

"A little of this and some of that. But you mentioned morphine a minute ago, and I got to thinking," Clay put on an expression meant to mimic contemplative thought. "I know some guys that could use that kind of thing for their pain."

"Of course, they must be in so much pain." Riley disliked these clients as they claimed pain rather than drug addiction. He tried to guess the rest of the story's plot. "You want me to get more pills like the ones I got you."

The table was silent while Clay pretended to consider this and shook his head. "No, I don't think that will do it. These particular clients are going to want something a little more personal. How do you think you'd do at finding them injectable morphine?"

Riley ran his fingers through his hair and tried to steady his thoughts before explaining. "You know why I did the first batch. I couldn't say no to that request. As for this delivery, I needed the money, but I can't keep doing it, especially if it's not on my schedule. It quickly gets hazardous."

Clay reached into his pocket and pulled out a roll of bills. It was twice as massive as the first, and he set it on the table. "Your choice, my friend. But if you're looking to make some money, this is the way to do it."

Riley's eyes fixated on the roll while his hand reached out to draw it back into his pocket. He needed to keep the heat on in his apartment, and this was the only option he saw. "Maybe," he started to say and trailed off as he thought about the problem. "We're finishing an inventory. I'll see if I can do any fancy math with what's left on the sheet. Who knows what will come up missing, and your friends might get lucky."

A smile creased Clay's lips, and he elbowed Glen, "See. I knew he was a team player. We'll be amazed what he'll be able to do once that old joker kicks it, and he takes over the store for himself."

The casual discussion of Dr. Green's death struck Riley, and he focused back on the now empty glass of beer. Riley had finished the business he came to conduct. He wasn't friends with Clay, so there was no reason to remain at the bar chatting with these two. "It's getting late, and I have work in the morning. Hey, Glen, think you could give me a ride back to the apartment?"

Glen fired back, "Call a cab. You've got money now."

Clay set a calming hand on Glen's knee. "Easy, killer. I have a couple of people I need to talk to, so this could be a good time to break up the band." He then turned back to Riley, his hand still on Glen's leg. "You know you're welcome to come out here to the bar any time to hang with everyone. Though you should look into finding yourself a car, so you don't go broke on cab rides. You can't expect Glen to help you every time you want a night out."

Glen hugged Clay and kissed goodbye before exiting the booth. "Let's get out of here. If the rest of the night is going to be ruined, I want to get home at a decent hour."

Riley winced as his stomach twisted into knots, hearing Glen refer to spending time with him as a ruined evening. Clay might have offered to let him hang out with the group, but the more Riley thought about it, the less it seemed like a good idea. "Thanks for the beer. I'll shoot you a text when I find out about the other stuff."

All he got in response was a smile before Clay pulled out his phone and no longer paid attention to the two leaving the bar. Riley exited the bar first, and it was nearly two minutes before Glen followed. Riley didn't care what held him up and never asked for clarification.

Glen asked, "You ready?"

Riley rolled his eyes as he had been ready and standing in the cold but held back a snarky comment. "I'm good. Let's just get back home. I am still not comfortable out here."

The car pulled off the gravel road and onto the interstate before Glen said anything. "So what spooked you back there?"

"What do you mean? I'm good; just Clay is asking me to do something crazy dangerous. I can go to serious jail, and I'm not crazy about becoming Bubba's best friend."

Glen shook his head without changing lanes. "Not what I was talking about. Before we went into the bar, you saw something. Is someone after you?"

How should Riley have answered that question? He wanted to tell Glen everything but didn't want to sound crazy. There was also Riley's attempt to tell Glen about his dream and the other man brushing the entire event off as unimportant. Would he think this just as silly?

In the end, Riley shrugged. "I don't know. Maybe it was an ex-girlfriend."

"See, now you're lying to me," Glen said and struck Riley in the shoulder. "But whatever, you can keep your secrets. We all have things we don't want to share with others. Just remember that I'm not the bad guy in this. We're all trying to live our lives."

The rest of the ride was without meaningful conversation as they talked about other kids from high school and where they ended up. It seemed most of them moved one town over in search of new jobs. This meant they were still close, but not always around. It was better than nothing. Glen's car pulled into the apartment's parking lot, and Riley got out.

No black dogs loitered in the distance, and he didn't notice any vagabond men waiting to ask him for insulin. Everything appeared as it should be. The night had a sense of peace to it, and as he considered the calm in the air, it began to snow.

"It is kinda beautiful," he said to himself before seeing the owl perched lamppost at the edge of the parking lot. Riley stared up at the bird through the drifting snow, and the owl looked down at him. It made no sound, not a cry or a fluttering of feathers, as it took to flight and disappeared into the night.

## CHAPTER 11
# 'IN FOR A PENNY

Friday night left, and Saturday morning arrived, both without fanfare. The sun rose to reveal a landscape blanketed in an inch of wet snow. The cold temperatures fought against any liquid water, which then became an ice-crusted shell covering everything. Riley had the foresight to set his phone and use the included alarm feature. He woke to what he thought was an incoming call. After trying to answer his alarm clock, he roused himself and readied for the morning.

There was always guesswork of what to do when the weather turned cold. Some places like to keep the thermostat down to save money. Others prefer comfort and raise the temperature to unbearable levels. Both options had incompatible clothing options. Riley could only guess what Dr. Green would do with his pharmacy. He eventually decided to wear the same attire he wore the day before and trusted that the temperature inside the shop would be constant regardless of outside weather.

As for coats, he had one option, and Riley pulled it over his shoulders while looking for breakfast. The cereal was running low. Despite that, the box had enough for a couple more days, so he filled a bowl and sat in front of his computer. Last night appeared to have been slow for news, and nothing locally was reported. National news continued to cover politicians arguing over how to improve America and which people had a right to live in the country. It didn't sound like anyone was making any progress.

Riley had developed a habit of reading the obituaries over the last few weeks, and he checked to see if anyone he knew appeared on the morning list. There were no familiar names, but a car wreck along the interstate caught his attention, and he read further. Around 09:30 PM last night, Joel Walsh, age 23, drove his Nissan Cima past a guard rail and impacted a tree on the side of the road. Paramedics transported Mr. Walsh to the County Community Hospital and pronounced him dead.

The time stuck in Riley's head as he read the article a second time. That was about the same time he and Glen arrived at the Iron Horse. The exact time he saw the demon dog. What did the man call those things? Ahemait.

Riley slapped the computer lid shut and, as he stood, closed his jacket tighter about his shoulders. "That's not something I need to think about. Maybe my mind is running away with crap again. Probably the emergency lights or something."

Riley left his apartment without another thought of the incident and walked to work. It was a dangerous journey as the roads were slick. After the first hundred feet, he discovered it safer to walk in on the snow-covered grass instead of on the icy street. Riley was late and out of breath when he reached the parking lot. Then everything came to a stop.

The doctor's car sat in its usual handicapped spot, but a second vehicle was in the lot that morning. No one ever showed up at the pharmacy that early, as they were not technically open. Riley walked closer to the unfamiliar car and glanced inside. This vehicle belonged to someone in law enforcement, as it had the quintessential radio mounted under its dash and a stack of paperwork in the passenger seat.

On any other day, the presence of this car would not have been an issue. Cops have as much right and reason to pick up their pills at a pharmacy as anyone else. The problem was this officer arrived before hours and on the day after Riley stole controlled medication for a second time. "I guess running home and hiding under the bed isn't an option."

He squared his shoulders and walked into the store. An electronic ding announced his presence, and he called out as he did every morning, "It's me, Dr. Green." Riley moved on autopilot to the employee break room to switch his jacket for the doctor's coat. He prayed that whatever purpose the officer had, it did not involve him.

These hopes dashed against the rocks when Green called to him, "Can you join us in the back? We have a man here who would like to ask you a couple of questions."

The ice that shot down Riley's spine did nothing to relieve the chill from the cold air. "Yes, sir. I'll be right back!"

Riley took several deep breaths to steady his nerves and tried to think if there were any lies he could tell that would let him off the hook. If this cop was here for him, then he might have nearly anything on him. Riley had no way of knowing how much evidence he had left for someone to follow. They had caught him in only a week. "Not much of a master thief, are you?"

Behind the pharmacy counter, Dr. Green spoke with a person Riley didn't recognize. This new gentleman was wearing a poorly fitted sports coat and slacks. He had a button-up shirt but no tie, and when he saw Riley, he offered the same type of smile Riley expected from real estate agents. "Mr. Brewer, good morning. How are you?"

Riley did his best to jump into the conversation. "I'm doing well, I suppose. The weather could be better. Things got a bit cold last night with the power going out."

The man didn't seem to notice anything Riley said, or perhaps didn't think any of it important. He didn't appear to care that Riley did anything more than respond. "That's terrific. So, I wondered if you and I could take a minute and have a conversation in private. I talked with Dr. Green, and he's filled me in on what's been going on. But I'd love to hear things from your perspective."

Nothing sat right. This man was overly friendly and had not introduced himself or said what he came to talk about. Every warning signal in Riley's mind fired and while he wanted to run, he had nowhere to go. "Yea, sure. We can. I guess. Walk up to the front. Not many private places in the store where we can talk. It's a small space."

"You know what, I was thinking about that," the man in business clothes said and turned to Dr. Green. "Would you mind if I borrowed Mr. Brewer here for a minute? I can bring him right back when we finish our little talk. Promise to have him back by the lunch rush."

No one bothered to ask Riley if he wanted to go anywhere, but he suspected his opinion did not factor into this conversation, so he remained quiet. "I suppose that is OK. Riley, just ensure you have my phone number so you can call if you're going to be late."

There was more in what Dr. Green said, and Riley heard the offer of support. He gave a nod of understanding and turned to follow the stranger out of the store. "So where are we going, and do I need to call a lawyer first?"

Riley expected the man would turn to Mr. Hyde as he caught him in the ruse, but his smile grew more prominent. "Oh, no. Well, not yet, anyhow. How about this? I'll tell you when you need a lawyer, and you tell me when you want a lawyer."

Riley expected to ride in the back of the car, but when the man motioned to the front passenger seat and cleared room for him, he climbed in. "Sorry about all the papers. I've been working out of my car this last week rather than the office."

He climbed into the driver's seat and pulled out a billfold with a gold badge on one side and what looked like an oversized passport on the other. Besides a photograph of the man, the card showed his name and agency. "Let me introduce myself properly. I'm Special Agent Charles Coronado with the Drug Enforcement Agency." He put the wallet back in his pocket and started the car.

"Am I under arrest? Because this is feeling uncomfortable right about now." Riley watched as the pharmacy slipped farther into the distance behind them. The car appeared to head toward Wytheville, or at least in that direction. It also would take them past the Iron Horse for an early morning beer, but that was unlikely.

The agent shook his head. "No. At least not at this point in the game. You see, we're in an interesting position with one case we're working and thought you might help put us back in the right direction."

Riley relaxed as it didn't sound like he was going to jail that Saturday, though it was still early and anything could happen. "How can I help? Is it something about the pharmacy? Dr. Green is above board. I haven't seen anything but professionalism and competency from him."

"Oh, no. He's been great. Other than paperwork legible and on time, I couldn't complain about him or his pharmacy. This is more about your new patient, Laura Willis."

As he said the name, it took a long moment for Riley's brain to trace back and find where he'd heard it. Then it occurred to him that this woman didn't exist other than as a fictitious name, created for him to steal Clay's drugs. "Son of a bitch," he muttered.

Charles let the moment hang before saying, "Now, before we go any further, I want to settle a few things. I've talked this over with the prosecutor's office, and they don't care about what you did unless you did something out-of-bounds crazy that we're not aware of. We're talking about if you murdered someone and you just decide to bring it up in a passing conversation. At that point, everyone would start to care."

Riley did the only thing his mind allowed him to do, which was to nod his head and follow along with the conversation. "But I'm not going to jail?"

"You're pretty fixated on that part. How about this? You're not under arrest and can leave any time you want."

This was close enough to not going to jail, so Riley accepted it and listened to the rest of what Charles said. "With that in mind, nothing you say is going to be held against you. When we reach the station, I'll have you make a statement of all the things you can tell us without us holding them against you. As I said, this is not your As-Seen-on-TV type of moment."

"So I'm not going to jail. I can leave, and you're not going to interrogate me. Sounds good, except you're spending a lot of time being very clear that this is not something. What is it?"

"Right, so the last piece to settle is if at any point you want to consult with a lawyer before you go any further, tell someone. Does all this make sense? Do you need any of it explained further or in another language?" At first, Riley thought the last part was condescending, but judging by the earnest expression on the driver's face, this appeared to be part of some rehearsed script.

"No, I'm good. So what is this all about?"

"We need you to sell drugs to your buddy from the bar one more time."

Everything made sense as the last piece of the puzzle snapped into place. They wanted Riley to do something they'd already caught him doing. But this time, it was to prove that the other person was involved. "Why do you care so much about him? I thought cops went after the dealers, not the users. It seems you know who the dealer is."

"You? Oh, no, not even close. Relax, kid. You're such a small fish in all this. The only thing you should worry about is losing your license. No, Clay has dozens of other sources of supply, and then he does his distribution. He's effectively a middleman for a sizable chunk of the drug deals in the county."

Riley quickly considered his motivations. It would be nice to believe that he helped law enforcement out of a sense of civic duty. Or perhaps to save himself from prison. That would be understandable. However, when he thought about why he would agree with the plan, he had to admit it was a way to hurt the man who had stolen his boyfriend. "I'll do it. Just tell me what I need to do."

Charles turned to judge Riley's level of commitment. "OK, good.

Now, this may be dangerous. I'll do everything I can to keep you safe, but there will always be some risk."

What was life without risk? Riley nodded. "I get it. But he's done some terrible things." Like assuming he could be Riley's substitute when he left. "One favor to ask, however."

Considerations were not unexpected, so Charles waited for Riley to make his demands before committing. "You'll not be paid if that's what you were about to ask. At most, I can comp a meal if you meet somewhere with food."

"No, nothing like that. Though it would be great if I could keep my job and keep the lights on, but that's not your problem, is it?" Riley didn't mean it to sound as bitter as it came out. Awkward silence filled the room as he waited to judge the response.

"There's always the option of going to jail. Three meals and a place to sleep. Tell me if you want to take us up on that offer instead."

"Forget I asked. But no, there's another guy, Glen. Is there any way we can make sure he stays out of this?"

Charles didn't appear ready to answer the question and asked, "Who's this new guy?"

"He's..." Riley hesitated. "He's a good friend of both of us, and I just don't want him getting mixed up in something like this. I don't think he knows anything about what Clay does, but I want to make sure he doesn't get wrapped up in everything."

"Again, no promises. You'll get very few promises from me, and if they're not in writing, take them with a grain of salt. At this point, I don't have any people of interest named Glen. It's unlikely we would suddenly add him to the case unless he was wherever the transaction took place or where Clay gets arrested."

Riley bit his lip. Glen could be at either location. There was no way to guarantee his absence, but this was the best he would get. "Thank you. Maybe I can persuade him to stay away."

The agent's car drove past the police station, and Riley turned in his seat. A brick building with its three street-facing garage doors rolled past his window. "Did we miss a turn?"

"Not exactly," Charles answered, and continued down the road. "We're going a little farther to the office. You never know who is going to be in lockup, and I'm not ready to advertise that you're in our corner."

They continued six more blocks and pulled into a parking lot with a large blue sign advertising the Virginia State Police Area Office. Riley exited the car with Charles, and together they entered the building from the back, where Charles ushered him into what appeared to be a seldom-used office. The only furniture that remained in the room from its previous occupant was their desk, a chair, and a very uncomfortable couch.

"Wait here. I need to check in with the chief before we go too far. Don't go wandering. I didn't get you a visitor pass, and I don't want to have to come find you in that little room they call a jail because they thought you snuck in."

The instructions were simple enough, and Riley nodded without thinking hard about his situation. It wasn't until Charles left that he realized he should have asked where the restroom was. There was always time to ask those questions later. Instead, he took a glance about the spartan office, found nothing of interest, and sat on the couch. The furniture was exactly as uncomfortable as it looked.

A clock above the door showed 10:45 PM for the fifteen minutes that Riley waited for Charles to return with another officer. This new individual wore a standard police uniform, though he did not have the utility belt and body armor that Riley usually saw officers wearing on the street. "Mr. Brewer, this is Sergeant Moon. He's officially running the investigation with the DEA's support."

Riley climbed to his feet as fast as the couch allowed, though it looked as awkward as a calf's first steps. "Sergeant Moon, a pleasure to meet you," Riley said, and offered his hand.

The look returned by Moon was less than friendly, but he shook the hand just the same. This stoic, nail-eating facade stood in sharp contrast to Charles, and Riley took a moment to adjust. "Yes, well, I understand there may be something I can help with?" Riley tried asking.

"Take a seat, Mr. Brewer," Sergeant Moon directed, and took the chair behind the desk. With the barricade between himself and Riley, he set a closed manila folder on top and gave the other men time to sit. "I assume Agent Coronado has filled you in on the situation and your options if you choose not to assist our investigation."

Nothing about this man's demeanor was friendly or outgoing, and Riley swallowed hard while attempting to adjust himself to a new style of encounter. "Yes, sir. I help or go to jail or something to that effect."

"That's a succinct way to put it," the sergeant said, then pulled a typed memo from the folder. "This is a letter written by you, which you will sign, describing the criminal activities in which you are involved. It says you are giving this information in exchange for immunity from the statements you are providing."

Moon took a deep breath and seemed to relax a bit. "Look, I'll try to sum this up without going down the lawyer rabbit hole. We need to know what you do, and we want your help to do some things that would, in normal situations, not be legal. This acknowledges we will not use your statements or actions against you provided they are limited to this operation. You step outside what's written on the sheet, and all bets are off."

Riley was no stranger to reading documents in a hurry and had finished with the first two pages by the time the sergeant concluded his explanation. "This makes sense," he finished reading the rest of the statement and waited for instructions. "Do you need me to sign it now, or do I wait?"

Moon stared at him. "Now, please."

Riley signed the document and slid it back across the desk. "Now, what information are you looking for from me? From the agent here, it sounds like you already know more than I do."

"I don't think you're paying attention to the situation. You may be educated, but don't for a second think you're smart," Moon began his statement. "Your friend is using you to buy drugs that he sells to addicts. Clay sits in the middle and collects money with minimal risk. He has dozens of cherries just like you all over Wytheville and the surrounding area. What we need from you is what drugs he is looking to buy, when he needs them, and where the deal is happening."

This was not surprising information, but being told he was stupid took the wind out of his sails. Not that he hadn't considered the same fact when he was selling drugs to make the rent after graduating from pharmacy school. "He wants injectable morphine but didn't specify which type; he probably doesn't know the different types, which makes it that much more dangerous."

The sergeant wrote this information on a notepad pulled from his breast pocket. "Did he give a day by which he needed this or a quantity?"

Riley shook his head. "Nothing that specific. He just left it up to me to see what I could come up with. I didn't know he was running a drug empire. He didn't appear to be on any timetable with customers or whatnot."

More notes appeared on the notepad. Charles asked, "If we acquired an amount of these drugs, could you facilitate another trade with Clay?"

"I suppose so. It was pretty easy the last time. I just called him up and asked to meet with him, and we made the trade, then went home. You sure you want me doing this? I'm not the best poker player in the world."

Charles glanced at the sergeant, and they appeared to consider their options without speaking out loud. After a moment, the sergeant nodded, and Charles turned back to Riley. "OK, here's what we're going to do then. I'll drive you back to work, so you're not missing for too much longer. I can also talk with Dr. Green about the medication. You'll get a text about which drugs and how much to take, then you go about doing the exchange the same as you would if we weren't involved."

Things sounded simple, but that did not always mean a good plan. It only meant there were fewer moving pieces to go wrong, though one of those parts could still be a problem. "What then? I tell you guys where he wants to meet and you go arrest him?"

"Not exactly. I mean, yes, text us and let me know where and when, but you'll need to be there to sell Clay the drugs. None of this will work if he doesn't buy from you."

"Will I have to wear a wire?"

"Oh no, we have a workaround for that. It's an app now. Think of it as police pocket dial," Sergeant Moon offered with a smirk.

Riley took a deep breath and let it out slowly. "I suppose there is not going to be any better offer. Let's get this over."

# CHAPTER 12

# MAGIC HOUR

The text Riley received was straightforward and to the point, with an exact lot number for each vial the police wanted Riley to remove. Regarding Green's involvement in the situation, Riley was unsure how much Agent Coronado had briefed the doctor on the operation and decided not to bring it up. If Green wanted to know something, he would have to ask. Riley had no intention of volunteering to give any information. After thinking things over, Riley realized his boss likely was trying to decide when to fire him for the original theft.

Riley would need to deal with the repercussions of his actions after all this was over. Sure, law enforcement said they would let him go, but that didn't mean his boss would do the same. It then occurred to him. The police never said they wouldn't prosecute, only that they wouldn't use his testimony against him. This still had the potential of ending in an arrest.

Riley finished the day with this lighthearted thought. Dr. Green left for lunch as expected, and during this time Riley moved the medication identified by the police into his jacket pocket. The rest of the day proved to be more waiting out the clock than productivity, and as of 6:00 PM, Riley quickly switched out his coats and left.

Before he made his way out the door, Dr. Green caught up with him and put a hand on his shoulder. "Hold up a moment," he said, his voice calm and measured. "I don't know everything going on in your world right now. If you make it through everything and come out the other end alive and a free man, come talk with me. Everything here at the shop has been building to something more. I didn't hire you just to stock shelves, and I'm not going to keep doing this job forever."

Riley didn't say what he thought, but he nodded his understanding. "You got it, Dr. Green. And sorry about all this coming down right after I started working here. I thought for sure you were going to fire me the moment you found out."

"I may still. We need to find out about your license, but I know what you tried to do for that family. You screwed up about as big as anyone can, but your heart is in the right place. I would rather trust someone who made mistakes and learned than a person who's never taken a risk in their life." He said this last part and gave Riley's shoulder another squeeze before letting him go, then walked back to the store.

Under normal circumstances, Riley would have waited until he arrived home to text anyone, as his fingers were at risk of freezing in the cold. Instead, he shot a brief message to Clay, "I'm ready when you are." Riley stuffed his hands and phone into his pocket and continued the walk home over the crunching snow.

The phone buzzed, and Riley pulled it out to read the message. "Great to hear. I'll let you know later when we can meet."

That did not help. Riley wanted to be through with this entire situation, and it sounded as if Clay had better things to do than spend time with his petty drug dealer. Riley stuffed the phone back into his pocket and hesitated before turning onto the walk to his apartment. He continued straight and walked the distance to The Kitchen. "If I'm going to go to jail, I'm eating first."

What accounted for an evening rush hour was finishing up, and several tables were still open as Riley entered the diner. A woman from behind the cash register called over to him with, "Pick any spot, hon. I'll be with you in a minute."

Even with plenty of spaces to choose from, the place did not attract enough of a crowd to boast an ample selection of tables. Riley sat at the closest approximation of a back corner and took up the laminated single-page menu. The same woman from the register, whose name tag declared her to be Kate, approached the table and asked, "So what you want, hon?"

"I'll take whatever the soup is and a water, please." Even with the money from Clay, he still needed to live on a tight budget. So he stuck with the items he knew he could afford.

If Riley had dressed to match his income rather than his job, he might have garnered enough sympathy for a free meal. Instead, Kate just stared at him and departed without another word. The rest of the meal was without fanfare, and when he left, he only left a fraction of the expected tip. She was kind enough not to offer profanity, and while Kate did not ask him to 'come back any time,' staff did not chase Riley out of the diner.

With the sun now altogether below the horizon, Riley walked back to the apartment in a huff. "I can eat canned soup in my home without being called cheap and worthless. Next time, I'll stay there instead of going out for the public to judge me. What can I expect? None of them care. Who would care if I froze to death in my apartment? No one, that's who, not until the landlord came to evict me."

He slammed the door shut behind him and left his coat on in the hope that he would eventually warm after the snowy walk. Riley pulled out his phone and noticed he had missed a text after leaving the diner. It said, "Let's meet tonight. Meet me at the Tractor Supply on Lee Hwy at 3 am."

The time made Riley do a double-take. That was not so much this evening as tomorrow morning, and part of him wanted to reschedule for another night if it would be that late. The other part told him to agree to anything, so he texted back, "OK."

Riley's following text went to Agent Coronado. "Tonight, 3 AM at the Tractor Supply."

No text came back from Charles for the longest time, and he wondered if he should text again. It was possible the message was lost, although it said 'delivered' on the trim line under his text. Before he sent anything more, a message came back with, "Approved."

Riley's eyebrow shot up as he looked at the screen. "Oh, I didn't realize I was asking for permission on that one. I thought I was telling them what was happening. Good thing it's approved then. I would hate to piss off the drug dealer I'd just agreed to meet, given that he knows where I live and everything. How do people do this for a living?"

Either way, there was little more for him to do before meeting Clay. Work was over, he had the drugs, he'd eaten. The last thing for him to do was to catch a few hours of sleep before waking way too early in the morning. "At least I don't have to work tomorrow. I think I would call in sick if I did. There's no way I'm showing up to work after going through all this bull."

Riley set the alarm on his phone before he curled up on the couch with his jacket still held tight about his shoulders and drifted off to sleep.

The phone alarm went off at 2:00 AM, and Riley resisted an urge to toss the source of aggravation across the room. He swiped the screen and dragged himself from the couch. Originally, the plan was to doze on the couch, so it would be easier to wake at the ungodly early hour, but the plan had failed, and he was as tired as if he had slept anywhere else.

Riley threw cold water in his face and drank what remained of a flat Dr. Lightning in the fridge. It wasn't a lot, but it was better than nothing. Riley pulled out his wallet and counted the bills. "This may be a gas-station morning," he said to himself before replacing the wallet and bouncing on his feet twice to get the blood flowing.

Outside, it was miserably cold. On the plus side, a fresh dusting of snow fell from the sky and gave traction to the otherwise slick, ice-crusted mess left from the night before. Riley first stopped at the gas station where he purchased a Mega Caffeine beverage, and despite it being cold when he'd have preferred warmth, he drank it. "That and a walk should get things going."

He checked the time, 02:30 AM. The walk from his apartment to the Tractor Supply took roughly a half-hour on a good day. He was cutting it close. Ideally, he would have biked the distance, but that remained out of the question with the night's weather. Regardless of the odds, he braced into the wind and headed out into the cold.

No cars were on the roads. Riley could only guess whether that was because of the weather or because no one else ever wandered around awake at that hour. He never explored the town at that time of night. There was no reason for anyone to be here so many hours before sunrise.

As he feared, the walk took forty-five minutes rather than thirty, and he arrived far later than he would have preferred. The Tractor Supply was a simple metal building with rows of bucket loaders, bulldozers, and other tractors in front and on both sides of the road. With all the farm work done in the area, they made good business selling to local farmers who relied on these machines for their livelihoods.

One car idled in the otherwise empty parking lot. Though the engine ran to keep the car warm, its lights were off. "Why on earth, if he had a way to drive, did he not pick me up at the apartment? He had to know he was forcing me to walk out here. Was he just being a turd?"

Once Riley made it into the light of the parking lot, both side doors opened, and two men exited the car. The driver was Clay, and he had a look of irritation as he tapped an imaginary watch on his wrist. The other was someone Riley had not met. He stood half a head taller than Clay, with broad shoulders and the type of expression worn by American football players before they snap the ball.

"You're late, doc. What the hell took you so long?" Clay yelled out over the empty parking lot.

Riley continued to close the distance before answering. "Weather slowed me down, but I made it. You know, you could have picked me up. It would have been the nice thing to do rather than make me hike a mile in the snow."

Clay did not appear to care and shrugged. "Whatever. I guess I didn't feel like seeing my car at your place that often. It's bad for business." He let that one sink in before gesturing to the man on the other side of the car. "Speaking of which. I thought I would bring my good friend. You know what, let's leave his name out of it. We'll just call him Bob. I brought my friend Bob with me tonight."

Something in Clay's tone of voice or how he closed the door behind him before he and the other man advanced made Riley suddenly aware of how isolated the situation was. No one was anywhere near the Tractor Supply. It was a small building far away from homes or any other business that might have been open. The three of them were alone in the parking lot.

"You know I have customers in Rural as well as Wytheville?"

Riley shook his head and took a half step backward. He tried to judge his chances if he ran for it. Where to run? The other man knew where he worked and lived. At least, the cops already had all the information Clay had used to blackmail him.

"It's true. So a suit walked into your shop yesterday, and then you left with him and were gone all morning. I'm thinking, what is my good friend Riley doing with a stranger that early in the morning?"

This is where Riley wished he had practiced lying earlier in his life. Maybe he could have developed a story that others would believe. Instead, he said, "It was about a girl, the one I killed. They wanted to ask me questions about her."

Clay feigned understanding and acceptance. "Oh, of course, that makes sense. So they believe you murdered a small child, or perhaps just accidentally gave her illegal drugs that killed her. And after asking questions all morning, they let you go back to work. Do you see why I'm having trouble with that story?"

Riley's eyes shot between the two men as Bob deliberately withdrew a semiautomatic handgun and began screwing on a round piece of metal to the end. The object resembled a skinny beer can but was flat black. Clay asked, "Did you know silencers were legal in Virginia? True story. So now we're going to play the abridged version of twenty questions."

Bob finished attaching the silencer and aimed his firearm at Riley's chest. Clay asked, "First question, what did you tell the cops?"

Riley did his best to control his bladder while answering, "nothing about you or us. They only wanted to know about the little girl, Haley."

"OK, OK, that's fair. So, when I check you over, you won't have anything on you I shouldn't expect to find." Clay's voice was calm, but his eyes were sharp and cutting.

"Same stuff as always, wallet, keys, and phone."

Clay moved forward and checked Riley's story with his hands, searching into each pocket and pulling Riley's shirt up to reveal his chest. He only possessed the prescribed items he'd listed, save for one small bottle.

"You're worthless," Clay said and looked at the one thing that Riley didn't list. He held the vial of morphine. "All this over one bottle? Are you kidding me? Why are you wasting my time?"

Things were spiraling out of control, and Riley raced to pick the pieces back up. "You asked me to get that for you, so I did. That's it, right there. It's what you wanted. I can't get large amounts all at once. People will notice if lots of that stuff goes missing."

There was a moment's consideration as Clay turned his back on Riley. "They might, but would anyone care if you went missing?"

Riley took a step backward and attempted to sum up the situation. "Hold on a minute. I did what you asked of me. You wanted morphine. There it is. This isn't worth getting shot over."

In Riley's pocket, his cell phone heard the mention of a firearm and the change in conversation. When that happened, a set of blue lights lit up down the road. It was hard to judge distance in the drifting snow, but they were not close enough for anyone to see what was happening at the exchange. They drove up to the scene slowly and cautiously.

The lights progressed towards the group, and Clay shot his eyes at Riley. "You set us up! You little shit."

He could have tried lying, but with the gun and the cops, Riley didn't want to risk it. Instead, he attempted to back away from what he suspected would become ground zero for a law-enforcement standoff.

The man called Bob did not shoot Riley but instead tried to hide the oversized pistol in his jacket. However, with the silencer attached, the gun was too long for its holster, and he had no option but to hold his hand under his coat and try to look inconspicuous.

Over patrol-car loudspeakers came an officer's voice, "everyone, stop where you are and place your hands above your heads!"

Riley misinterpreted the distinction between 'everyone' and the 'two guys who threatened him with a gun.' When combined with a surge of adrenaline, this caused the young man to attempt running away from Clay and Bob.

Law enforcement tends not to distinguish between good and bad guys when approaching a potentially hostile scene. The poor weather and lighting only made this worse. No one could see who anyone was, and when one of the three suspects broke from the other two and began running, the officers hollered again. "Halt, stop, don't move!" all said to find the word to keep Riley from running at their car.

Clay saw his opportunity to flee the area and ran the opposite direction from Riley. Bob didn't appear to be adept at judging situations for himself and simply ran after Clay.

With the patrol car stopped, two officers exited their vehicle, the driver with the radio still in his hand and the passenger with a shotgun. The driver's amplified voice over the car speakers called out, "stop, show me your hands!" Unfortunately, it was unclear to whom he was directing his instructions as several people were running in different directions.

Each person would later describe what they remembered seeing in somewhat different ways. The driver said he observed one of the two men who ran from the scene pull a pistol from his coat and aim it at the patrol car. This officer then shouted, "Gun!"

Riley stretched his arms out towards the police car to show empty hands, but all anyone could see was his outline against a white backdrop of snow and illuminated from behind by Clay's car.

Armed with a shotgun, the second officer followed the pair of suspects with his eyes as they fled the scene. When he heard his partner yell "gun!" he pivoted and saw Riley with his hand pointed directly at the patrol car. Body-camera footage confirmed that the suspect had no firearm, but the officer insisted he saw a pistol pointed at the two of them when he pulled the trigger.

Everything hung still in the air as the snow stopped falling and the scene froze as the shotgun fired.

Bob tucked the pistol back into his jacket and ran as fast as he and Clay could exit the area. Their car remained in the parking lot, so it was easy for the police to discover who one of them was. But for the moment, they were gone.

As soon as he fired the gun, the passenger realized what he'd done and turned his sights to follow the two suspects who fled the scene. With them gone, and no other threat visible, he shoved the shotgun into the car's vertical rack and grabbed an aid bag. "Damn it, kid, why'd you do that. You're so stupid," he said while running forward and ripping open a trauma kit.

The driver switched channels and called dispatch, with the radio already in his hands. "Break, break, break; this is Charlie-Three; request immediate medical transport. We have a gunshot victim, single adult male, at the Tractor Supply, beginning first aid." He let go of the microphone and waited for the response while watching his partner cut open the man's shirt.

The radio was silent as no one interrupted the critical communication, and everyone waited for dispatch. After a minute, they came back and said, "Charlie-Three, EMS en route to your location, secure scene and prep for transport."

"Wilco, Charlie-Three out," he hung up the microphone and stepped around the car to join his partner. "Anything I can do to help?"

"Not unless you're a trauma surgeon. How about you grab the gun and keep an eye out for those hoodlums? They may try to come back for their car." The passenger then slapped a large white square of cloth on top of the wound, and Riley cried out under the pain. "Hold tight. Someone's coming."

With the suspects gone and only a critically wounded informant still at the scene, Agent Coronado's car pulled up. He exited and looked across the parking lot at Riley. "Sorry, kid. That's not how any of this was supposed to go down," he said to himself and then pulled out a camera and began photographing everything within sight. He could do little more other than document the scene, but he would do the kid that much kindness. He'd make sure they held Clay responsible for what happened here.

Rural Retreat's fire and EMS had their own ambulance, which was helpful because there were no other trauma medical services within the town. The nearest hospital was the Wytheville County Hospital, and with the weather continuing to be a problem, it was anyone's guess how long the trip would take. When EMS arrived, the officers briefed them on the situation. There was little to explain other than being hit in the chest with a shotgun.

Paramedics are outstanding medical professionals, but some injuries are beyond their level of care. Once things reach a critical stage, their only option is to transport a victim to a trauma center and trust that they make it in time. Many people talk about the magic hour, or the limited window medical staff have to save a victim. Sometimes this hour is an optimistic number.

The medics placed Riley on a stretcher, and as the doors closed, the two officers stood in the snow, watching the flashing red lights disappear into the night. They then did the only thing they could do. They assisted Agent Coronado to secure the scene and collect evidence. None of them wanted to deal with the tragedy of what just occurred. There would be time for that later.

Under normal circumstances, the ambulance would have driven the twelve miles to the county hospital. Riley's wounds made this situation other than average, and their only option was attempting to reach Bloomfield some fifty miles away. Again, if the night had been any different, the weather would have allowed for a helicopter flight to emergency lift Riley to the medical center. The ambulance crew then attempted what would typically be a one-hour drive in less-than-ideal weather.

The crew did their best. They were well trained and had the most modern medical equipment available. No one could fault the EMS staff for what took place. But during the two-hour drive, they declared Dr. Riley Brewer, age twenty-nine, dead.

Riley arrived at the Bloomfield Regional Medical Center at 6:00 AM Sunday, where the attending physician pronounced the time. Medical staff confirmed his identity by a driver's license carried in his wallet but found no immediate family to notify. Law enforcement arrived thirty minutes after Riley's body and requested they sequester the remains for autopsy and preserve his personal effects as evidence.

Two additional subjects were brought into the hospital later that morning in critical condition. Two men were involved in a high-speed wreck following a law-enforcement pursuit. The individuals had returned to the Tractor Supply to retrieve a vehicle, which the police now held as evidence. One had in his possession a semiautomatic handgun with a silencer.

Even with all the deaths and injuries, the medical staff at the emergency center saw nothing unusual. The weather was terrible and last night was Saturday. There was, however, one person who showed an interest in what occurred that night.

A man of Mediterranean descent flipped through the fashion magazines and waited patiently. His foot tapped to the sound of a ticking clock on the far wall. Death turned another page and glanced at the clock. He then grumbled under his breath, pulled out an ornate pocket watch, and checked its gold dials. "It's about time. Does he know nothing about being early for an appointment?"

It was at that moment that Riley, the man who had died moments before, stepped through the operating-room doors. To clarify, he did not push open these doors, but passed through them. His eyes darted about the faded green and white room with its plastic chairs and general absence of people. He tried to say something or ask anything, but nothing came to mind, and his mouth opened, then closed, several times.

"You may wish to have a seat, Mr. Brewer," the man with the magazine said as he set it aside. "You've had quite a night."

Stumbling as if drunk, Riley found a seat and dropped into it. He faced Death and questioned why he was there. "What's happening? Did that man shoot me?"

There was a moment's consideration, and Death asked, "Would you prefer a sugar-coated answer or should I rip the bandage off in one swift go? I find it easier if we just get things over with."

Riley did his best to pull start the motor of his mind and nodded his agreement to a multiple-choice question. "Yes, that's fine."

"You were shot. Please don't hold it against the man who pulled the trigger. He was doing what he thought was right. There are evil people in the world, and he's not one of them, but that is not the point. Your body ceased to continue living while they drove you to this hospital."

The wordplay did not go well with Riley's addled mind, and he tried to understand what Azrael said. Riley asked, "Then I died? I'm dead?"

"If you want to go with an overly simple explanation of the conditions of existence, then yes. However, I've interrupted the normal course of events to ask for your help. The world has become larger and more complicated since things started, and I require assistance."

Riley shook his head to clear the cobwebs. "You need my help? Who are you?"

"Right, how rude of me. I am Azrael, the current Angel of Death."

# CHAPTER 13
# HOSPITAL ROUNDS

Riley did not meet many celebrities or high-ranking government officials. To say that he didn't expect to meet the Angel of Death was an understatement. Riley sat for ten minutes, or perhaps longer, with his mouth open, trying to put together his next words. "Aren't you the guy from the bar?"

This brought a smile to Azrael's face, and he chuckled at the simplicity of the moment. "Yes, I spoke with you at the bar. We talked twice as I tried to know you better as a person. I'm sure you can understand why I didn't introduce myself at that time. That would have been," he considered his next word, "disruptive."

A fog settled on Riley's brain and refused to allow him to think correctly, though, from his expression, he was making a masterful effort. "Why would Death want to talk to me at a bar? Were you going to kill me?"

His companion in the waiting room winced at the implications. "I thought I mentioned once before that I don't kill anyone. My title is a bit of a misnomer. The first night I escorted Rosa to what is beyond this world, and the second night I was waiting to find out if you'd come back."

"So you were at the bar for me," Riley accused the man who patiently let him work through his emotions.

"When someone dies suddenly and unexpectedly, the transition is complicated. I lose more under those conditions than any others," Azrael attempted to explain. He stood and motioned for Riley to follow. "Here, let me try to show you. It may be painful, but it will make things easier."

Riley hesitated before pushing himself to his feet and following the specter of death out of the waiting room. In defiance to consistency, Azrael showed no difficulty passing through the surgical doors, while moments before he held a magazine in his hands. "Come, stay close."

Riley thought about his options and tried to develop a plan, but nothing came to mind. In the end, he decided that staying alone in a waiting room with none of his questions answered for all eternity was not the most desirable option. With three quick steps, he followed Death into the other room.

In the surgical suite, the doctors had all left, and the abandoned blood-soaked scene became the domain of the nursing assistants. The two hospital staff employees cleaned the blood and switched medical instruments, all to prepare for the next patient who might need the room. Neither of them took any notice of the two new guests who arrived.

Death gripped the sheet and pulled it back to reveal Riley's face staring blankly up to the ceiling. Riley gagged and attempted to throw up, but as his spectral body no longer allowed for such functions, his efforts resulted in only coughing. His only alternative was to turn away in horror upon seeing the face of his death.

Azrael replaced the sheet, and none of the hospital staff noticed when Death came around the table to place a comforting hand on Riley's shoulders. "That was unkind of me. I considered my options on how to prepare you for the truth, but our time was limited."

Riley took several deep breaths while attempting to steady himself. "OK."

Azrael waited for Riley to recover before going any further. "Are you leaving anyone behind? Any last message you need to send?"

It was an odd question, as Riley suspected the dead rarely received a chance to communicate with the living upon their death. "Only my boss and my ex, but I don't believe they'll miss me."

"This next part is a bit disorienting, so hold on to me. Soon you will be able to travel on your own." Azrael gave no other warning or instruction, but Riley took a firm hold of Death's arm and waited for anything. His mind wandered to pictures of hell, heaven, and oblivion. Was there a way to guess where his life would lead him in the next world?

One moment they were in the hospital, then between the ticks of the clock, they were sitting in the back of a car. Riley's mind stopped working for a moment to process what had occurred. It seemed as if they had always been in the car. With no feeling of travel, no rush of wind or blur of lights, it was as if he were in both places simultaneously. He stopped existing in the operating room and began again in the back of the car.

"What the hell was that?" Riley exclaimed while attempting to articulate his surprise.

"We'll cover things like that later. Right now, I want you to understand where you are and what is happening."

It was difficult to ignore the fact that he appeared in the back of someone's moving car, but Riley did his best. Instead, he focused his attention on the vehicle's details, and as his mind took inventory he understood where he was, and his eyes continued to the driver. He said, "Glen."

"You had three numbers on your phone. Glen's was one of them, and the police called him, so now he's driving through the snow to the hospital."

Riley was in shock upon seeing his ex with such a look of dedication on his face. It must have been some ridiculous time in the morning, though the sun was peeking up on the horizon. "He'll make it, won't he? He's not going to get in a wreck just trying to visit my dead body, will he?"

Azrael shrugged, and Riley raised an eyebrow. "He's not scheduled to die today. But not everything happens according to plan, even the truly grand plans. Sometimes They make a last-minute decision, and there is always free will."

The answer didn't satisfy Riley, and he shouted, "Not good enough! Will he die?"

"Someday, yes, but likely not today. We're not here for that. This is your chance to say goodbye to one of your few fetters unless you want to count the lover you two shared, but he's about to resolve himself."

Riley swallowed hard but didn't argue, so he turned to face the reason he had returned to Rural Retreat. If it weren't for Glen, he would go anywhere in the world other than his hometown. What would he possibly say to this man if he had one last chance? Everything inside him wanted to tell him he forgave him for everything, but that felt wrong. Glen did nothing wrong. All this was of Riley's doing.

Eventually, he sat back beside Azrael without attempting to speak with Glen. "Let's go back. He doesn't need to hear anything from me."

Azrael gave a knowing nod, and the two were again standing in the waiting room of Bluefield Medical Center. "Their lives will go on without us, and we will go on without them until They unite everyone in the end. Now come, we still have much to do before the day is over."

Rather than vanishing and reappearing wherever Azrael was leading him, the two walked through the hospital. Death checked in on the sick and wounded with the expression of a loving caregiver. Occasionally he'd check a pocket watch, then tucked it away.

Azrael led Riley to the roof after their slow procession through the hospital. What remained of the winter storm sifted light snowfall over the city. At the far edge of the horizon, the sun crested at the edge of sight, and a deep orange glow filled the morning sky. A chill wind passed through Riley's face.

"Why did you bring me up here?" he asked while taking in the sights of the city below.

Azrael walked to the building's ledge as he peered out in deep thought. "Do you know the last time I stopped to enjoy a sunrise?"

This question from the Angel of Death caught Riley off guard, and he hesitated before answering. "I'm not sure I thought anything about it. No one thought you were a real person, just an idea, something from a storybook."

Azrael gave a muffled chuckle. "I can understand that. Who would want to think that hard about Death? But, no, the years are getting to me. I've been doing this job for more years than I can remember. Billions of people guided to their last resting place, but it never ends."

Riley was unsure how to respond to this confession. What was Death trying to tell him? "I suppose everyone has their place in the world. You have to keep doing what you're meant to do."

"Do I?" Azrael asked. He turned his gaze back to Riley and questioned if the deceased man had an answer. "Is there any great rule book that dictates what I must do with my existence?"

Riley shifted his weight while searching to see whether a third person might appear to rescue him from the conversation. "You know I can't answer that. I'm more lost about this kind of thing than you are. Hell, I don't even know what I'm doing here, let alone what you're supposed to be doing."

This seemed to bring the immortal being around to the matter at hand, and he straightened himself. "Yes, of course. You're here because you have a choice, one that most people don't get."

It would be nice if Riley could find a place to sit, but the roof was barren except for the industrial air conditioning units, and nothing looked like a seat. "What makes me so special that I have to choose something?"

"I'm getting to it. You are going to need to learn patience if this is ever going to work."

Riley nodded. "Yes, I'm sorry. What choice is it?"

"Will you become Death?" Azrael let the question linger in its vague simplicity while Riley attempted to comprehend what it meant. He said, "I'm done with it all and almost to a point where I would let the Ahemait take every last one of them so that I might have some peace."

This was a word Riley had heard before, but only once, and he still did not fully understand. "Who are the Ahemait?"

Azrael appeared to realize how much he needed to explain for his plan to work, and he took a deep breath. "Those creatures that resemble skinless dogs are the Ahemait. They scour the penumbra hunting for lost souls to devour and corrupt." Azrael needed to fill in another blank. "You're in the penumbra, the place where souls reside before crossing to what comes next."

Riley followed along with the conversation and nodded at the appropriate places. It was relatively straightforward, with an occasional word he'd never heard. Large demon dogs were hunting ghosts, check. "Where do you, or I, fit in with all this?"

"It is the responsibility of the Angel of Death to guard the lost souls against the Ahemait. There are different ways to do the job, but that is the job at the end of the day. You can find each soul and lead them to what follows, or you can hunt the daemons. The choice is up to you. I've tried both with mixed results."

Riley felt like he was spiraling out of control as Azrael switched from talking about Death as a title he held to a job that Riley would be doing. "I never said I'd do this. What makes you think it should be me? Why can't you keep doing it or let someone else do it?"

Azrael took several long strides to stand in front of Riley and scrutinized the young man's face. His eyes considered the deceased man's face and tried to judge whether he'd made the right choice. "The job's becoming too much for me. It needs a fresh set of eyes. As for picking you, no, I could pick someone else. That brings us back to your choice, which needs to be made."

The rising sun grew brighter, and its light-filled the horizon with a brilliant glow. Radiance extended from the center of the orb as a bridge to connect with the roof.

"There is your proverbial light. If you follow it, you will find the Elysian fields. In Elysium, you will know peace and happiness for the rest of your existence." Azrael stood aside so Riley could walk freely to the bridge and leave the mortal world behind. He could abandon all pain and would be free. But something nagged at the back of his mind, and he hesitated.

Riley took one step and then stopped. "If I go, you said you were ready to let the dogs kill everything they found. Is that true?"

Azrael shrugged his shoulders. "I'm not sure. I wouldn't do it on purpose, but it gets harder to care what happens to people every year. Some nights, it's easier to let them take the souls than to keep fighting."

Hearing those words, Riley took no further steps toward the light. An image of the animals at the bar tearing apart the older woman crept into his mind and haunted his vision. If Death had not been there, would they have destroyed her soul? But something more occurred to him. What would happen to the children like Haley? Riley took a step away from the light and the bridge faded.

"I can't. I would never know peace if I knew it was my fault that others suffered and died because of my selfishness."

The light faded, and as it did, Azrael offered Riley one last chance. "If you don't go, the bridge will not appear again. This is your one ticket. And I may still find someone willing to do the job."

It was not enough to convince Riley to make a run for the bridge. He stood his ground as his chance at eternal peace faded into the distance. "I would punish myself forever because of the choices I made. It would become hell when it should have been paradise," he said as a single tear rolled down his cheek.

Death put an arm over Riley's shoulder, and together they

watched the last rays of Elysium fade into the rising sun. One light replaced another as the new day brought with it a promise of things to come, even while questions of opportunities lost vanished from sight.

With the dawning of the day, Azrael gently said, "Come, there is someone I want you to see." He then turned and guided Riley off the roof. The two walked the long halls, tracing the same path that led to emergency surgery.

"What is down here that I need to see? I really don't know that I want to see myself again."

Death shook his head and continued to lead Riley through the halls. "Not what I had in mind, and they should have moved your body to the morgue by now. People have a thing about not wanting to be surrounded by dead bodies. I think it reminds them of their own mortality."

Regardless of what Azrael said about his intent not to see Riley's body, they continued to walk toward the emergency wing. Once there, Azrael appeared lost and pulled out his pocket watch as though to consult it for directions rather than time. Once oriented, he motioned Riley to join him inside one of the private patient rooms.

A curtain blocked any view through the glass front, and Riley hesitated before passing through the door. "Who's in here?"

"The source of much of your frustration, Clayton Harris," Azrael said and checked his pocket watch once more. "He has little time left upon the earth."

Hearing the name of his tormentor fueled a new resolve, and Riley pushed his way into the room. There he saw the broken shell of the man who had threatened him in the parking lot. Clay's face was checkered with black and purple swelling, while a tube ran from his arm and another from his mouth. "What happened to him?"

Azrael followed at a respectful pace and stepped to the side. Once there, he pulled a chart from the foot of Clay's bed and read the notes left by doctors and nurses who had come before. "It appears to have been a car wreck. If I had to guess, law enforcement found him, and he attempted to flee on ice-covered roads."

Azrael replaced the chart, and Riley tried to put together pieces of a puzzle that appeared to be from different boxes. "Are you like me? Here where I am, with the other dead people? How did I talk to you before, and how are you picking things up now?"

Death checked his pocket watch once again. Whatever event he anticipated was imminent. "You and I are the same now that you have turned away from the light. But, no, we're not the same as the recently deceased who exist only in the penumbra."

That was another word Riley needed to put into the proverbial notebook and have Death explain in detail. Instead, he chose not to interrupt, and Azrael continued, "We move between them, and part of us will always exist in both. With concentration, you will learn to do it as naturally as walking."

In college, one of Riley's friends attempted to describe the concept of fourth-dimensional travel. The idea hurt his brain, and now that Azrael told him he could do it, a headache began to develop. "That's some science-fiction crap. Anything else I need to be aware of, like how you sometimes seem to know what's happening everywhere?"

The question appeared to stump Azrael as he thought about how best to answer. "You don't have to exist in only one place. Without a body, there is no longer a rule requiring you to tie yourself to a location." Azrael then said, "It's also how we traveled. Try not to worry too much about it. You have lifetimes to learn how to do these things and hundreds of years more to debate why they work."

Riley would have preferred a more direct answer, but as he thought about it, nothing could satisfactorily describe what had happened. This would be one of those things he needed to take on faith.

With the matter of his new reality addressed, Riley turned his attention to the man in the bed. Clay had tormented him in life and, by all accounts, was the reason for his death. Or was the blame

Riley's alone? How much responsibility did he need to bear for his own choices and actions? Riley asked, "How much time does he have?"

Death checked his pocket watch but thought better of himself and held out the ornate gold locket on a chain. "Have a look."

Riley hesitated, but then reached out and accepted the gift from Death. As it touched his palm, he could feel the weight of the object in his hand and upon his soul. On the outside of the fist-sized locket were intricate reliefs in a script he could not read. A symbol in the middle reminded him of the light and the bridge, but without the beckoning call. Inside was a three-dimensional swirl of stars, as if looking into a miniature galaxy.

Riley had no words for the longest of moments. He stared in wonder at the rotating lights as some grew brighter and others faded. "What do I do?"

Azrael said, "focus on the pocket watch and the man who is Clayton. Search for his star."

Riley did as instructed until one flickering point of light came into focus in the middle of the scene. As he focused, a clock with Roman numerals appeared around the light. "I see it, but how do I know what any of this means?"

"Relax and watch. You'll understand its meaning."

It took a few moments, but then Riley understood what everything meant. He saw the time of Clay's birth and the imminent nature of his death. The gold letters emblazoned the man's name across the sky, and he foresaw the man's death here in the emergency room.

"You can't be everywhere, so look for the ones where you think the Ahemait may hunt a lost soul," Azrael explained. "They feed on those who died unexpectedly. A soul that did not expect the end will not always find the light. Many of the others will find their way home without a guide. That or the Strix will help them."

Riley nodded as he listened to the explanation, but he was watching Clay's light flicker until the clock's hands came together.

The monitor alarms attached to Clay went off, and seconds later, nurses rushed into the room to try to save the man's life. Riley stood to the side with Azrael, but they already knew what would happen. Many of the medical staff knew as well. They could not save the man.

The doctors covered Clay's face with a sheet, and the staff then left. Azrael turned to Riley and said, "free him from the body. You know as well as anyone how frightening it is when you can't escape your death."

He remembered it was an experience he would not wish upon his worst enemy. Given the circumstances which led to that night, Clay would meet this description. Riley reached forward, grasped the man's hand through the ether, and helped pull his spirit into a sitting position. He then stepped back, expecting Clay to lunge forward and attack him for everything that happened.

Instead, Clay sat there and looked at his hands. He then looked at his body. "Well shit," he said. "I guess that means the car didn't make the turn." His voice was reserved and accepting.

Azrael stepped forward and spoke. "You did not. Can you see the way from here?" He turned and motioned out past the curtains and the glass wall.

Riley observed the dawn appear once more, but there was no bridge this time, as it did not call for him. Clay saw the light as well and said nothing more as he left his body. He stood from the bed, then walked on a surface unseen by Death or Riley to vanish into the distance.

# CHAPTER 14

# DEMON TREATY

The last rays of dawn faded into the fluorescent light of a hospital emergency room, as Azrael turned his attention back to Riley. "Come, there is someone you need to meet."

Whatever questions Riley may have had, he did not ask. Instead, he fell in step beside the Angel of Death. Together, they traveled to the ambulance entrance. This time, when Riley left the building, he felt the chill cross his face and reached to pull his jacket closer about his shoulders. It was then that he realized all he wore was his shirt, pants, and shoes.

"Where is my jacket, or my phone, for that matter?"

This did not appear to be a question people often asked Death, and it took him an extended moment of thought. "You are wearing what you thought you should wear when you died. Everything about how you appear reflects how you see yourself. As for a phone, I doubt you would get a good reception in the penumbra. I would hate to know what currency was required to pay for that plan."

Riley smiled despite himself. It was hard to admit that Death had a sense of humor, but he was funny, even if it was not intentional. Perhaps the ancient creature did not want to be laughed at. This second option occurred to Riley, as he strengthened himself and attempted to remove the grin from his face. "Yea, good point. Can I do anything about the cold?"

Death took a minute to consider what to say before speaking. "Not that I know of. If it's cold, you'll feel the cold. You're not going to get frostbite or freeze from it. It is only your way of knowing the surrounding temperature."

The answer was less than encouraging, and Riley shivered while attempting to pull his t-shirt tighter about his shoulders. "Still would be nice to have imagined I wore a nice warm jacket. So, what are we doing out here?"

"We're looking for someone," Azrael said, and turned his eyes up to the hospital's roof. "They're normally up there." He pointed to the corners of the building.

Riley joined with Death in his search for whatever he tried to find, and because Riley did not know what he searched for, Azrael found their friend first. "There she is," he said and waved a hand up towards what appeared to be a brown and white owl.

The distance made Riley question whether they were visible to an animal that far away, but their head swiveled around, and they stared down at the two of them. The owl took to the air on silent wings and glided down to perch on a lamppost. All of this was remarkable, but when the owl spoke, Riley felt off balance. "Good morning, Azrael. Have you brought me the one you talked about?"

"It talked?" Riley blurted out before he thought better of what he said.

Death glowered at Riley and turned his attention back to the owl. "I have. This is Riley. He is learning the trade, and I am showing him around." Azrael then introduced the two of them. "Riley, this is Strix. She (or they, depending on your point of view) is a guide for the departed."

Riley offered a wave up at the owl and a "good morning."

Rather than engage in pleasantries, the owl looked over the

deceased man, then turned to Azrael. "You sure about this? I suppose talking you out of this would be a wasted effort."

"We'll just have to see, won't we?" Azrael challenged back.

Azrael stood under the owl, looking up at the creature. In every other situation when Riley had seen the Angel of Death, Azrael towered over the subjects before him. Here, this simple owl held dominion, and the power dynamic of the afterlife came into question.

"Anyhow, Strix is one, or many, depending on how comfortable you are thinking about such things. While you and I can guide the recently dead to Elysium, Strix are responsible for most of the passages in the world."

Everything continued to come at Riley through a firehose of information, and he did his best to soak it in. "So we're special teams, then?"

Azrael considered this option for an explanation and turned to the owl for her opinion. The two appeared in agreement, and Death spoke. "That is a way to look at it. We must protect those crossing over. Strix is the guide. Most deaths only require a guide, and some find the way on their own."

The unasked question appeared to reach Strix, and she answered, "No one is in charge in the way you're thinking. We are all given our duty, and that is what we do, or They will replace us."

No sooner had her last statement come from her beak than Riley had yet another question. This appeared to be a night of endless questions. His entire world had been upended, and while he believed in a vague concept of an afterlife, he did not actively think about it and was unprepared to go there. In retrospect, everyone should be prepared for their own mortality, even if death itself comes as a surprise.

"Do I even want to know who assigns these tasks and fires people if no one is in charge?"

Strix closed their beak, and Azrael shifted uncomfortably.

Riley observed the body language of the two as realization

dawned upon him, and his eyes widened. "Oh. You mean. Forget I asked," he said and closed his mouth.

Breaking the silence, Azrael spoke. "I have an excellent idea. Let's change the subject."

Riley snorted a laugh as Death quoted a children's book; he couldn't hold back before collecting himself. "Yes, sorry. So what do we do from here? This is my first time being dead "

The owl ruffled her feathers as though left out of a joke. "Whatever you two do, I'm not involved. You know how to reach me if the need arises. Otherwise, I'll be here, doing my job." In this last part, she spoke with venom towards Azrael and his current course of action.

The two specters returned to the hospital's interior as Strix flew back to the roof. Azrael said, "If you search near a hospital, you will always find her, or one of her. However you want to think about it. But as for calling her in an emergency, I have no idea what she's talking about. You'll learn to love her, honestly a great person."

After describing Strix as a person, Azrael hesitated, but shook his head and let it go. "Anyhow, we have a lot more work to accomplish before the next sunrise. You've chosen to remain behind, but I need you to go one step further and take up the mantle of Death."

"Come, I want to show you more of Death's tools." Azrael led Riley to a round table with four uncomfortable chairs. It was never clear why hospitals went out of their way to make families waiting for loved ones as miserable as possible. These chairs and this table were an example of such furnishing.

Azrael reached into his coat and pulled out the same oversized leather-bound book from the night before in Riley's apartment. "So I didn't dream that thing up," Riley exclaimed upon seeing the artifact.

"You are the only one who said it was a dream," Azrael said, and opened the book. It again showed the duplicate rows of handwritten names and dates. The constantly shifting dates made the book seem alive as the ink crawled over the pages. Some names changed so frequently they were difficult to read.

Death reviewed the ledger as he ran a finger down the long list of names. He spoke mostly to himself, but also for the benefit of Riley. "The Strix will handle most of these. It takes patience to learn which ones you need to watch."

"What are you looking for?" Riley asked, trying to make sense of the book as other than a row of names and dates.

Azrael reached up and guided Riley's hand down to the rows and let the new specter's fingers trace the page. As Riley touched each velum surface, the people appeared before him where they were, as if he were standing with them as things were happening. Azrael explained, "Distance and location don't matter. The book gives you a connection to the person. You're looking for someone alone who was not expecting to die. It's not a rule, but good practice."

The experience was disturbing, with the scene shifting as fast as Riley's hand brushed past each name. He wasn't sure there would be a time when he could do this without being disoriented. Perhaps with unlimited time, anything was possible. "What about this one?"

Earl M. Reed, born June 16, age 49. The date of death was for that night and only moments away. Azrael touched the entry and joined Riley in viewing the location. Then the two of them were standing on the side of the road. Tire tracks ran from the street through the snow, off a guardrail, and into an oak tree. Azrael considered the location. "This is an excellent find. The Strix tend to remain near where people congregate, so Mr. Reed may be stranded for some time."

Riley puffed his chest at the commendation of finding someone in need of saving on his first attempt. Perhaps he was well suited for this line of work. Filled with the confidence of the young, he began striding across the snowy field to the crashed car. But Azrael grasped him by the shoulder and whispered, "hold up."

Nothing appeared out of place, but the tone of Azrael's voice was clear. They were near danger. Riley froze in place and perked his ears while scanning with his eyes for anything that could have triggered the experienced specter. That was when Riley beheld the third and final deathly relic. Azrael withdrew from nowhere a bronze-bladed sword that reflected no light.

The air hung still while the two specters held their breath and waited for any sign of what had caused the alarm. From the car, they heard a mix of sounds. The radio was still playing a garbled pop-music channel, and fluids from the engine were hot enough to continue sputtering. Neither of these was what caught their attention. The sound of an animal gorging from the front seat drifted out of the car and across the snow.

Azrael's face hardened, and he circled the driver's side of the car while motioning for Riley to do the same. It was fine for Death to be brave in this situation with his experience and armament, but Riley showed genuine fear. He hoped the sounds came from a wolf or other terrestrial animal and could be ignored. But part of him knew what he would see when rounding the back window.

Through the passenger door, Riley saw the skinned form of an Ahemait. It stood on the empty seat feasting on the driver. Though none of the animal's teeth touched the man's body, he continued to eat just the same. Everything within Riley wanted to hurl, but specters can't do that.

On the other side of the vehicle, Azrael moved slowly with methodical steps, drawing him closer. The beast didn't notice Azrael until he was nearly upon it, then it crouched back and screamed. A terrible sound of rusted metal and tortured animals reverberated across the field while Death attempted to strike the Ahemait.

His blow was not quick enough, and the creature pulled back further into the car before breaking the passenger door. He scrambled out into the snow and turned to face Riley, who stood exposed and weaponless.

With nothing to defend himself, Riley did the first thing which came to mind and screamed back at the creature. The newly created specter attempted to puff himself up as large as possible and yelled to the best of his ability while lunging at the terrifying beast. If this plan did not work, Riley had no backup or idea what he would do next.

It startled the creature, who turned from Riley, glanced at Azrael, and ran. The thing traveled twenty meters before it disappeared in a wall of heat that left the snow melting in the real world. With the threat gone, Riley collapsed to his knees.

Azrael joined his protégé and put a reassuring hand on his shoulders. "You did well. You'll learn to do better, but that was good. I'm going to go check on Mr. Reed."

Sitting in the snow with none of it melting and his clothes remaining dry, Riley remained where he fell and waited for Death to return. Azrael came back with an expression of defeat on his face. He didn't describe what happened to the man they came to save. There was no need to say anything. Riley could tell from the expression that they were too late to do anything for the first person he had tried to help.

Azrael sat next to Riley in the snow, put an arm about the young specter, and pulled him into a comforting embrace. "It's OK," he said in a soft voice. "We don't save them all. The goal is not to save everyone. We do this job to rescue one soul, anyone. If you can give eternal peace to just a single person, you can forget about any of those whom you lost."

Riley let his head rest upon Azrael's chest as they sat in the field of snow and stared out at the wrecked car. "So I guess I need to keep trying until I can save at least one. Because so far, I'm batting a zero."

"Not true. You started your second life after guiding the man responsible for your death. That was not about his redemption. Strix could have shown him the way. I brought you to him because you needed to be the one to do that for him."

Azrael pulled himself up. "Now come. Let's leave this place and get back to what we were doing."

The two specters brought themselves to their feet. But before Azrael could explain how to travel back to the hospital, a shimmer of heat manifested, and two Ahemait stepped through. Riley had no way to distinguish one from the other, but suspected he'd already seen the smaller of the two. That one had fled the scene moments before. It was the more massive beast that drew his full attention.

This disproportionately massive creature was the same Ahemait Riley had seen at the bar. He knew little about these creatures, but from what he understood of their canine brethren, that must be their alpha. "Are we in trouble?" he asked Azrael.

"Maybe," came the less-than-favorable response as his mentor attempted to take stock of the situation. "What do you want?"

After the exchange with the owl, Riley would not have been surprised if the monster spoke English with a British accent. Instead, it barked and yapped in defiance of the Angel of Death.

Azrael listened to the sounds and observed the creature's posture. He said, "That's less than reassuring," loud enough for only Riley to hear. Then, for the benefit of the Ahemait, he shouted, "Yes, I know! We were leaving!" He shoved the sword back into whatever dimension it originated from and took Riley by the arm.

"Come on. We need to get out of here. I'll explain after we're at the hospital." There was a shift in Riley's vision, and they were again standing in the waiting room over a table looking at Death's book.

Riley pulled out a chair and dropped into it while trying to wrap his mind around what had occurred. "What was all that? What did you tell that thing?"

Azrael put the book away and sat beside Riley. A look of pride crossed the older specter's face as Riley moved the chair from the real world, but he said nothing about it. "I wouldn't call what we have with those things a truce, but there is an understanding. The alpha seemed to think we would not honor our side of the agreement."

Negotiating with those creatures was a foreign concept to Riley, so he looked blankly back at Azrael. The older specter tried to explain, "Mr. Reed was gone by the time we arrived. There was nothing we could have done to save him. If we attacked the smaller

Ahemait, the only purpose would be to destroy one of those loath-some creatures."

"I don't see the problem with that plan. Maybe if you got rid of enough of them, we wouldn't have to keep running around trying to save everyone."

"It's not as simple as that. We don't hunt the Ahemait, and they don't hunt the living. They also won't come inside our hospitals or places of healing."

Riley glanced about himself at the sterile walls, and his mind raced to think of how many people must die in hospitals all around the globe every day. The weight of the number showed on his face, and Azrael nodded. "Now you understand why we don't break our side of the agreement. Think of the destruction if those things ran rampant in places like this, nursing homes, or when someone's receiving hospice care."

The anger at what he'd witnessed deflated from Riley as he thought of how much more terrifying the world could be. "OK, I get it. So we left those two, and they finished," he trailed off. It was too much to complete his thought out loud.

"Correct. But try not to dwell on it. There was nothing more that we could do for or to Mr. Reed. Also, please don't ask me where he is now because I don't know. If a spirit dies, I can only take it on faith that it must continue its existence in some other form. It's too much for me to believe in oblivion. I don't know how the atheists do it."

Time passed, and Riley regained his strength, eventually bringing himself to his feet. "You picked the wrong person. I'm not cut out for this. I'm just a failed pharmacist. You need a soldier, a warrior, someone who can fight."

Death rose from the chair and stretched his hand out to Riley. "Come, let's go for a walk. I want your opinion on what we witnessed."

He had nowhere else to go, and as he was unsure if the terms of his existence hinged on continuing to perform his functions for Death, Riley followed. Azrael took them out of the emergency room and into the urgent-care wing of the hospital. Beds lined the walls with only curtains providing privacy to the various patients. A woman dressed in floral-print hospital scrubs stood over a desk and flipped through charts while glancing at monitors on the station's wall.

"Let's play a little game. Who is she, and what is she doing?" Azrael asked, indicating the overworked woman who didn't have time to sit.

Riley suspected he knew, but he walked closer to see her name badge to confirm before answering. "She's the charge nurse. I'd say this is the start of her shift, except she looks too tired, so probably at the end of yesterday's." It occurred to Riley to look around the room. There was no one else. "Where are the other staff?"

"That is Eloise Brandy. The snow forced her and the rest of the staff to shelter in place last night, and their replacements have not made it in because of road closures. You already saw how dangerous the ice was from Mr. Reed. The other nurses are taking an hour break to try to sleep while she holds down the fort."

Such stories of overworked hospital staff were not alien, but Riley spent most of his time in a hometown pharmacy, so he never experienced this kind of stress. Azrael asked, "Would you describe her as a warrior and a fighter?"

He had to admit this woman showed dedication to her profession, the same as any soldier on a battlefield. "You're right. She is, but even if I'm supposed to be a fighter, how do I face a demon dog?"

"The Ahemait are not demons, but that's a technicality for another day. Your physical form does not define your strength and power as an agent of Death. That body died and is gone. All that remains is your spirit, determination, and resolve."

Riley did his best to listen to what Azrael told him, and it began to make sense. He took up his hand and looked at the fingers as he rotated it to view from all sides. "I am what I think I am," Riley said to himself, while trying to put the pieces together. An idea occurred to him, and the jacket he had worn before his death once again appeared on his shoulders. The fabric wove together from nothing.

Death smiled as he watched his protégé take his first step. "Now you're seeing the larger picture."

The coat fit more perfectly than it ever did in life and no longer had the rip at the bottom where it caught on a nail and tore. It was a rare moment that Riley took pride in his accomplishments, but this was a moment for him to beam and show off what he had done. "OK. So now all I need to do is fashion myself a dog-catching van, and we should be in business."

"Let's start with the basics first."

# CHAPTER 15
# OLD DEBTS

Azrael left the *Book of the Dead* sitting on the waiting-room table and attempted to make himself comfortable on a hard plastic chair. "Search through the names. Do any of them stand out to you? No one holds us to a work schedule in the traditional sense, but it is best not to let the dust settle. The Ahemait do not sleep, and every moment we're not in the trenches they claim another soul."

The weight of Azrael's words pulled on Riley's shoulders as he attempted to comprehend working from then until the end of time. Could he never take a break without questioning whether he was condemning someone to some version of hell? He opened the book and turned a page.

Names did not appear in any logical order. They were neither chronological nor alphabetical, and he could not guess how the book sorted them. Everything was overwhelming as he stared at the shifting writing.

"Try not to force the issue. Think of it more like listening to a noisy room," Azrael attempted to explain. "You're trying to find that one voice in the crowd that stands out from the rest. What's written on the page is only a visualization of what the book is trying to tell you."

"I'm not sure that makes things any easier, but I'll try." Riley closed his eyes. He took a deep breath and opened them again. The exercise became more like trying to decipher a magic-eye picture than searching for a black grain of rice. As Riley became more comfortable relaxing into the search, names stood out from the page.

"Why so many?" Riley asked before he thought better of the question.

Azrael shrugged. He was not reviewing the book and could only guess the number Riley saw. "It's normally not so many you can't sort through the names. In the United States, we're looking at about seven thousand a day, and the Ahemait are not so numerous that they exist all over the globe. We follow their pack and stay focused on our assigned purpose. Strix will hand most of the wandering souls."

"Does the book have an index?" Riley asked dryly, while turning pages on an ever-increasing list of names.

The concept of looking up names in an index must not have occurred to Azrael, and he considered the question for a minute. "No, but perhaps your version of the book could have one. The three artifacts of Death become more personalized the longer an angel possesses them."

Riley's mind hit the proverbial brick wall, and he held up a hand. "Two points. One, I'm not an angel, and two, this book is yours."

"English is a poor language at times. Please don't confuse words you recognize with how I use them. Angels are agents of a higher power. It would be the same if I described myself as the Agent of Death, but then I sound like I should be in a spy novel."

"So not," Riley started to say before Azrael cut him off.

"We don't talk in detail on that subject. None of us pretend to understand Their intent or nature, so let's move on, shall we?"

It wasn't easy to decide where to take the conversation after being shut down, so Riley went quiet and turned back to the book.

His hands continued to run over the pages as he searched for anyone who called to him as the one they needed to visit. The name Glen Kinder struck him. And next to his name was the current day as the date of death.

Riley shook his head and checked the name a second time before focusing on the location and seeing his former lover. The sight of the man he knew intimately caused him to recoil, and his eyes snapped back to stare at Death. "This has to be wrong!"

Azrael was unfazed by the outburst. He said, "It attempts to gauge the intent of the Fates. I don't know that I would say it's ever wrong as much as they change their minds. You can't know the future, only predict it."

"It says Glen is going to die," Riley accused the purportedly inanimate object.

With a shrug of the shoulders, Azrael attempted to understand where the distress was originating from. "Everyone is going to die. Is something more specific bothering you? Or did you not expect to find his name?"

"Tonight. The book thinks he is going to die tonight!" Riley shouted. If they were in the real world, someone would have called hospital staff to calm down the irate patient. But as no one listens to the dead, he continued to holler without interruption.

After pulling himself to his feet, Azrael joined Riley at the book and reviewed the entry. "It does," he confirmed. He looked closer and touched the line. Riley wasn't sure what he expected when Azrael viewed the other location, but nothing was unusual other than Azrael's hand on the page.

"It also appears to be a situation that could attract the Ahemait. Their alpha may have recognized you from the car wreck and the bar. If he also knows Glen was important to you, they may use that as an attack." Azrael reviewed the situation dispassionately.

"They need to face me head-on, those cowards. They run away from a fight and then attack the defenseless," Riley said while the anger continued to build.

Azrael nodded before saying, "It's their nature. They will kill where there is no fight and scavenge rather than hunt. As powerful as they may appear, they are cowards at heart. My guess is they believe if they destroy Glen, then you cannot continue your fight against them."

Bile crept into Riley's throat as he thought of those monsters eating his friend's soul as they had done with the stranger in the car. "We're not letting that happen. I'm not going to sit here; they are going to suffer if they so much as touch one hair on his head."

Death grinned as he watched the young specter work himself into a fervor. "That is the passion this job requires. Remember this moment and how you feel and think. The same thoughts and feelings affect every family of every soul of those people they destroyed."

Riley screamed. "I don't care about those other families! We're stopping them. They're not killing Glen!"

"Now hold on to that feeling but try not to let it get the better of you. Stay focused." Azrael ran his hand along the book, and Riley followed suit before the two of them appeared in the parking lot of the Iron Horse.

The only people who frequented the Iron Horse during daylight hours were employees cleaning and preparing the place for the next evening. Given the night before was Saturday, they had a lot of work to complete before everything was back in shape. As was customary, the owner gave the staff until the afternoon to go home and rest before coming back in to reset for the next night.

In the parking lot were two cars. One was Glen's hatch-back, and the other was a rusted-out sedan that had once been painted red. The occupants of the two vehicles stood with their coats held tight about their shoulders on the leeward side of the building.

"So what did you want, knuckle dragger?" Glen asked of the man known as Bob.

With his coat held closed with one hand. Bob tucked his other hand inside the jacket and kept it close to his chest. Presumably, his hand was inside the coat to stay warm, but the significant bulge made this seem unlikely. "Clay's missing. Your boyfriend's been shot. It seems you're running out of friends, buddy."

Glen sniffed back a stuffy nose and spat into the snow. "You think this is news to me. I lost the two people I care about. Now I'm talking with a Mensa reject like you. My day's in the toilet, so let's get this over with."

The two specters appeared near one another, a short distance from the two mortals as they engaged in conversation. Riley took a moment to decide what was occurring with the discussion. He turned to Azrael and asked, "Is he going to kill Glen?"

Azrael appeared not to be interested in the exchange between the two men. Instead, his attention focused on the surrounding area. "Probably, but it could be anything. He could have a heart attack for all I know. The *Book of the Dead* tells us who and when."

This confused Riley as he glanced about the parking lot. "It also showed us where."

"No, this is our thing. We chose to be in the same place as the person from the book. It didn't need to tell us where."

Bob snorted in disgust. "You think you're pretty funny. How about you figure out a way to get me the money Clay still owes me? I'd love to learn the punchline to that joke."

The simultaneous attempt at a threat and humor left Glen confused, but he shook it off and addressed the threat. "I don't have whatever money he owed you. And that was him, not me. You and I don't have any arrangements. You'll have to take it up with whatever estate he left behind."

"See, another funny joke," Bob said, though the smile on his face showed the sick type of humor one reserves for pulling legs off insects. "I'm pretty sure he left you in charge of his will. So time to pay up. He owed me ten grand, so now you owe me, plus interest."

Despite his better instincts, Glen rolled his eyes. "Why do thugs always include interest? Does anyone actually compute the interest or is this a random fee? I told you. That's not my problem. Now, if we got nothing else, I have places to be. Two of my best friends both died on the same night, and I'm pretty sure you caused at least one of them."

Riley stepped closer to the two and spoke to Glen. "He has a gun! Don't threaten him! He's going to kill you!"

There was no response from Glen, though Death walked up behind Riley and put a compassionate hand on his shoulder. "They won't hear you."

"You said we could interact with the living as you did at the bar. Why can't I tell him this?"

Azrael tried to think of an answer that would satisfy the emotional specter. "We're too close to a fated event for us to interfere. If this were a random act such as with the boy on the Ferris wheel, there would be a chance of changing the course of events. But here, you already know the outcome. Only the Fates can change what will happen next."

Riley gave one more attempt at screaming, "Leave! Run home! He's going to kill you!"

Glen did not so much as flinch with the banshee in his ear. He did, however, catch sight of the motion from Bob's hand and came to terms with the new reality of his situation. The revelation was a moment too late as Bob pulled his pistol, this time without a silencer, from a shoulder holster and aimed it at Glen's chest.

"No. Both of them had their minor accidents. I had nothing to do with them. Now, unless you want me to be responsible for one specific death tonight, you'd best come up with the money."

The gun attracted everyone's attention, and Glen fixated on the small object, which posed an enormous threat. When he answered, the cocky attitude disappeared from his voice. "Come on, man. You have to know I don't have that kind of money on me. I don't even have that in my bank account. How do you expect me to pay you ten grand?"

Bob shrugged his shoulders without taking the pistol from Glen's chest. "I don't care. Your stupid friend got my cash daddy killed. We had a good thing going until he showed up, and best I can tell, you're the only one still breathing who gets to catch the blame."

With his hands held up in front of him, Glen took a step backward towards his car. "It's cool. Look, I'll figure it out. We can make this work. Let me go back to the house, and I'll find a way to get you the money."

"No. You're going to tell your friend something. Let him know he's lucky he died before we learned he flipped us to the cops."

The severity of passing a message to a dead friend struck Glen, and he attempted to shield his body with his hands as Bob fired the gun. Four shots rang out into the cold mid-day air. The bar was so isolated that no one was near enough to think it was anything more than hunters or kids shooting at cans. Glen fell forward, staring at the holes in his hands and the blood flowing onto the snow.

This was too much for Riley to watch, and he turned his back while they murdered the one man he cared about. If this was what he had to look forward to for the rest of eternity, this exceeded his emotional capacity. He heard footsteps running to a car and tires crunching gravel.

The parking lot became still, and no other sounds invaded the isolated space. Riley turned to find his friend lying still on the ground, a faint glow about his body. "Can you do it? I don't know if I have the strength. This is all just too much," Riley said, while looking down at his best friend.

Death considered the request and reached down to free the soul from the body. Glen stood and glanced at his surroundings in a haze of confusion. Azrael said, "Be calm. All is as it should be, though there is someone who wishes to talk with you one last time."

Riley stepped from behind Azrael. With his face held low, Riley whispered, "I'm sorry for all the trouble I caused. This was not how things were supposed to happen."

To describe the expression on Glen's face as shocked would lack nuance but still sum up the emotion. He stood there with his mouth hanging open and eyes wide while looking between his recently vacated corpse and the man he had identified in the morgue only hours before. "What's going on here, Riley?"

It took every effort he had to speak, but Riley said, "It's a long story." This was unhelpful, and Glen shook his head, hoping to make things fall into place.

Azrael prepared to allow the two of them the time and space they needed to come to some form of final closure. But then, across the frozen air came a wave of heat and the sound of rusted metal and tortured animals crying in pain. Both Riley and Azrael froze in place and exchanged glances.

Death drew his sword of bronze and ordered Glen to "find somewhere to hide. If you see a clear path to the light, take it. Riley, do you know where that came from?"

There were no places to hide in the parking lot. It was an enormous expanse of gravel, with the only obstruction being Glen's car. The newly deceased specter ran for cover, with the vehicle his only option.

Riley stood beside Azrael, and the two of them scanned the surroundings. It was unclear where the sound came from, but Riley pointed to the melting snow that led to the Iron Horse. "They're inside."

A second howl echoed from the end of the driveway, and Riley spun to see the alpha standing in silhouette facing down the three of them. "There's the big one," Riley said and then caught sight of a smaller Ahemait exiting through the bar's door. "Any ideas?"

"Protect your friend! Get him to the bridge. I'll try to keep one or both of them off you."

This was not the pep talk Riley hoped to receive, as it included reliance on faith and luck, but it was a plan and gave him a direction. Without waiting for more detailed instructions, he pivoted on the gravel and ran to join Glen at the car. "We're getting out of here."

Death screamed at the two wolf-shaped monsters and brandished his sword. They turned to him, and he snarled in anger. Whatever words or message he conveyed appeared to have insulted their lineage and implied unmarried parents. The smaller of the two lunged forward and attempted to bite the back of Azrael's legs.

Azrael turned and struck with his sword across the wolf's furless snout. There was a crack as it hit bone and a yelp of pain before the creature turned away. It circled to regroup before attempting another bite.

The alpha waited until Azrael turned his back with the swing of a sword, then closed the distance with three leaps. Before Azrael could come round with his sword, the monster was upon him, forcing Death to the earth. Azrael rolled to his back and lay prone, using the blade to keep the beast from finishing its attack with a series of bites to his face.

"Where are we going?" Glen asked while his eyes darted back and forth between the Ahemait and the friend he'd seen dead. "Those things are going to kill us."

Riley tried to calm Glen by saying, "He's got that, but I need you to stay focused."

Glen turned his attention back to his friend and did everything he could to keep his eyes locked.

Though Death had shown Riley the bridge when Clay made his journey, he did not detail how to lead someone to the light. This left the two of them huddled behind a car with the threat of the Ahemait eating them before he figured it out. "Damn it, Riley, get it together," he said to himself.

With the alpha on top of the prone figure of Death, the smaller Ahemait stalked the other two specters. The vocals of that monster sounded a deep growl, like rocks crushed under tremendous weight. Riley stuck his head up to catch a view of where the other three were and pulled back down the instant the Ahemait circled the car.

"Come on, Glen, I can't lose you. I need your help," Riley pleaded.

This confused Glen, as he could see the fear in Riley's face but had not worked out what was taking place. "What do you want me to do? You're the expert here."

Riley wanted to cry at the description of himself as the most qualified person, given that he did not know what he was doing. The Ahemait came round the car and stood behind Glen with its legs braced, ready to lunge. "Get down!" Riley yanked Glen to the ground.

The Ahemait lunged, and Riley rose to meet it above his friend's prone spectral body. There was a searing flash of heat, and Riley pulled his hand away in pain as if he'd dipped his fingers into molten metal. What he hit was not liquid. It was the solid frame of the Ahemait, and the impact did more damage to it than to Riley. The hit flung the creature backward to crash into the spectral side of the Iron Horse.

A window in the real world exploded from the impact, and the Ahemait passed through into the bar. Riley stared at his hand until he realized the creature was gone. The victory was short-lived as there was still another, and he reached down to pick up his friend. "Look for a light, find it. There will be a bridge between the brilliance and where we are standing."

Glen appeared confused, but as he looked around, he saw the light that Riley mentioned glowing at the far edge of the parking lot. Riley gave his friend a little shove. "Now go. We'll take care of it from here."

The two of them wanted to say all the things to one another, but they didn't have the time. Glen hesitated, but then ran for the bridge and, in a flash, disappeared into the setting sun. The light was gone, and Riley turned to face the alpha and the other Ahemait as it emerged limping from the bar.

Death pushed the monster clear and made his way to his feet so that he stood with Riley against the two Ahemait. But the Ahemait's prize was left along the bridge. They had no reason to remain. The alpha barked at the smaller one, and the two ran off in a wave of heat.

Riley stood stoic, just long enough to ensure everyone left. He then cradled his hand and sat on the ground. "Holy shit, that hurt."

Azrael wore a smile of pride as he said, "It was still a good punch.

You did well, and your friend is now at peace. Come, let us go back to the hospital. There is nothing more we can do for anyone here."

The scene shifted, and once again, they stood in the hospital waiting room. The *Book of the Dead* sat on the table in front of them. Riley looked at his hand and saw it burned with red blisters covering its surface. "I don't suppose there are ghost doctors that can patch this up?"

Death shook his head, "No, but you'll heal. Next time, we'll try to find you something other than your fist to hit them with. Now let's see where they may have gone to. You injured one, and they will now become more desperate."

## CHAPTER 16
# FLYING SOLO

A chill wind found its way through the hospital as emergency-room doors opened and admitted a team of paramedics. They pushed a gurney with a woman whose chest they covered with thick bandages and rushed into the trauma center. The team ran past with their patient. The spectral form of the injured woman followed behind them.

"She's not going to make it, is she?" Riley asked Death as he continued to nurse his singed hand. The blisters were no longer weeping, but he covered them in the cloth of his shirt. It didn't stop them from hurting but made him feel better because the shirt prevented him from looking at the wounds.

The excitement surrounding the injured woman's entrance did not attract the attention of Azrael. He turned from the book when Riley spoke. "Who?" The ghostly image passed through the door at the far end of the hall, and he nodded in understanding. "Oh, her. No," he said with no emotion and returned to reviewing the *Book of the Dead*.

The indifference in his voice increased Riley's irritation. The young man continued to carry excess emotional baggage from the last few days and had not worked through everything that had occurred. "How can you be so dismissive about this? You don't care about any of them, do you?" he shouted at the Angel of Death.

Azrael closed the book and set it aside before patting the seat beside him. Anger fueled Riley, but he had nowhere to direct it, so after fuming for another minute, he sat beside the angel. When Death spoke, his words were patient. "I care about every soul, all of them. The people who lived their lives as sinners and millionaires or saints and paupers are all worthy of love."

He paused, but Riley would not allow the gap in the conversation to go unfilled. "Then what about her? What are you going to do about her?" He gestured vaguely in the direction of the trauma ward and the spectral woman.

"Margaret," Death helped by filling in the missing name of the woman.

"Whatever. What are you going to do about her?"

Death's hand came up, and he stopped Riley from saying anything more. "No! They have names, lives, and I care about all of them." Azrael allowed a moment of silence to hang while this concept developed. "Do not confuse inaction with lack of feeling."

For a long moment, the only sounds came from the back of the emergency room. Riley lowered his eyes to the book and attempted not to stare Death in the face. "I'm sorry."

"You love them. I can see that. It's why I asked for your help, though you still need to learn to keep your emotions in check. They are a source of great power for you but can distract you from your goals." Azrael slid the book over and opened it to a seemingly random page.

The more Riley observed the book, the more he realized that the pages did not matter when looking for a specific name. With all the people and dates changing, he was as likely to find what he searched for on any given page. Azrael left the book and asked, "What do you see?"

This was not the first time Riley had attempted to read the

leather-bound tome, but he was still new at the task, and it took focus and effort. The names this time highlighted themselves, and he ran his fingers along the rows. As Riley did this, his perceptions shifted, and each person appeared as a flickering image. He stopped on one, which caught his attention.

"Here, Edward Woods." The man was climbing a frozen ladder with a stack of shingles over his shoulder. Snow draped over the roof of his two-story home and a single melted patch showed in the center where heat escaped the attic. "He's on an icy roof. I don't see anyone helping him."

Azrael considered the option and touched the name so that he gained an image of the man and his situation. "It looks promising. This time it will be just you, so let's talk for a moment."

Residency in pharmacy school was thirteen months, but now Azrael expected Riley to go out alone after one half-successful try. "You're joking. You'll back me up, right?"

No answer came from Azrael, so Riley pulled back his vision and turned to look at the Angel of Death. "I can't do this on my own."

"You can, and you will do fine. Trust yourself. This job is more about confidence than about knowledge." Azrael then pulled the familiar bronze blade from a pocket next to nowhere and offered it to Riley.

"What's this for?"

Death waited for Riley to answer his question, but as the silence continued, he said, "So you don't punch another creature from the pit with your exposed skin. You can hurt them by hitting them either way, but they are *incestus*." He paused for a second and said, "Perhaps the better word is polluted."

It took time before Riley accepted the sword, but it also bore an unexpected weight when he did. The heft in his hands pulled against his soul. "Thank you. I'll give this right back when I finish."

"Don't make promises when you can't predict the future. We will all do what we can and try to do our best."

Riley nodded and put the belt of the sword around his waist, and though the weight of the blade remained, the object disappeared from view. He reached his hand down to touch the pommel and found it a simple process to draw the blade from whatever ethereal hiding place in which it existed.

"Are you sure I'm not going to mess this whole thing up completely? I don't know that I'm going to live with myself if they destroy someone's soul because of me."

Death reached out a hand and gripped Riley's shoulder in a reassuring embrace. "You will do your best. We never know if we will succeed or fail, so all we can do is our best."

The book was open, a sword was on his hip, and the watch was in his pocket. Riley held every trapping of Death and stood ready to walk out on his first attempt to save a soul without the help of Azrael. Fear showed on his face as he bit his lip, though he kept his chin high. There was nothing left to say, and Riley ran his fingers down the names until he found Edward's once more.

Between the ticks of a clock, the scene shifted, and Riley found himself alone on the snowy lawn of a suburban home. Houses were upper-middle class, and most stood two stories tall with brick exteriors and blinds covering each window. Every suburb Riley had been in showed the same feature, which was a lack of people. Whoever lived in these sections of a city only ventured outside when necessary, and on this day, only one man needed to be away from his central heat and fireplace.

Mr. Woods laid the unsupported ladder against the gutter and climbed up its length with a bag of shingles. At some point a leak had formed in his roof, and though it was not apparent in pleasant weather, the water came in once the snow arrived. A contractor would do a better job later, but for now, he needed to stop the leak.

The scene was beautiful in its own right, and Riley took a moment to enjoy this moment of stillness. Part of him wondered how the Fates could transform such a moment into a time of horror, but he knew better. Any point held the possibility of being peaceful or terrifying, and the shift between the two took less than a second.

As he continued to watch the man work on his roof, Riley decided this was the worst part of his new employment. Every aspect of him wanted to warn the man of what was to come. The man must have known the inherent danger of working on a snow-covered roof, but Riley knew the likely outcome. How could Riley force him to the ground without waiting for the man to fall?

Riley held a terrible contract with fate and waited for the inevitable end to play out before him. As he waited, a wave of heat washed over him and turned a patch of snow to slush. This was not the first time Riley had experienced heat from the Pit, and he pulled his sword from its hiding place. He stood ready and scanned the scene, looking for the infernal creatures.

At the end of the driveway stood the Ahemait alpha, judging from the creature's size. Riley needed them to stand shoulder by shoulder to know for sure. The monster showed no fear, only a predatory calculation as it attempted to decide if Riley was a threat.

What was Riley supposed to do? Should he stay focused on the creature that threatened him or turn his attention back to the man on the roof? His first instinct told him to defend himself and worry about the man later, but something was wrong with the plan. As he continued the thought, it occurred to him what the problem was. These creatures were cowards.

As frightening as they were to Riley, they fought by circling behind their victim. When Azrael confronted them, they ran at the first opportunity. Their tactics were to distract and nip at the heels of weaker targets. If this remained true, then where was the other one? The alpha must have been their distraction.

With great effort, Riley pulled his attention from the massive wolf in the drive and looked back at the man on his roof. He was no longer on the slanted shingles. Casting his eyes down, Riley found him crumpled on the ground with a bag of slate on his face. Inwardly, Riley winced at the position in which the home handyman landed, and part of him was grateful he wasn't watching when the man fell.

The other thing he saw while looking over his shoulder was the smaller Ahemait. This placed Riley at the tip of a triangle and the man along the distant edge. He cursed under his breath at being in the worst possible position to intercept both monsters before either reached the recently deceased.

Riley hesitated. That moment of indecision was when none of his plans were good enough, and he was unwilling to choose a less-than-perfect option. The Ahemait took advantage of this, and both screamed their terrible rusted howls while the alpha broke into a run aimed at Riley. Its powerful hind legs forced the thing to bound and close the distance. There was no time to contemplate a new idea.

Riley did his best to brace the sword between himself and the creature, bringing the weapon up. He'd never trained in swinging sharp objects more massive than a scalpel. The hope that this blade confirmed a mystical knowledge of fighting was dashed to the ground, and the monster plowed into the young specter. Both of them collided with the earth and slid across the lawn.

Riley's skin burned beneath his clothes where the thing stood on top of him. But his concern was more with the mouth full of fangs trying to tear apart his face. The sword gave Riley a barrier to hold between him and the alpha, but he struggled to find a way out from under it.

Somewhere on the other side of the yard, the smaller Ahemait ran towards the defenseless soul of Edward. It was only a guess what happened to the man and Riley prayed there was still time to affect the outcome.

Everything held still in the air as time stopped. It was difficult for Riley to describe later what occurred, but a glow formed near the center of his chest. The more frustrated and angry Riley became over his impotence at his prone position fighting with the alpha and his fear for Edward, the more radiant the glow became. Eventually, everything became overwhelming, and Riley screamed in the creature's maw.

As his voice lashed out and the glow released, the alpha tore away. The creature flew across the yard and landed on the far side of the driveway, its chest smoking as it struggled to regain its feet.

Without waiting to understand what occurred, Riley pulled himself up and searched for the second Ahemait. It was easy to find the thing as it stood over the form of the fallen soul. There was nothing to do. This was his first chance to show Azrael that he could trust Riley to save someone, and he'd failed. Another soul had died because of him, and Riley retched as the monster gorged itself on the existence of the man's spirit.

Riley's anger while struggling against the alpha was nothing compared to the murderous rage he focused on the creature feasting on the dead. No light existed in what Riley did next. He stalked around the edge of the driveway and drove his blade deep into the side of the lesser Ahemait. A sickening hollow sound of escaping wind echoed out of the wound, and Riley's hand erupted with heat and fire.

Every fiber of Riley's hand filled with pain, but he kept the blade deep into the monster's side. He then twisted it and drove the dull bronze deeper until all sounds from the Ahemait stopped, and it fell to the ground. Riley withdrew his blackened and blistered arm to stare at his kill. It wasn't until the alpha's scream of rage jerked him back to reality that Riley paid the world any attention.

Snarls and yips came from the older Ahemait before it spat burning liquid on the ground. The monster ran and disappeared in a wave of heat. Riley's anger continued to course through his body but had nothing on which to focus, so he slammed the sword into its sheath.

He looked at what remained of Edward's soul and mourned for the departed. "What a waste. Those creatures have no right to destroy people. I won't let them do this again. If Azrael wants my help, he will see a change in how I do things. We're not letting them get away with whatever they want anymore."

There was nothing he could do with what remained, so Riley retracted his focus and returned to the hospital, where he opened his eyes and glanced about the waiting room. He saw the same pale walls and plastic chairs. What he did not see was the former Angel of Death.

There must have been some mistake. Where would the angel have gone if he were not waiting here? Riley walked through the emergency ward of the hospital. In every room, he poked his head through the wall and attempted to catch sight of the familiar specter he had befriended. Once confident that Azrael was not in the hospital's emergency section, Riley prepared himself to search the rest of the building.

Riley stopped his search when he entered the waiting room and found Strix standing on the table with the *Book of the Dead* in front of them. "He's gone," they said once Riley came out of the emergency exit.

"What do you mean, gone?"

"Is that a hard concept to understand?" The owl tilted its head to its side. "At one time, Azrael was here. You and he spoke. Now he is no longer here." Strix said none of this condescendingly, but the creature talked as if addressing a small child. Perhaps that was how they viewed Riley, or anyone of mortal age.

Riley glanced about the room, attempting to see someone who was not there. "There has to be a mistake. He wouldn't just leave. He's supposed to be teaching me what I need to know."

Strix took a slow breath to calm themselves. "Azrael trained you to be the Angel of Death so that you would no longer need him. However long you expected the training period to be, it was shorter. Take the book and become the new Death."

The *Book of the Dead* sat on the table, and everything in the room appeared to rotate around it as Riley attempted to adjust his life's compass. He took a step forward and put his hand on the same leather surface he'd touched several times before and felt the spiritual weight of the book. "Is everyone sure? I just let someone die. How can I be Death if I screwed up already?"

"I can't explain how little that made sense," Strix said in response.

Though Riley never literally picked the book up from the table, its weight passed to him. With it came the responsibility and the mantel of being the Angel of Death. He didn't fully know everything that went with the position, but he understood its value.

Strix watched the exchange with something best described as boredom and waited for Riley to stop making odd expressions before they spoke. "Are you done? OK, good. Now about your minor issue on that last time out. We need to talk."

This was like any other job Riley had while he was still alive. He had not worked for a full day, and they were lining up to reprimand him for poor performance. What would happen if they fired him from being an angel? "I already told you I messed up. The guy died. Those two monsters got the better of me, and I couldn't save him."

"No. First, the man was supposed to die. That's why you were there. Also, the Ahemait eat the dead. That's what they do. It's in their nature as much as it is your responsibility to protect the newly departed."

The choice of words confused Riley, and he asked for clarification. "They're monsters. Why are you permitting them to go around killing people? We should destroy them so everyone can be safe."

Strix had learned a close approximation of an eye roll and demonstrated this for Riley. "You need to learn a new lexicon. Your morality does not guide existence. What you think is right and wrong does not define how They should put the universe together. The Ahemait exist for a purpose. Maybe one day you will understand what that is."

"And I have this job for a reason. I can kill them, and if given a chance, I'm going to do just that," Riley said.

"How about you stop using any word related to death unless you know what you're talking about. As the new Death, you sound ignorant."

In the books and movies Riley knew, the Grim Reaper was always on top of the totem pole. Never had Riley assumed that Death would be the low man in the office of some larger hierarchy. Clearly, from the way Strix was talking down to him, this was a new reality to which he needed to become adjusted.

"Try this. If employment is the reference you want to use, your job is to defend the dead from the Ahemait and guide the dead to the Elysium Fields. After they destroyed Mr. Woods's soul, could you fulfill your assigned duty?"

There was nothing he could have done at that point. The man was dead, not just in a traditional broken-neck type of way. He'd gone wherever souls go when they die, and nothing Riley did could have brought him back. Riley shook his head. "No. I failed before I got a chance to do anything for him."

"Forget him," Strix snapped and bit Riley's hand with their sharp beak. "Once Mr. Woods was gone, you had the obligation to leave. It didn't matter that the Ahemait stayed and devoured what remained of his soul."

This still made little sense to Riley, and he defiantly shook his head. "I don't believe that. It always makes a difference what you do."

"OK, yes, you made a difference." Strix took several long breaths as they continued to try to remain calm. "You killed one of the younger Ahemait, and there are many. You also denied the alpha her meal. She is now upset at the death of a cub and starving. How do you think this is going to play out?"

Realization sometimes strikes like a bolt of lightning or a clap of thunder. This time it was a slow glow of a light turning on in a dark room. Riley's eyes widened as he considered all the possibilities of destruction he'd unleashed on the penumbra. "How bad could it possibly be?"

Strix opened the book with their foot and let the pages flip past until Riley saw numbers and names changing in rapid succession. "You must have noticed that they influence the real world, same as you and Azrael. If they can't scavenge the food they need, they are going to hunt for it."

The names were changing so quickly that many would not finish before the ink wrote over it with another. Riley said, "There has to be something we can do."

"We?"

Riley's eyes snapped up from the book to look at Strix. "You're a guide for the departed as well, aren't you? Can't you help with this?"

"Everyone has their role. I'll continue to do mine, but this," they motioned to the pages, "is your mess, and I recommend fixing it."

The book closed, and Riley sat in one of the hard plastic chairs with his head in his hands. How did things come to this point? How much worse could it get? What would these things do in their search for food? Who would they go after?

Ideas formed in Riley's mind, and he looked up, ready to discuss his plans with Strix, but the owl had left, and he was once again alone in the waiting room. Riley returned his head to his hands and did everything he could not to give up and cry.

# CHAPTER 17

# COUNTING COUP

Time passed, as night and day blended into a complex gray of light and moving people. At best guess, Riley sat in the waiting room for a day and a half before an older woman took up the chair beside him. She appeared to be in her nineties and wore a patient expression of someone who had seen two lifetimes of experiences.

"I've seen that face before," she said as her way of introduction.

Riley brought his head up and glanced about the room to see if she perhaps was talking to anyone else. No one sat near them. He made another guess and checked to see if she had died. She was old, but alive. How did she talk to him? Riley had no answer for her.

"It's OK," she continued, "most people pretend they can't see me either. They want nothing to remind them of death. Somehow, they think I was never a teenage girl because I'm now an old woman. So tell me, what has caused such a young man to try to balance the weight of the world on his shoulders?"

With the departure of Azrael and Strix, Riley assumed he would be without a companion or confidant for the rest of his days. Perhaps the isolation was what drove the previous Angel of Death to search for a replacement. But there must be something more nuanced behind the divide between the living and the dead. Someone close to death had just spoken to him as a friend. Then he remembered the man from the carnival.

His conversation with the carnival man had happened only a week ago. It seemed as though a lifetime had passed since the night he spoke to someone who was near death or already dead. What was the man's name? Riley tried to remember. He would need to learn people's names better if he were to stand in for the previous angel.

To the woman, he said, "I didn't do my job right, and someone died. I did something terrible, and now I'm afraid more people will die. This is a new job for me, and I'm afraid I already put uncounted numbers of people at risk."

Riley expected any number of responses from the woman, but when she smiled and patted his knee, this surprised him. For one thing, Riley did not expect tactile contact with a person from the physical world. But he was even more surprised when she said, "Son, people are going to die, especially in your line of work. You're Death."

The look on Riley's face must have been clear to read as the woman chuckled to herself. "Oh, come now. A person does not reach my age and not know such things. You will need to stop letting yourself be so easily surprised. It will make more sense when you're as old as me."

Riley nodded his head and attempted to wrap his thoughts around what she told him. "I'll keep that in mind, but I didn't just mean they died. I wasn't able to protect them like I was supposed to."

"Do you know what ineffable means?"

Riley shook his head. The woman explained, "It means something that is too grand to be explained. There are other deeper meanings, but that one works for us now."

"What's your point?"

"Patience, little one. You have all the time in the world, and you still haven't learned patience. The answer is coming." She deliberately paused and took a deep breath before saying, "Many believe an ineffable plan exists to govern the creation of all things."

This sounded a bit too much like Sunday school. Riley resisted the urge to allow his eyes to roll back into his head. "That's a great idea and all, but even if this was some glorious plan for me to fail, I still failed."

Again, she forced Riley to wait for what she said next. The room was still except for the buzz of a fluorescent light. Riley held his breath and his tongue. "If you intend to reach greatness, the failures you suffer in the beginning are to teach you. So ask yourself if the Angel of Death is intended to fail, or is this a learning experience? Those are the two options if you believe in an ineffable plan."

Riley pulled himself to his feet. "I'm sorry. Things are getting to be a bit too philosophical for me. I messed things up. This wasn't a minor problem I caused. This was something terrible, and I don't know how to fix things. I can't just hope that everything will get better just because some play says it's supposed to."

The woman sat quietly and allowed Riley to talk to himself while speaking in her direction. "I have some thinking to do, but thank you for seeing me. It is good to know I'm not alone, if even for a moment."

"You're welcome," she said, but did not rise with him. "Now go do whatever you need to do. I'm sure it will be the right thing."

Riley had little more to say to this woman, so they parted ways, and Riley took up the *Book of the Dead*. He had not practiced travel without using the book, but he needed somewhere to think, and he was in no mood to remain in the hospital.

When he opened his eyes, his mind, and by extension his body, had wandered back to the carnival where he'd saved the young child, William. Things had changed so much in only a week, but people continued to fill the rides and buy ridiculous snacks. As much chaos as the carnival presented to the world, the risk of death was surprisingly lower than many other places he considered visiting.

The Ferris wheel stood on the far side of the parade field, and

Riley made his way in that direction. At first, he did his best to avoid bumping into anyone. This was challenging as no one paid any attention to his existence, and he ducked, then dodged each wandering pedestrian. After a hundred yards, it became clear that everyone subconsciously avoided bumping into him. The more he observed their behavior he realized the living worked hard to avoid touching Death, stepping clear of him every chance they found.

Once he arrived at the massive rotating wheel, Riley took an empty car. He rode alone in an extended lazy circle. Everyone appeared so happy down below. Many in the crowd risked death, but it didn't appear Riley would work any of them tonight. To be sure, he pulled out his pocket watch and looked at the swirling myriad of stars.

The blaze of tightly packed dots spiraled from where he was sitting and expanded to show the entire carnival. It then revealed itself as a terrifying horror as dozens of lights flicked in seemingly random patterns. Something was about to happen there, and he had no way to predict what. The only thing he knew was it meant he needed to be ready to go to work.

If Riley had taken the time to think, he would not have stepped out of a moving Ferris wheel.

At the top of the rotation, he stepped from the car and stood on the rotating edge. The wheel turned below him, and he remained motionless, with no rule of physics keeping him in place. From this position, he searched the carnival with his eyes.

What had happened? The pocket watch appeared to show that a singular event would occur to kill several people at once. But this may have been misleading, as the lights did not all go out. They pulsed. Some went out, and others continued to burn. These people all hung on the edge of life and death, but maybe not everyone would cross over.

Riley wished he had a way to contact Azrael to ask his former mentor for guidance. He had so many more questions about the way things worked, but he received no answers. Why had the man left him so quickly? He had to know that situations above Riley's capability would develop. How did he expect him to deal with them when they arose? It didn't matter now. Riley was on his own.

To take inventory of the situation and try to determine where the problem might be, Riley looked at what the people were eating. This was by no stretch of the imagination healthy, as vendors fried much of the food and put it on sticks for no apparent reason. These gastric atrocities also contained enough grease to lubricate several small engines. It seemed unlikely that these would threaten dozens of people at once, so Riley considered the rides. The Ferris wheel stood taller than the others, and if people fell from it, they would suffer significant injury, but this didn't feel right. The pocket watch seemed to be showing a mass casualty event.

Something about the object on which Riley perched was more like a rock in a storm. Everything might move around him, but the wheel was not going anywhere. Perhaps this was another ability Azrael forgot to teach him how to use. Riley looked out at the other rides. What about the kid rides? Those also didn't seem like the source of danger, as they moved slow enough to be of negligible risk to anyone.

Then he saw it. No glowing banner or arrows pointed at the ride to tell him that the destruction would occur there. At the same time, he felt deep within his gut that the ride in front of him threatened the lives of everyone near it. Riley took out his pocket watch and held it facing the ride and those standing around the rotating base.

The longer he focused on the swirl of lights, the better he identified which light belonged to each person. That steady beam on the side was the little girl with the cotton candy. The faded red light was the overweight man eating his third corn dog while eyeing the dessert vendor. Then there were the blinking lights that traded in and out, which would switch off tonight. Those all gathered near the spinning spider thrill ride.

The spider was a favorite attraction for young adults who lacked excitement in their daily lives. Here, a five-spoked hub extended out from its center to hold three cars each. The cars rotated around one another, and the hub rotated and tilted about in the middle, and everyone screamed. As dangerous as everything appeared, it was far safer than the drive home many of these kids prepared to undertake after being out late and drinking.

Someone had changed the rules and stacked the deck against the carnival patrons tonight. Riley put the pocket watch away. There was nothing to do to change the blinking lights, and watching them caused him anxiety. Should he try to do anything? As the Specter of Death, his responsibility was caring for the dead, not worrying about the living. People will die. That no longer concerned him, or that's what everyone expected him to believe.

Riley wanted to do anything in his power to change the course of events. If he had known how to prevent the accident from occurring, he would have interfered. Time passed, and he talked himself to a point where he accepted what was to come as inevitable. The ride gave an unnatural shift.

Everyone on the ride screamed as it veered below them. None of the spectators noticed the difference in screaming. The riders had been shrieking to various levels since the ride began. Now that they shouted for the ride to stop, they lost their voices in the night. Riley observed the shift. He expected just such an event, and his body tensed in anticipation of when screams of joy became terror.

The only person who realized something went wrong was a young girl who tugged on her mother's hand. The two were walking towards the ride, but the little girl insisted that she wanted to go in the other direction. There was arguing between the girl and her mother, but the child won, and they headed back towards a game with little rubber ducks.

When the inevitable occurred, things happened quickly. The hub shifted again. Its massive spinning section dropped off-balance from whatever mechanism it sat upon. Once the base broke free, the cars on the low end drove into the dirt. The screaming from anyone in those cars ceased. The hub stopped its rotation with the impact but fell in on itself with the loss of momentum. Each remaining vehicle hit the ground with successive collisions.

One ride at a time, the carnival came to a standstill as everyone stopped and focused on the destruction at the spider. The silence lasted for a second or an eternity, then people began screaming and running. Most fled the scene. What they feared would occur after the ride came to a stop was hard to comprehend. Others pulled out their phones and began recording videos of the event. Miraculously, one employee of the carnival called the emergency medical services.

A small contingent of volunteers ran into the wreckage to search for anyone who might be trapped under the rubble. Soldiers, nurses, firefighters, cops, and five others began sifting through the broken pieces of the ride. They were unable to move most of the pieces, but at least the wounded would know someone was there and help was on the way.

Someone else needed to go to work; Riley stepped from the top of the ride and fell at the speed of a feather to the ground. It wasn't until the new Death landed and began walking that it occurred to him that stepping off tall objects might be dangerous. Thankfully, he had yet another ability Azrael failed to mention, and instincts allowed him to find it.

The entire scene was confusing, and Riley was unsure which souls might need him. From everything Azrael taught him, his role as the Angel of Death existed for unattended deaths. The Strix did the heavy lifting for everyday deaths and collected at the hospital for the unexpected ones. This was unexpected, so likely an ambulance would pick up these souls and take them to the hospital where the Strix would care for them.

If all this was true, he had no purpose in being here. He only came because he needed a place to think. The event with the ride was just a coincidence. Though the more he considered it, the less he believed coincidences occurred. He remained on the outskirts of the wreckage and watched the mortals. They worked to find survivors and identify the dead. Riley kept his eyes open for any new specters who might try to wander from the area.

Searching the scene, Riley caught sight of the occupants of the first car. There were three of them, and all of them were standing near the crash. A general look of confusion remained locked upon their face, as they stood together to discuss what had occurred. "Poor guys. At least they have each other to help them come to terms with things. The transition can be rough," Riley said to himself.

He prepared to stroll over and join them when the massive form of the alpha Ahemait stepped from the spider's base. Riley froze in place. The alpha bared rows of teeth and gave a guttural growl. As much as Riley wanted to believe he was becoming accustomed to the sound of these creatures, he doubted it would ever happen.

He reached into his jacket, grasped the sword's hilt, and withdrew the bronze blade. "We don't have to do this," Riley said while attempting to sound like the tough guy. Nothing inside him felt like the big scary man he wanted to portray, but he hoped to fake it.

They say that dogs can smell fear. This adage likely extended to demon hounds from the Pit as the Ahemait showed no sign of backing down from Riley's threat. Riley stepped to his left and attempted to circle the creature. If only he could reach the three specters, then they could flee. Novel-Death didn't need to fight this thing and win. All he needed to do was help them escape.

Riley moved slowly, and the alpha jumped to land between him and the destroyed cars. The demon barked in defiance and snapped twice while advancing on the young reaper. Riley held up the sword and ensured it remained between him and the creature. What could he do?

He continued to face the alpha. Riley saw behind the Ahemait three more exited the portals of heat. Every fiber in Riley's body tensed as he prepared to fight a losing battle against impossible odds. He had a hard enough time facing one of these creatures at the last encounter, and now there were going to be four against one.

The thing he would not do was back down. Riley decided if his story was going to end, it would end in bravery. He planted his feet and shouted at the alpha. "Come on. You want me! Come get me!"

Part of the rational thinking side of Riley hoped the monster would waver at his defiance. So often in movies, this was the part where the bad guy reconsidered what he was doing and ran away. Maybe the hero had some secret weapon that no one knew about. His other thoughts reminded him that this monster did not watch many films.

The alpha lunged. Its massive form bounded across the distance before jumping to the side at the last moment. The monster evaded a collision with Riley's blade and planted itself to the far right. Riley held the sword ready for the impact and hoped to skewer the monster, but when it changed directions, he pivoted. This forced him off balance and took his eyes away from the other three.

"Oh, come on. That's cheating," Riley complained, though no one listened. As soon as he rotated ninety degrees from his starting position, the creature continued its movement and landed behind where he originally stood. This forced Riley to turn so that his back was to the spider and the three other Ahemait.

"I don't suppose I can take a mulligan and try this over?" he asked, knowing the answer. Even if the creature spoke words, that would not provide any type of relief, but then it did something unexpected. Riley thought when he turned around the alpha would leap straight at him. This did not happen.

The alpha didn't attack and Riley glanced over his shoulder to see what the other three were doing. It was fate that he did, as one of the three was in mid-leap. This forced Riley to rotate once more, completing a three-sixty, and he braced the sword for the creature's impact.

The thing came in high, and while it was not as large as the alpha, he might have confused the two if they were not standing near one another. If Riley braced the sword the way he had attempted on the alpha's original lunge, then the beast would skewer itself on the point. Instead, it met him in the middle of its lunge, driving Riley to his knees with the sword held horizontally between them. They were now at a stalemate.

It's OK to reach a neutral position with your opponent when fighting one-on-one, but with multiple attackers, it is untenable. Riley heard behind him the scrape of claws against dirt as the alpha lunged at his exposed back. He braced for death, or whatever the next closest alternative would be for him at this stage.

The creature did not make a killing blow. Instead, it bit hard into his left ankle. Teeth sunk deep, and Riley cried out in pain as the searing hot razors bit through flesh and into bone. Alpha gave a pull and yanked Riley from his feet, then tossed him aside. The world was flashes of red and black as Riley did everything possible to remain conscious through the pain.

Then the Ahemait barked at one another and Riley expected them to end his existence. What were they waiting for? This was how monsters did things. He killed one of them, and now was their chance to exact vengeance by destroying him. But the attack didn't come.

Carefully, Riley forced his eyes open and saw that one of the smaller Ahemait stood guard over his body. While prone, it was difficult to judge size, and they all appeared far too large. Riley pushed himself to a sitting position, and the Ahemait growled a low-throated warning against moving any more than that. The pain from this simple movement was warning enough, and Riley wondered if he had the ability to stand if he wanted.

What stopped their attack? For a fleeting moment, Riley hoped it was the return of Azrael or a flight of Strix. As he looked at the scene of destruction, it was clear neither of these had occurred, and the Ahemait wandered freely to do as they pleased. The horror of the situation was that what they pleased was dragging flailing specters from the wreckage.

It was too much to watch passively. Riley still held his sword in hand and, despite the pain, forced himself to his feet and threatened the Ahemait. "You can either move or get cut. Your choice."

This time, the creature hesitated. It appeared unsure at the level of resolve in someone so injured who would face these odds a second time. None of the Ahemait would have done the same, and it did not register in their minds that this type of behavior might be typical for anyone else.

First, it tried to growl, but this did not dissuade Riley, so next, it barked over its shoulder at the others. The alpha heard the call, and though it did not answer back, it stopped what it was doing and trotted over to join the smaller creature.

The two exchanged barks, but then the alpha took a bite out of the smaller Ahemait's ear, and it ran off. Alpha then turned to Riley and communicated with a series of barks and yaps. Unlike Azrael, Riley could not understand the words from the infernal being. He shrugged his shoulders. "I don't speak mutt."

Alpha barked once and snapped his teeth. Riley needed no interpretation to see the anger at being called a "mutt." The creature advanced two steps closer and snapped its teeth. Spittle from its maw dripped on the ground, where the dark liquid bubbled and burned into the earth.

Riley brandished the blade at the alpha and repeated his threat. "You can stand in my way or not, but I'm going to help those people."

Another guttural growl echoed from deep within the beast's throat in response to Riley's attempt at intimidation. Whatever threat Riley thought he presented, he failed. Instead, he stood exposed with only a thin piece of metal to defend himself against the alpha.

The alpha lunged at Riley's right hand and its bronze blade. The young specter had no experience handling weapons and was ill-prepared to defend himself. When the Ahemait reached his arm, its teeth bit once more into his flesh. The pain destroyed his grip, and he lost the sword to the ground. The alpha slammed its shoulder into Riley's body and knocked him to the ground.

Riley curled in a ball with his arm torn at the wrist and his ankle mauled. He wanted to cry but was doing his best to remain stoic. The alpha reviewed the angel's condition and seemed satisfied with what it had done.

From the ground, Riley yelled, "Go ahead, finish me! Just get it over with!"

The day before, Strix had approximated an eye roll for Riley. Here, the alpha did its best to show the same trick. Its patience with this screaming biped was thin, but the creature was young, and the former human would learn if given time. The alpha leaped toward Riley and gripped his neck in its powerful jaws, then held him there. Riley could feel the teeth threatening as if burning hot razors, but none punctured his skin.

After holding him for ten heartbeats, the alpha released Riley and shoulder-checked him to the ground. He then barked and ran to join the other Ahemait, leaving Riley in a huddled pile, wounded, humiliated, and confused. Then things got even worse. He could do nothing to stop the monsters as they dragged the souls of the recently departed away from the ride. Tonight they were not eating them where they fell. Whatever their intention, they appeared to be taking the dead back to their warren.

Each of the four took a soul, and they disappeared in a wave of heat. Riley pushed himself into a seated position and leaned his back against a piece of the broken ride. "Azrael, if you're out there, you could not have picked a worse person as your replacement. Look at everything I've done. I'm causing suffering everywhere I go, and now I have nothing left to give these people."

An ambulance arrived through the parting crowd to help with the wounded and check on the dead. Riley had forgotten about the others who were there, the ones who did not die. He hoped they would survive, or at least that the Strix could save them at the hospital. There was nothing more Riley could do for them. He had spent everything and was now an empty husk.

He looked at his arm and the deep gash where the teeth dug into his flesh. There was no blood, and blackened char showed rather than clean cuts and blood. How long did it take for an angel to heal? Or would he be fired and now become just a specter? If only he could go back to his choice on the roof and go on the bridge. Why did he decide to save the world?

The paramedics could only fit two of the wounded in the back of the ambulance, as they both needed to lie flat. They then drove from the scene. There was still an extensive number of injured who needed help, and signs showed Riley that some of those who remained were not guaranteed to survive.

# CHAPTER 18

# COUNT TO EIGHT

T he Angel of Death's duty was to protect the souls of the departed and guide them to their next world. Azrael told Riley this path they presented led to Elysium, though he never heard Azrael accurately describe the Elysian fields. He assumed they stood in for heaven in whatever religion angels followed. If that were the case, then the creatures of heat, pain, and tortured screams must come from the place corresponding to hell.

No one remained for Riley to ask these types of things. Perhaps Strix would answer the questions, but Riley was afraid to confront the owl. He had screwed up stuff beyond recognition. The last time he and the ancient avian spoke, the bird reprimanded him for his mistake. No. He would not crawl back and ask Strix to teach him after things became complicated. He would fix them first.

As for fixing the situation, Riley did not know how to do that. He pulled himself to his feet as best he was able, though his injured leg barely supported any weight. Some broken debris littered the ground near where he had fallen. This included bits of wood from an old fence, and Riley used a piece to fashion himself a crutch.

Riley maneuvered closer to the injured and dying, using the cane and limping heavily on his good leg. At first glance, the scene was nothing more than confused mortals running among the casualties. Novel-Death took a deep breath and attempted to focus. After opening his eyes, the aura of life that distinguished the souls from corpses was not visible.

"Have they demoted me out of a job after less than a day?" Riley asked himself. He pushed his hand into his jacket and pulled out the pocket watch. After opening it, he consulted the stars and better understood who was before him.

The confusing mass of people stopped flickering and blinking after the ride crashed. What remained was a steady-state of bright light or pale glow, and he judged which ones stood closer to death. "I thought there were more." He continued to look around the wreckage.

The truth occurred to him that a count of bodies did not correspond to the number of souls. Eight bodies lay lifeless near the spider. Riley had seen the Ahemait drag four souls away, but that should leave four. Instead, he observed just two specters sitting together on the side of the crowd. They attempted to comfort one another while waiting to accept what had occurred.

Where were the other three? Riley left the two together and went in search of the three. The debris and his leg slowed his efforts, but the longer he looked, the more desperate he became. "They can't be gone. They only took four."

Riley cast his cane aside and began moving bits of broken metal to search for any of the spirits trapped below. If he had considered his actions, he would have known an object could not physically trap a soul, but he was desperate and needed answers.

One searcher glimpsed the lone figure on a pile attempting to dig through the wreckage from below. "Hey, you find something?" he yelled up to Riley.

It wasn't until the man joined Riley in moving large pieces of debris that he realized someone was helping him. This forced him to stop and look at the mortal in confusion. "You can see me?" he asked.

In retrospect, he did not pick the best way to start the conversation. But Riley was dealing with many issues, and he did not fully engage his brain. This question caused the man to pause and inspect his fellow digger. The mortal glanced at the injuries on Riley's wrist and leg. "Oh, shit, man, you're hurt. Here, come with me. We'll get the medic to check you out."

Riley wanted to disappear. If he knew how to turn invisible, he would. He would leave the man guessing what happened to his phantom visitor. As things stood, Riley did not know how to become visible or invisible. Did they not see him for some other reason? It appeared somewhat random when people noticed him. This was another item he would have appreciated Azrael explaining before he left.

"No. I'm good. They are just little dog bites. I'm trying to find someone." Riley tried to distract himself and focus back on the search. "Let's find them first."

The mortal hesitated, but as there was little anyone could do for the injured man, he allowed him to continue digging for as long as he was able. No other bodies existed. Riley knew where they rested. He was searching for their souls but couldn't describe this to his fellow searcher. After a half-hour, he found the first and guessed what had become of the others.

She was a woman of perhaps twenty years, and beside her was what Riley presumed was her date. Only fragments remained after sharp teeth had torn the souls apart. The creatures had not devoured this couple as they had done with all the ones before. They did this to kill someone and nothing more. No longer did Riley think of the Ahemait as animals. They thought as clearly as any rational creature. They were evil monsters, but still rational and capable of retaliation.

Riley fell to his knees. The pain was immense along his leg, but he ignored it. A scream issued forth, not out of physical discomfort but resulting from the injury to his soul upon seeing these two destroyed specters. The man who'd been helping him search stopped what he was doing and watched with confusion and concern.

"You OK, man? You need me to find someone?" But he did not wait for an answer and started waving down a pair of paramedics at the far edge of the wreckage.

"They killed them," was all Riley said. This would make more sense if he knelt over the pair's bodies rather than their souls. As things stood, he was presumably the only one who witnessed the desecration. "Why would they do this? What is the purpose of this?"

"Hold tight. We'll get someone up here to look at you. It's OK." The man moved forward to intercept the paramedics and give them a brief description of what he'd observed.

Riley ignored them and fixated on the souls. He attempted to pick the woman up to cradle her in his arms. Her form then broke apart, and cold air released from where she once existed. Nothing of the woman's soul remained except his memory of her. Her lover followed soon after, and the two disappeared.

The paramedic reached Riley, put an arm about the angel, and guided him back to his feet. "Come now. Let's get you somewhere away from all this. Everyone's had a rough day, and there's no sense dwelling on things you can't change."

Something in the back of Riley's mind wanted him to throw the mortal off him and scream his defiance. This part of him lost the battle against the piece that wanted to huddle in the corner and cry over his wounded arm, leg, and ego. He gripped the offered arm, and together they hobbled to the makeshift aid station.

At the far edge of the broken ride, a tent that once held the ring-toss game was cleared to make room for the injured. Riley counted eight bodies, though the ride injured many more when it broke apart. These wounds ranged from broken bones to cuts and scrapes. Many of the casualties suffered from dust inhalation. The carnival staff laid them out and used the ambulance's oxygen to keep them comfortable.

Initially, the medics believed Riley to be an emotional victim, so he received the lowest level of care. They pushed such people off to the far side and gave them a quiet place to sit where no one bothered them. It was enough if they stopped bothering the staff who tried to help the other injured in this isolated location.

What made Riley different were the wounds to his wrist and leg. These savage rendings confused the paramedics the moment they saw them. Not only did the injury have no apparent connection to the ride, but they implied that a giant wolf was running loose at the festival. This created a new logistical nightmare that none was prepared to deal with.

The other problem was the wounds were not only bites, but burns as well, and both looked infected. How does someone manage to burn themselves and simultaneously become infected? For that matter, what animal leaves burn marks?

"What the piss?" came the official diagnosis from the first paramedic. "Tell me this is some kind of bizarre mechanical crushing, and I'm just interpreting things wrong."

Riley didn't have it in him to argue, so instead, he told the young woman the truth. "Nope. Hellhound bit me while I was trying to save the souls of the departed."

She laughed at the apparent joke. "Good one. OK, yea, we'll get that bandaged up, and you'll get in line for the bus back to the hospital. I won't lie to you. It is going to be a long night of them shuttling people."

Medics covered the wounds in white gauze, though the leaking fluid from the infections caused them to discolor within minutes. Riley was at least grateful not to have to stare at his failure in gory detail. He walked with a limp and could not flex his hand to fight with his sword if the Ahemait came back.

The medic released him, as they could do nothing more than apply a clean bandage. Riley wandered off and leaned back hard against the side of a ride's trailer. From the screams exiting the makeshift building and a repeated loop of recorded clown laughter, he'd found the funhouse. Riley went into a funhouse once. It was not fun and cost him as much money as any other ride. He refused to repeat the process.

Seeing that this was the ride against which he came to rest summed up his defeat. "Eight. I let those monsters destroy eight innocent souls. You're freaking brilliant, Riley." He muttered with disdain.

No one was close enough to overhear his quiet mumblings, and if they had heard him, no one would stop to question someone in his condition. People who come across the injured, the desperate, and those at the end of their rope do not want to reach out and help. Perhaps it's a fear of becoming too involved in their problems.

"But those weren't the only ones, were they? Nope. Who else have you killed?" Riley ran down the list of everyone he had killed since arriving in town. "I gave Miranda the wrong medicine, and she died. The Ahemait ate Earl. Who else? Oh, right, Mr. Woods. They also ate him. These eight. What am I forgetting?"

He tried to recall who else had suffered in his blaze of destruction. He'd only been at work a short time, but there must have been more. This was not all that he'd done. What was he missing? Then he remembered, and tears stung his eyes. "Clay and Glen. How did I forget to include them?"

"Maybe not Clay. He probably deserved what he got, but Glen. That was my fault. How did I allow that to happen?" Riley put his head in his hands and cried. Tears flowed from his eyes, but no one who passed paid him any attention.

Riley didn't know how much time passed, but when he stopped crying, he felt empty. Nothing was better, but he had emptied all the tears he possessed. "I'm sorry, Glen."

Everyone continued to walk past, and Riley saw the ambulance returning to pick up more wounded. He hobbled the short distance to see who they loaded in the paramedic's vehicle. This trip included those who suffered lung injuries, and the crew sat four of them side by side to max capacity. "How many more trips will they make before they tell people to take their personal vehicles?" Riley asked himself.

Riley considered climbing in the back with everyone else for a moment, then hesitated. Did people still see him? Did he have a safer way to find out before he attempted to board an emergency vehicle? The debate ended without consideration as they left no room inside the truck, and if he wanted a ride, he'd have to attempt holding on to the top. As much as he fancied himself a supernatural creature, the wounds he had suffered that night told him to be more careful.

Instead, he found a bench and dropped down on it. "I'm no good to anyone. Why can't someone just come here and fire me? It was such a ridiculous idea to think that anyone else could do this job. You can't prepare to do this. It would take hundreds of years, and maybe then I would be ready."

The self-deprecation was unhelpful in all aspects, except it appeared to confirm that people were once again ignoring him. Why didn't death come with a manual? If someone thought to make a *Handbook for the Recently Deceased*, they would be a genius.

Lacking such guidance and reassured by no one paying him any attention, Riley moved his hands and let his head swing forward. It impacted the table with a resounding thud. He suffered no pain from this action, but it was satisfying to pantomime to the world how he felt.

"Now what?"

He sat and waited for someone to answer his question. No one spoke up, which didn't surprise him, so he leaned back and began unraveling the bandage around his arm. It had swollen and turned a frightening black-red. Riley touched the arm further up from the bite and found it hurt everywhere. "Oh, good. I'm going to die of a hellacious infection. Of all the pharmaceutical training I received, I don't think any of it covered something to help with this."

A quick check of the leg confirmed the same with the lower extremity. "Can Death die?" It was a strange thought, but he couldn't help but wonder as he sat alone. "And the best part is that no one will notice me when I'm gone. I've already killed or driven off anyone who might have given a shit."

It was not the first time Riley had considered the end of his life.

In college, sometimes the stress of tests became overwhelming, or friends abandoned him and life tumbled out of his control. There were firm rules against such drastic actions, but it didn't prevent the thoughts. He should have talked with someone about how he was feeling.

In school, there had been counselors available with whom he could make appointments. They supposedly keep everything confidential. There was, however, the fear that if you said the wrong thing, they would call your parents. The kids were over eighteen but had only recently left home, and no one knew the new rules of adulthood. Were their parents allowed to call the school and ask about their grades? Everyone had a different answer.

Riley scheduled an appointment to speak with the counselors one time. It was after he'd heard word from home that his grandfather had passed. That was the same week he failed a midterm and wasn't sure if the school would approve him for next semester's student aid. Nothing had gone right. Two of his friends had already taken the stretched limo home, and it seemed like everywhere he turned, Death stalked the students.

If only he had known then that Death was someone he could talk to. Maybe it would all make more sense. Then again, did Riley speak with Azrael occasionally at the student center? He wouldn't have known the angel or why he was there. How many times did Death sit amongst the living and watch them, asking the universe for answers?

That was a question Riley would like someone to answer for him. Why was he sitting alone on a bench in the middle of a field of destruction? Even if Riley did not actually cause the deaths by his hand, he drove the Ahemait to this desperate act. Would it be better if he had been the one who died instead of all these innocent people?

Again, the wave of confusion and torment washed across the young angel. He died. His former body lay in the ground, and only his soul roamed the earth. Why did the Fates allow him to live and not the others?

Another question for Them if Riley ever asked questions of all creation, "Do the Fates control the deaths of souls or only of mortals?" Everything continued to pile on Riley's shoulders, and he clasped his hands about his head attempting to hold in the tormented thoughts. "Why didn't Death let me die?"

Then darkness fell across Riley as if a shadow overtook the bench. Riley contemplated a path to redemption that did not lead to the Elysian fields. He reached his hand down and grasped the pommel of the bronze blade and drew Death's sword. It held a dull red shine, as if reflecting pools of blood by firelight. Riley stared into its pitted and scratched surface, trying to form his thoughts around a single idea.

Can Death die?

# CHAPTER 19
# DEATH'S RETURN

What would happen if the world was without Death? Would people no longer die? That seemed unlikely. Riley considered this and realized that his sacrifice would not prevent the Fates from ending mortals' time on earth. They could live for only so long before their souls passed to the penumbra. Despite everything he believed about Death, he was not responsible for the transition from life.

No, Death served one purpose, and that was to defend the lost and wayward souls from creatures of the Pit. It was a hard job title to understand as Riley had encountered only one such monster, the Ahemait. He made things worse with his poor performance in causing so much death and destruction with a first attempt to save one soul. He hadn't saved anyone. The demons destroyed three, and he endangered four others.

Perhaps if the current Death disappeared, the Fates would appoint someone to the position. The idea pushed itself around in Riley's mind and seemed to fit. The trappings of death would still exist; the need for the job wouldn't go away. Why would the Fates not then appoint someone new to take his place?

Whom would they appoint? Would the job go back to the previous holder of the title? It would not please Azrael to receive back the tools of the trade. What if a random soul received them without warning or training? Was that what had happened to Azrael? Had his predecessor died, and no one remained to train him in the new position?

It was bad enough that Riley had minimum training and explanation. He shuddered to think that They might thrust the responsibility upon him with even less. Could he morally accept doing that to someone? Why was none of this easy? All he wanted was an answer, a sign that pointed in the direction he needed to wander to find his way out of the desert.

Riley set the blade down on the bench as his mind continued to tumble and trip over dark thoughts. What about talking with someone? He had moderate success speaking with someone in college. He looked back on his problems. They did not seem as bad as what he was dealing with now, but at the time, they appeared monumental. They were enough to cause him to question life. But who would listen?

A mirthful chuckle found its way from Riley's lips as he considered the image of the Grim Reaper lying on Dr. Freud's couch. Riley could almost hear the Reaper say, "I suppose the scythe symbolizes my father's farm." It felt good to laugh, even if only through tears.

Was it possible? He'd been able to talk with people in the past. Could he find a therapist and chat about what was bothering him? Or would the burden of death overwhelm the doctor, who would then refuse to acknowledge his existence? That or try to lock him into a psych ward because he believed himself fighting demon hounds.

What about Azrael? Riley considered if there was a way to find the previous Angel of Death. Suppose he had a way to contact his former mentor for help to solve problems. The Ahemait were not the only creatures Riley would encounter, and he would have questions. But, beyond the practical, he needed a companion. Riley realized he desperately needed someone with whom he could share his existence.

He felt pain as he thought of his mentor, Azrael, and his lover, Glen. He didn't want to continue through all eternity alone. Having a purpose in his work was something, but it wasn't enough. Riley needed to be with someone he loved and understood. When Azrael left, he had lost more than a teacher. He'd lost the only other soul who knew he existed.

"Why did I let you go? Was there a choice? Could I have convinced you to stay?" Riley asked of the crowd, who ignored his every word.

There was little else to change the way he cast the dice. Riley picked up the sword from the table and slid it back into its sheath, letting it fade from view. "So now what?"

Every path seemed to lead to his destruction. Even if he turned away from the dark road to self-destruction, he still needed to face the Ahemait. They were organized and stronger than Riley. He did not know how many there were, and every time he met them, they left him hurt and humiliated except the one time when he enraged them enough that they murdered eight people. How do you win that type of fight?

Then he looked down at the wound on his leg. "That's assuming I live long enough to reach the next fight." He touched the wound with a gentle finger and winced from the pain. It had worsened while he went through his self-pity and despair. "I don't suppose the hospital would be able to treat this. I know I don't remember demon dog bite infection on any of the final exams."

"Come on, Fate, throw me a bone here," he said to the sky before letting his head fall forward to smack against the table once more. "So about that first question, can Death die?"

Someone sat on the bench but Riley paid little attention to the person. He expected they would ignore him the same as everyone else. No one acknowledged Death sitting alone crying and feeling sorry for himself. However, this new companion was different.

"That's an interesting question. I would say it depends. The current angel might die, but the job still needs to be done by someone, so Death will always be a part of life." The voice was familiar, and Riley realized it spoke to him as it talked.

Riley lifted his head, looked at the new companion, and recognized the familiar form sitting beside him. "Azrael! Oh! My God. Where did you go? I've messed things up terribly since you left."

The other specter held up his hands to keep Riley from climbing him or attempting a hug. "Calm down. You'll scare the locals. Tell me what's been unraveling you this bad."

It took everything he had, but Riley sat back and attempted to compose himself. He then explained what had occurred with the man who'd fallen from his roof. He described the events at the carnival and the destruction of all the souls involved. Riley did his best not to leave out any details, any of which might be vital.

"It sounds like you had quite an experience. I'm not sure it could have gone worse, but it wasn't catastrophic," Azrael reassured his companion. He reached out an arm around Riley's shoulder to pull him in close. He cradled the young specter like a protective mother and let him cry for a second time.

Riley would have preferred to describe how brave and stoic he was, but now he broke down in the arms of another. Those bottled-up tears found their way out, and he began to feel better. Azrael's hand stroked Riley's head while he grieved over the losses that had piled up at his feet.

"There will always be times in our past that we wish would change. The best we can do is learn from them and not let them occur again. I had one question, however, if you can collect yourself for a minute."

Something in the tone of voice let Riley know this was business, and he needed to pay attention. He wiped at the corners of his eyes and sat up. "What is it?"

"You mentioned eight whom the Ahemait destroyed." He

counted them off on his hand, "four they took with them. They killed and discarded two."

Riley waited for Azrael to finish the count, but his mistake dawned on him when he said nothing. "Two more still out there."

Azrael nodded his head. "You didn't fail all eight. There are two who have been by themselves, scared and alone. You can make all the difference in the world to those two by guiding them home."

In all his self-hatred and anger at what he'd failed to do, Riley never considered that someone might still be alive. At some point, he would find a better word to describe their post-mortem condition, but how did he forget about those two? Novel-Death remembered seeing them when he first came upon the wreckage. Riley stood and limped his way back to where he had last seen the two with newfound determination.

The forgotten souls remained in their same spot, separate from the searchers but close enough that perhaps someone could find them. They wanted to be found and told everything was OK. The longer time passed, and people continually left them behind, the more hope they lost. Riley hobbled across the field to join the two. "Excuse me. I'm sorry for not seeing you earlier. Today has not been a good day for me."

The dead have tempered emotions, but even with muted aggravation, the taller of the two stared hard at Riley and his bad day. "You're kidding. I don't want to hear how your day didn't turn out how you wanted."

Riley winced at the truth of the statement and looked about the field. He searched for the faint flicker of light that hinted at the distant Elysian Fields. The blinking lights of the carnival made this problematic and were likely why the two had not found their own way. After a minute of searching, he saw the hint of dawn.

"There." He pointed. "Can you two see that light over there? It's different from the rest. The light is brighter but further away."

It took them less time than Riley, as he pointed them in the right direction. "I see it," the taller one said and instinctively began walking towards it. The other picked up her feet and followed as a bridge formed between them and the increasingly bright light.

Once they left, Riley remained in the carnival's artificial lights, absent the glow of peace and redemption. When he turned, he saw Azrael standing at a stone's throw from where the three had been. "Those two were your first. Without help, you guided them home. Never forget them or their names."

A pain gripped Riley's stomach as he realized he'd never asked their names or checked the book. But then it came to him. He knew who they were. "Cynthia and Dennis."

Azrael wore a smile of pride as he nodded his head. "You've learned a lot in a short time."

It wasn't enough. Riley said, "I still can't forget how worthless I was when those monsters came for the others. I can't protect anyone. If the job is to save people from the Ahemait, I'm a complete failure. You need to find someone better."

"Perhaps, but we're past that point. You are now Death. There must be a reason that the Fates chose you."

How could Azrael not know the reason if he was the one who chose him? "You picked me. You have to be the one who knows why."

"Yes, and no. I was becoming burned out. The job was too much for me," Azrael said, while motioning for Riley to follow him somewhere they could be away from the mortals. "Strix said I was insane for wanting to leave the job. They told me as much frequently. But I'd been doing this job for more years than I can remember. It's a lonely, thankless job."

None of this helped inspire Riley while the man who hired him disparaged his new position. "Great, so you're saying I got a dead-end job with no benefits."

Azrael chuckled at the reference and nodded. "Essentially, yes. But you were the one the Fates presented when I put out to the universe that I was overwhelmed and couldn't handle things anymore."

Riley sat on the ground. The pain in his leg was unbearable, and he worked to take the bandage off the ankle. "Well, if this doesn't fix itself, I'll need a replacement soon myself."

"You're distracted," Azrael said, as if that explained everything. When Riley did not spontaneously heal, he detailed further. "I'm not sure how many times I need to tell you, but you don't have a physical body. Nothing bit your leg. There is no leg to bite."

The leg appeared red and swollen with vicious black charred marks and draining fluid. "I'm having a hard time believing you at the moment."

Azrael considered how best to explain the situation. "That's a bad or distracting idea. The Ahemait attacked you so you would not finish your task. It put you out of commission."

"I'm almost there," Riley said. He was trying to understand and work the ideas over in his mind. After a moment, it occurred to him. "This is one of those spoon moments, isn't it?"

It was Azrael's turn to appear confused. Riley waved off any question about flatware that his mentor might have had and explained his thoughts. "My leg's not hurt because I don't have a leg."

Whatever the new specter was trying to explain, it appeared he was on the right track. "Yes, that's it. All you need to do now is realize you're looking at the memory of having been bitten. I know it's esoteric, but you'll get it by accident the first time and then learn to do it intentionally after that."

The pair of them sat together for another hour while Riley attempted to forget about the wound on his leg. It proved to be a stubborn and complex issue, but suddenly he hit the right switch. Once Novel-Death touched the correct wires together, the bite misted and disappeared. To be sure, he poked it several times and then repeated the same on his arm. It took less time to find the magic combination, but that wound also vanished.

"Those kinds of wounds are more a distraction than anything else. That said, they can still keep you from completing your mission and saving the wayward souls," Azrael said.

Riley nodded his understanding and tried to think of how to word the next part. He'd been thinking of more than the wound over the last hour. Perhaps that was why it took so long, but he had many ideas in his mind. "You said the universe, fate, or whatever you want to call it, showed me to you. But it did it after you put out there that you were overwhelmed and couldn't continue to do the job. I then heard you say it was lonely and thankless."

Healing his wounds impressed Azrael, so it caught him off balance that Riley was doing two things at the same time. "I'm not following you. Where are you leading me to?"

"One more question. I could still be wrong about my whole idea," Riley said. "How is someone defined as the Angel of Death? I don't remember a ceremony or official with a certificate. So what was it?"

Azrael thought about how to best describe a concept he'd never put to words. "It's not a position that is conferred. The thought has been that the angel who possesses the trappings of death is Death."

"But there are three objects. I have a watch, sword, and book. What if the universe only intended you to give one of these things to someone? I know I'm new, and this takes time to learn, but I can't imagine that it becomes less overwhelming."

Azrael stopped. He'd never considered two angels standing as Death. Was there any rule against it? Who would tell him "no" if he did it anyhow? He continued to muse over the option when Riley spoke again. "We previously shared the objects during training. I took them one at a time. Only at the end did I have all three."

He was right. Azrael had to admit that nothing from the force of creation came out of the walls to demand that the same angel possess all three. "I don't know," he said and appeared stuck in a decision.

Riley moved forward and picked Azrael's hands up to place into his own. He held them against his chest and spoke directly. "You don't have to do this job alone. No one does. I don't think the universe ever intended a single soul to bear the burden of Death. Please. I can't do this without your help."

A tear hung from the corner of Azrael's eye as the first person in modern history held his hand without fear. He didn't have the strength to do the job alone. What made him think someone else would be any stronger? Azrael nodded his head. "Let's do it. Give me back the sword and book. From everything you told me, you are terrible at fencing, and we should separate the book and watch."

The weight lifted from Riley's soul was literal and spiritual as he passed the *Book of the Dead* back to the original Angel of Death. When he gave the sword to Azrael, he stopped himself from tossing it in disgust. "That thing has caused me nothing but trouble."

"I thought you knew," Primal-Death said. "Weapons are never anything but trouble."

No one was certain what They would do next. So the two of them waited, but the universe did not tear itself apart with the declaration of two Angels of Death. Minutes ticked by, and nothing happened. Azrael took a last look around. "It appears we did not destroy creation."

Novel-Death, as Azrael came to call Riley, agreed, and they returned to the issue at hand. Though Azrael named him the new Death, Riley always thought of himself as Death's assistant. He admitted that in the wrong context, someone could become confused and think he was a euthanasia doctor, but none of that related to the matter at hand.

"Something tells me that if They didn't want something to happen, we couldn't do it. Kinda like how They made a rule about people not flying without the aid of machines." Riley had tossed the idea over in his mind and wanted to see how Death received it.

Azrael thought it over and nodded. "It makes as much sense as anything, and until They answer letters from the post, that's the best we'll get."

## CHAPTER 20

# INTO THE PIT

Death pulled the *Book of the Dead* from his pocket and held the tome in front of him and Riley. The pages flipped open to a random leaf with four specific names scripted on the top line.

The names were not familiar to Riley. Their dates showed them to be the ones who died on the amusement park ride. These were the same souls the Ahemait dragged away.

"When a soul is destroyed or moves on to the next world, the Fates remove it from the ledger. This book only contains the names of those souls that need to return to Elysium. The first date," he motioned to the only number that remained static for every entry, "is when the soul departed the sacred grounds. The second changing number is when they are eligible to return."

This was not what Riley expected of the book when he first read it, and if Azrael left him again to fend for himself, he only guessed how long it would be until he learned the truth. "So it doesn't tell you when someone will die?"

As he tried to think of how best to explain it, Azrael tapped his finger against the page. "A soul cannot return while their body is living. So the person will die before the time shown. Normally, the times are moments apart. It is rare, but a body can live beyond nirvana, and there are instances of souls that are not at rest. But those are not normal conditions."

Riley did everything to file this information into little pockets inside his mind. He was having flashbacks to pharmacy school and memorizing compound formulas. After another few minutes of cosmology class, he raised a hand for questions.

The act of a hand going into the air confused Azrael enough to force him to stop in mid-sentence. "Is something up there? What is it?"

"No. I just had a question. Why are you telling me all of this now? These things are all interesting, but how does this apply to those four?"

"Right, I was getting to that. So when these four died and their bodies stopped living, they should have returned to Elysium." Riley nodded but did not interrupt. "The Ahemait arrived and stole them away. Two issues need consideration, but let's focus on the first problem. If they destroyed the souls, then the Fates would cross off the names and move them to the back."

Everything was making sense as Riley saw what Azrael attempted to explain. "They're still alive. The alpha didn't kill them. She kidnapped them. Why would these monsters do that kind of thing? They're just animals. What type of animal kidnaps its food?"

"People, for one," Azrael answered with brief consideration. "The Ahemait are not mindless beasts. You can't assume that someone is ignorant because you don't speak their language. Their alpha is older than I am."

Shock stamped itself on Riley's face. "How can that be? Surely you killed enough of them while you were Death to reduce their numbers. How is there still one that is older than you?"

"We don't destroy one another. There is a truce between us. Or there was before you killed their pack-mate, but hopefully, we can sort that out later."

Azrael noticed the hurt expression of overwhelmed confusion on Riley's face and put his arm around him. "It's OK. I didn't prepare you for all this. What you got was the same basic set of instructions I received when given the job however many thousands of years ago that was." He thought for a moment. "I can't even remember when that was."

Riley leaned into Azrael's shoulder. "You never should have left. If we do this, you need to promise you won't do that again. We're in this for the long stretch."

The pause that followed Riley's request was not encouraging. Eventually, Azrael said, "I won't. I mean, I promise not to run away. You're right that this was a job for two. If I couldn't do it on my own, I should not expect someone else to simply take my place."

They remained in each other's arms in the blessed silence as they tried to pretend the rest of the world was not burning around them. This moment lasted only five breaths before they leaned back and brought up the book. "OL. So we need to decide on a plan. Do we have a way to find out where they took these people?" Riley asked.

"Yes, and no. The book provides a connection to their location, so we, in a sense, yes. We can travel to where they are. It is no different from what we do with any of the others near death. The Ahemait can do nothing to prevent that."

This put a smile on Riley's face, and he said, "So, what's the problem? We jump over to the souls. Point them in the right direction, and we're done. Same as any other time, only now it is the two of us, and we're prepared for a fight."

Azrael did not share the optimism of his younger companion. "You asked me before why they would keep these souls." He paused for Riley to acknowledge the question. "They have few reasons not to eat them. Their pack must be hungry with how many we saved these last few nights.

"So what, they're saving them for a late-night snack?"

"It doesn't work that way." Azrael took a moment to consider his words. "The alpha knows we can travel to these souls' location. He believes you to be young, reckless, and alone. But more than that, you broke the truce and killed one of her pack."

A realization came to Riley slowly, but when it arrived, the story of his death played out in vivid detail. "She's setting a trap for me. This whole thing, from the accident at the ride to stealing the souls, is all to drag me into a fight I can't win."

"I can't think of a better way to explain why they did it. Ahemait don't gain benefit by saving food for later. They gorge on what is available until there is nothing left to eat. I've described them as sentient creatures, but their eating habits are best not repeated by humans."

This last comment generated a chuckle from Riley, though he stifled himself quickly. The two looked over the scene at the carnival. Few people remained on the grounds as most took their opportunities to leave. The traffic in the dirt parking lot became a nightmare of honking horns, with a handful of police officers attempting to maintain order. "We're still going to go after them, aren't we?" Riley asked. It was a question, but he believed he knew the answer.

"That is in the job description. I don't know that we could continue calling ourselves Angels of Death if we were not willing to save those who had died."

The change in wording gave Riley a moment's pause. Angel meant so many things. It was funny how one word, passed down through generations, changed its meaning. "Someday, you'll tell me the story of where all this began," Riley said.

Primal-Death appeared confused and waited another minute before Riley said, "What started everything. Who are the Fates? What are angels? It just seems that the longer I'm, well, not alive, but with you, the more questions I have."

A smile creased Primal-Death's face. "Those are endless stories. Maybe someday we'll take the time to chat by the fire, but for now, let's focus on the lost souls."

Riley nodded his agreement, and they turned to the book. "So we can travel without an issue, but you said they are waiting for us.

Well, they're waiting for me. I guess I'm the one who killed their pack member."

"None of them will know I'm back. We didn't even know that until a few moments ago. We weren't even sure we could be a team until we tried. It's a safe bet that this will be a surprise to them."

"You don't think they spied on us, do you?" Riley asked. He glanced around the carnival, the memory of the lone creature at the Iron Horse firmly in his mind. It had watched him from a distance, and Riley didn't put it past them to repeat the same process.

Azrael followed Riley's eyes as they searched, but they, too, found nothing. "I find it highly unlikely. The alpha won't want to distract you with another fight before you learn you can find the four souls. She likely is only guessing how long it will be before you fall into her trap."

"Can we wait her out?"

None of the depictions of Death from paintings showed a man with his head cocked to the side and one eyebrow raised. "That's a joke. You're trying to make me laugh again." He waited and saw that Riley had intended to be serious. "No. We can't 'wait them out.' If they think this failed, they'll eat the souls and move on to a new plan."

Monstrous wolves pacing around captive souls before devouring them by campfire emblazoned itself into Riley's thoughts. "Ouch, OK, no. So, can we spy on them? What about when we used our book thing at the hospital to look in on people?"

Azrael allowed Riley to describe what he was saying but couldn't hold back a chuckle. "'The book thing,' yes, well, we can use the *Book of the Dead* to travel to their location. I think what you're trying to describe would be clairvoyance, and it is not something we can do, though I can understand the confusion."

"What do you call what we were doing? We touched the book and saw the other places where the person was about to die. You and I did it several times."

"Trick is we existed in both locations. To see a place, we need to be at that place."

Riley considered what Azrael described. The ideas rotated in his mind, and he attempted to put the pieces together. "So if we use the book to check in on the kidnapped people, then the Ahemait can still attack us, and we become trapped."

Primal-Death nodded his head. "That is a good enough explanation. And again, they may have also come up with a way to trap you there once you arrive. As I mentioned, their alpha is older than I am, and I don't know what she is capable of doing."

The more Riley thought about their options, the more impossible the mission became. He looked at the names and their fixed dates of death. Was he missing something? Riley tried to focus his mind on the problem but kept returning to the image of four souls eaten by wolves.

"I'm not giving up. We have to find a way to do this."

"It may be one of those things where we must step forward and cast the bones. They know we are coming. Or rather, they believe you are coming, but not that I am with you. We may be able to use that to our advantage if you go first."

Riley flinched at the idea. "Not a chance. They'll kill me before you show up. What makes you think they won't pounce and feast the moment I'm in sight?"

Azrael considered how to express himself. "A hunch, although if that's not enough for you, the alpha said as much. When she wounded you, she could have killed you. Nothing prevented her from ending your existence, but she continued with her plan. No. I think they planned something else."

Preferably, Azrael would have given him a more definitive solution than a casual observation of a fight he heard secondhand, but it was what he had. Riley took a deep but unnecessary breath and squared his shoulders. "I've lived long enough. Let's get this over with."

The book sat before the two angels, and Azrael gave a final pep talk. "It may be dark where you're going. Remember, you don't need light to see. It may take years, but you'll learn not to trick yourself into believing you're still in an actual body. I don't know where they took the souls, but the book will put you close enough that you can perceive the one you selected."

A realization hit Riley as Azrael said this last part. "What if they're not all together?"

"Then you'll find only the one you chose, and we'll need to keep looking for the others. I'm not expecting they made this easy for us, but if they split them up, they won't be able to guess which one you'll pick first. It could work to your advantage."

This was true. The alpha could stand guard at only one location, and if they split the souls, then they had a three in four chance that Riley would be somewhere else. Alternatively, if she kept all of them together, it guaranteed him to come face to face with the massive creature.

"One last thing we need to discuss before you check on them."

Riley waited for Azrael to drive in the wrong bit. The worst part of information always held itself until the end. It was some type of cosmic joke. "There's a chance that the light of Elysium won't reach where they have the souls. If that's the case, you won't be able to send them on their way."

"Perfect. I can find them, but then not know what to do with them. How about I wait for you to show up after setting off their trap?"

"Whatever we decide to do, we need to do it soon. These souls may not have much time before the Ahemait loses patience. There is an insatiable hunger inside them, and this is against their baser instincts," Azrael said. He turned the book so that Riley faced the names.

The four stood at the top of the page, and neither was more remarkable than the other. Riley judged from the dates of birth that they were all somewhere near eighteen or twenty-two. He wasn't ready to do the math to know precisely. How did Primal-Death always know their exact age? "I suppose I pick one at random, then."

Azrael shrugged. "Unless you have a preference. Any of them is as likely as the other to be near the alpha, if that was what concerned you."

It was the primary fear for Riley. On his first attempt, he had no desire to land beside the massive demon and hoped there would be time. Perhaps his mentor would arrive before then, so he would not fight a losing battle.

Riley steadied his breathing and reached his hand out to touch the scripted name. Everything was darkness. Somewhere in the distance came the sounds and intensity of eternal fires burning. An oppressive, heavy heat pressed down on him while he tried to gain his bearings. What did Azrael say about sight?

Vision did not require light. Riley closed his eyes and tried to think of how this riddle helped him in the pitch black of the tunnels. He only observed the world with his eyes and ears. As he kept his eyes closed, he saw the structure of the surrounding room in his mind's eye.

It was not a perfect vision, and Riley assumed it would only become better with time, but for now, the outlines of the tunnels remained etched in his mind. He was in an underground series of channels, each dug by a massive animal with terrible claws. "So I'm here. But where is that?"

Letting his eyes sweep the limited space, he found a cut that branched up into a pocket. Roots covered the hole's entrance as a set of natural bars. Behind this cage was a woman. "Hold on. I'm here. Stay where you are."

Riley wanted to kick himself for saying such ridiculous things. This girl did not know who he was or if he was there to help. She also could go nowhere, so why ask her to stay there? The worst part of his shout was the bark he heard in response from the other direction down the tunnel. "Well shit, that didn't take long for me to ruin everything. I hope someone's not keeping score on my life."

The barking continued to echo through the tunnels as other Ahemait picked up the call and passed the message. This was too much for Riley, and he decided to abandon the mission. There would always be a chance to try again later, but if he stayed, they were going to kill him. Focusing on the book, he tried to recall his perceptions.

Nothing changed. He felt no connection to the book or the carnival. Riley attempted to leave the warren and travel to any other location he knew. Nothing was within reach. Azrael had warned him that the alpha might have a way to block his movement, but he hoped it wasn't possible.

"Oh, come on, Azrael. I'm going to need your help." Riley said these things under his breath, but Azrael had no way to hear him. The only way the other Angel could talk with him was if he came to stand beside him in the tunnels. But would they both become trapped, then killed? "How did I dig myself into this hole?"

Riley scrambled up the trivial incline to the cell and the trapped woman. "There's someone else coming too. He'll fix everything when he gets here."

She didn't answer immediately but eventually asked, "Then why did you show up first?"

"That's a good question. I'll be asking myself that same thing for years to come." Riley only hoped to live that long.

The bars on her cell appeared to have grown naturally from trees or other rooted plants. They couldn't form that way in such a short time. There was no way to enter the cell as earth enclosed it from all other sides. Riley observed the construction and attempted to devise a plan to pull her out. "Guess I'll start with the simple answer before trying something hard."

Riley looked in the dark for the faint hint of light that would show Elysium. There was no way to know how soft it would be this deep into whatever realm he'd embedded himself in. "I'm looking for a light. Have you seen anything since you've been down here?"

She shook her head although she believed no one could see her.

"There is no light down here. Those monsters move by smell and sound."

He expected as much. If the light reached this far, they would have left on their own accord by this point. But there was no harm in the attempt. In the far distance of the tunnels came the baleful howl of the alpha. Her voice rang out in defiance and challenged the intruder to face her. Riley could not understand any words she spoke but knew the meaning behind what she said.

The woman retreated to the far wall of her cell. While huddled there, she covered her ears until the noise of the terrifying howl ended. "It's going to kill us. They've brought us here to eat us," she said.

Riley attempted to talk to her again, but after the howl she did nothing more than huddle in the corner. In retrospect, explaining that the creatures would have already eaten her if that was their plan, did not seem well thought out. "It is OK. I'll go, and we will release you." He hated lying to someone, but the only other option was to leave her more terrified than she already was.

The tunnel sloped gently down from the cell, and Riley followed the path. No branches went to either side, and he was alone in the dark. Whatever these creatures' intentions, they meant for him to come to them. Riley considered his options and decided that continuing past this point alone was not the wisest course of action. But there were no good choices.

He turned back into the tunnel and went far enough to see the cell and then waited without calling out to the woman. It was twenty minutes before Azrael arrived, and Riley waved him over. "Were you waiting for them to eat me first? Dear God, how much longer was it going to take?"

Azrael held up his hands in defense of his position. "You're not dead. Perhaps I could have come sooner, but what was the point of our plan? Either way, I saw the woman at the end of the hall. I'm guessing no one else is down here. How about you fill me in on the rest of the situation?"

"The alpha is that way," Riley said and pointed the only other direction down the tunnel. "She's waiting for me to come to her. I don't know how patient these things are, but I'm sure at some point she'll send one of her friends up here to drag me outside."

"Well, let's not keep her waiting."

## CHAPTER 21

# HOMECOMING

T he passage continued downward at a gentle grade until reaching an antechamber at the base of a vast cavern. A lone Ahemait stood guard over the entrance to the main room, and when the Angels of Death emerged from the tunnel, it rose and growled. The menacing sound was deep, with gears grinding over broken rocks.

Riley held his hands in front, in the least threatening pose possible, and Azrael drew the bronze sword. The blade glowed a dull red of sunrise in the darkness, lit from an unseen source. Azrael spoke, "We're not here to kill any more of your kind, but I'm not leaving without the souls. Make your choice quickly if you want to stand in our way."

In all its ferocity, the creature attempted to intimidate the pair, but when it heard the ultimatum from Primal-Death, its resolve faded. Looking between the two angels, the Ahemait chose to flee into the cavern. The sound of its barking voice alerted others who may have been waiting in the darkness.

"At least that one did not expect to see both of us. I'm guessing that our element of surprise has now been spoiled, and he has told the rest that we're here." Azrael kept the sword in his hand.

Riley tried to follow the monster, but he lost track of it in the massive room. "I don't know that surprise was ever going to be our biggest ally in all this. Let's go back and get the one we found and take her out of here."

Confidence is a powerful force during times of conflict, and every soldier looks to their commanders for inspiration. Novel-Death turned to his mentor with such an expectation while in the antechamber. But the expression returned by the ancient being did nothing to reassure Riley, who said, "Please tell me you have a way for us to get out of here."

No answer came. Riley glanced into the cavern and back down the dead-end of the tunnel behind them. They either stood huddled in a hole for all time or faced the monsters in their den. "You're not building a lot of confidence right now. I need you to have a plan for how we're not all going to die down here."

In a flat tone, Azrael said, "We won't die. We're angels. We died long before we came into these tunnels. The most they could do is torture our souls for all time."

"Again, you're not helping. I'm not hiring you for the corporate pep talk next year." Riley paced in the small chamber as he tried to think of any answer that did not involve spiritual suicide. "Hear me out. We break her out of that cell and then bring her down here. What if we keep moving forward? Can we get out that way?"

Azrael inched to the cavern's opening and cast his eyes out into the void. He stared through the darkness for a long time while developing a plan. "The Ahemait need a way in and out. Nothing can stop us from reaching a soul when using the book, but they've blocked travel both ways to everyone else."

This answer lit a spark in Riley, and he beamed at the new idea. "That's perfect. We use the book again. Grab this one, then jump to the next one. It's so simple. All we need to do is hop from one soul to the other, and we're out of here before anyone notices something wrong."

"Other than pointing out that they know we are both here, we have one minor issue." Azrael had a way of crushing Riley's dreams, and his heart fell several feet to the floor. "The book is where we left it. We exist at both locations. Not normally an issue if you are only doing something interesting in one place, but if you start multitasking, it can become complicated."

Riley was not prepared to handle the concept of existing in multiple locations. The Ahemait made this more complicated because they trapped one of his projections in this underground location. If Riley hired a therapist as the Angel of Death, would ethics require them to keep confidentiality? Or would this fall into the category of danger to self and others?

"So what do we do?" Riley asked.

"I think our only option is to push forward and confront the alpha. She's the one with the keys to the gate. We're not getting out of here without going through her."

It was not the answer he wanted, but Riley saw that a better choice would not present itself. He squared his shoulders and attempted to summon what courage he possessed. "OK, let's do this before I run back into the hole and try to wait things out."

The Angels of Death faced one another and, after they agreed, stepped clear of the chamber and into the cavern. The massive room covered a space the same size as Dr. Green's pharmacy, though it was twice as tall and roughly circular. It branched out from the center and ran through multiple tunnels and chambers. Riley assumed that some of them led to the other trapped souls, but the warren had more tunnels than prisoners, and he could only guess which direction to run.

A pile of stacked stones, smoothed down by time, stood on the far back wall. Upon the cairn was the alpha. When the two angels entered her cavern, she rose to her feet in a fluid motion of power and authority. Four other Ahemait filtered in from the tunnels and stood to her side. They remained on the ground with the alpha's feet at their shoulder level.

Each of the Ahemait barked and snapped like dogs held back on the ends of chains. Their anger came as spittle across blood-flecked maws, and only by great restraint did they hold themselves back from attacking the angels. Each wanted to lunge forward, tear the two offending bipeds apart, and leave their pieces scattered on the floor.

Riley tried to think of a worse situation than with the Ahemait outmaneuvering them and trapping them in their warren. Azrael leaned over and whispered to his companion, "This is going better than I expected."

The younger specter of Death nearly struck his mentor but stopped himself. There was no telling what would happen if he started a fight in this place. As it was, the only thing he could do was roll his eyes. "I hate to think what your worst-case scenario was."

Barking and snapping continued until the alpha howled and the others silenced. She then bent over and breathed into the stones, which then glowed a deep coal red. This cast the first light Riley had seen in the chamber. He now saw its rough-hewn surface, dug by the claws of the Ahemait. The cave was ancient and reminded him of a time when humans huddled by fires to ward off vicious predators.

The other Ahemait scratched and clawed at the ground while they paced, but then they settled and dropped their bellies to the stone ground. They sat with their heads facing the two angels. The cavern became still, and the alpha barked once to the smaller Ahemait on her right. The monster left and returned with the body of the beast Riley had killed at the roofer's house.

Riley did not lose the ceremonial nature of these creatures' behavior. The barks and decisive movements of the Ahemait communicated between one another, sentience beyond animal instincts. Whatever Riley believed about these monsters was wrong. They were calculating rational beings who had lured him to the warren to make a point.

Riley glanced down at the body of the dead Ahemait. If they intended him to feel sorry for killing the creature, he didn't. That thing ate people's souls. How could he possess anything but contempt for a monster such as that? So why did they go to all this trouble?

As Riley tried to understand what was happening, Azrael turned the sword around and handed it to Riley, pommel first. "You may need this."

"I thought we agreed you were better at fighting," Riley said in confusion.

Riley was missing something, and he shot his eyes between Azrael and the Ahemait. The alpha stood on her stones; the pack flanked her sides, and the body lay in front. That was when the realization occurred to him. "She wants to fight me over this?"

The alpha answered before Azrael responded and barked twice. The wolf at her feet, the one standing near the slain Ahemait, yipped in response and growled at Riley. Azrael explained, "The younger one. Not the alpha, but the smaller one. It is challenging you. There's some relation between him and the dead Ahemait, and he took it personally."

"Yea, I kinda got the gist of what he said. Do I have any choice in the matter?" Riley already knew the answer but wanted to ask just the same. Perhaps there would be some loophole he could use to get out of this.

"Not likely. They trapped us in their warren and threatened to kill four innocent souls. We could run back down the tunnel, but what would that do for us? I think fighting the one is better odds than trying to attack everyone."

He had a point, and as Riley counted the number of enemies that stood against them, he agreed. There was little chance that he would win a fight, but it was a better chance than if he fought all of them at once. Riley took the sword and stepped forward into what had become a circle of enemies, plus Azrael.

No one called for the fight to begin; there were no referees or officials. The Ahemait lunged. Riley watched too many movies that included civil duels, and he thought things would proceed on different terms. So it was that the wolf caught him full in the chest and barreled him to the ground.

The only thing that saved Riley's life was bringing his sword up at the last moment and bracing it between the monster's teeth. Its claws raked his chest, but the beast could not gain purchase with its fangs. They grappled together on the stone floor.

Riley's sword bit into the Ahemait's jaw, and the creature pulled back with burning liquid dripping from the wound. There are two basic concepts in a sword fight, one of which is to defend yourself. He'd done that. The other was to attack. Riley swung the sword in a large lazy arc at the Ahemait's face.

There was no effort when the creature stepped to the side, and the blade passed harmlessly through the air. The wolf turned to watch the sword's passage, then back to Riley as if asking an unspoken question. Riley shouted at the silent creature to "shut up!"

The Ahemait paced a circle around Riley in a new tactic, forcing the angel to pivot or allow his opponent behind him. This continued for a complete pass before the Ahemait braced and sprang to attack, away from where Riley turned. With no duel training, Riley learned of the simple trap when the monster bit his right leg.

The searing and tearing flesh was familiar to Riley. He'd felt it so recently that he questioned whether this was a fresh wound or his old injury opening back up. Screaming, he reversed the sword and struck down upon the Ahemait's neck. With its teeth gripped on Riley's leg, it had nowhere to go. The creature thrashed. Its fangs pulled and rent the muscles in Riley's leg while throwing him to the stones at the alpha's feet.

Every inch of Riley's body hurt. His leg burned, throbbing pain in his head warned of pending darkness, and a voice inside him whispered that he should give up. Riley listened to the tormenting thought and stayed on the floor with his head lowered, waiting for the end.

"Get up, you idiot!" Azrael shouted. Riley brought his eyes up and saw all the Ahemait howling and barking. Azrael waved his hands frantically for Riley to stand back on his feet. He didn't understand the purpose. Things would end either way, but Riley brought himself to his feet.

The alpha howled, and the cave went quiet. Nothing made sense to Riley, and he searched the faces of the wolves for answers. Not until the body of his opponent lay where he'd left it did everything make sense. Had he won? Riley turned back to Azrael for confirmation, and the other angel only shrugged but pointed back to the alpha. No one knew what would happen next.

The alpha barked at the gathered Ahemait, and they dragged the bodies away. She snarled until Riley backed away from her and rejoined Azrael on the edge of the cavern. Everything hung in the air, and the massive wolf looked at each Ahemait who stood before her. She barked several times, but none answered her. Several turned away.

"What's happening?" Riley asked, after joining his mentor.

"I think they're trying to decide if they should kill us."

"Oh, come on, I won. That's not even fair."

"No one said things were going to be fair. They hold all the advantages, but there is one fewer of them now to worry about. We may have also intimidated a few of the smaller ones." Azrael motioned to the Ahemait, who refused to look in their direction.

Riley handed his mentor back the sword and prepared himself emotionally for whatever followed. The alpha stood facing them and barked several times with a few other vocalizations when she looked back.

"Any idea what she said?" Riley asked, after leaning closer to Azrael.

The older angel thought, while trying to put the pieces together for a moment. "Good news is, I don't think they're going to kill us. So probably going to let us go." It wasn't much of an answer, and Riley suspected his mentor couldn't so much translate the monster's language as guess what they were trying to say.

From three tunnels returned three souls, and an Ahemait pushed past the angels to retrieve the prisoner from the shaft behind them. With the four kneeling, their necks held in the jaws of the wolves, the alpha growled at the two angels. When she finished, they released the four and shoved them forward.

The sound of rocks splitting and fires burning opened a portal in the middle of the cavern. The angels could see the carnival through the waves of heat and pushed the four through without waiting. They then followed without a word to their captors.

They spilled out on the carnival grounds. The sights and sounds of emergency vehicles continued in the background. Rescuers pulled the bodies from the wreckage, and all that remained were twisted piles of metal. Law enforcement held the owner and operators of the ride off on one side of the excavation. The interrogation appeared amicable, but tensions were high.

The four souls and two angels stood on a slight rise that over-looked the scene. And as the heat faded, they breathed a collective sigh of relief. "I thought we would stay in hell forever," one of the rescued souls proclaimed as it fell to its knees on the soft earth.

"That wasn't hell. You did not even travel to the Pit. You were in the Ahemait's warren," Primal-Death said before judging the condition of his companions. "But none of you care about that distinction, do you?"

Each of them shook their heads and returned blank stares of confusion. "I should have figured as much. Just know you're safe but still have further to go before you are home. Riley, can you help them find the way from here? I need to talk with Strix."

"Of course," Riley agreed and motioned for the four to join him while Azrael disappeared. To best understand his departure, a person would need to consider two moments in time. Azrael was standing on the hill in the first, and in the second, he was not. There was no pop, flash, wave, or portal. The Angel of Death stopped existing where he once stood.

The souls did not show that they noticed his departure. Only Riley observed the event, and he asked about it later. "I need each of you to search for a light. It will appear as a sunrise from a distance."

He continued to talk them through the process, but the carnival lights made it difficult. After a minute of searching, Riley asked, "Can you forgive me for this?"

The souls turned from their searching and questioned what he asked. "Why would we forgive you? I thought you were the one who came and rescued us. Should we not thank you?" Another joined in and said, "Yes, it sounds as if you were our savior."

"No. I'm no one's hero," Riley quickly countered. "You were all trapped in the warren because of me. Those creatures came after you to hurt me."

The realization took its time before reaching the four, but when it struck, they collectively turned to one another and discussed. Riley had not previously come across souls who were so long away from their time of death. The unity between them was curious and their lack of aggression, or any powerful emotion, created more questions than answers for Riley.

The spokesman for the four said, "It appears you have learned from the experience. We believe the beasts taught you something that you will not forget or repeat." It then gestured to the other three. "We are also safe, and no one is hurt, so all is well."

"I don't know that I would agree that no one got hurt. Eight people died, and dozens went to the hospital in an ambulance, but thank you." What more was there to say? He did his best and had nothing more to give.

As they stood in silence, Riley observed the gradual light of dawn creeping over the horizon. It took him a minute before he realized what he saw was not the sun. "There, look in that direction. Do you see the light to the left of the building?"

The four turned and searched and soon found the light. Once they saw the rising dawn, the bridge extended to them, and they followed it to the next world. Everything then faded, and they left Riley alone on a hill with only the human authorities to keep him company.

Azrael didn't say where he would talk with Strix or when he might return, so Riley decided to remain at the carnival. Those in need of emergency medical attention left, and the ambulance was not returning tonight. Other less severely injured victims found their way to the hospital in private vehicles but expected a long wait. One EMT advised a woman that she "could consider waiting until tomorrow and schedule an appointment with her primary doctor."

Riley continued walking among the mortals as he made his way to the law enforcement officers and those responsible for the ride. He caught the last part of a man covered in grease saying, "Everything checked out fine before we started. I checked all the bolts myself with the torque wrench just like we do each night."

The man I presumed to be his supervisor said, "I have his punch sheet in the office. Nothing was missed. There is no reason the ride should have failed, and not in the way it did. Something lifted the pin off its post and dropped it on the rotating gear. I don't know anyone who could do that with the arms still attached. It's just too heavy."

The older officer took notes, and the other said, "And yet that is what you are saying happened. Needless to say, you will shut all the rides down until we can have a thorough inspection of everything here."

The first carny prepared to object, but the second stopped him. "Yes, sir, we understand. Do everything you can to answer to the people." He then said something in a language Riley didn't recognize but which he understood meant, "We let the police inspect our rides, or we watch as they take them."

Neither officer spoke whatever language the owner used, but its effect on the ride's operator forced him to back down. "Yes, of course. I'll show whoever you want, whatever they need to see."

Riley listened to the rest of the conversation but was more concerned about hearing a foreign language he understood. He'd studied a semester of Spanish, but this was something different. Without knowing the words, he had understood their meaning. "I don't know that I'll ever become used to all the angel's wackiness."

The older officer stopped with his notes and glanced up as Riley spoke. His eyes searched the scene until finding the angel. It would not have been hard to see him standing in plain sight except that most people choose not to see or acknowledge Death. "Did you have anything you wanted to add? Otherwise, I'd like to ask that you give us some privacy while we conduct this interview."

Three mortals turned to look at the fourth in confusion. He then became confused and motioned to Riley. "That guy? Do we want him hanging out while we talk to the owner?"

The three pivoted and looked where the fourth pointed. The man who presumably was one of the deputies asked, "Sheriff Wallace, are you feeling OK? There's no one there."

Wallace didn't back down from his words and stared Riley in the face as he said, "Yea, probably nothing. But I'm guessing someone may know more about the people who died here tonight, though I never had much luck getting any information from the other guy. I've tried to ask him those kinds of questions before."

# CHAPTER 22

# EPITAPH

The two angels returned to stand upon a hill overlooking the carnival. All the cars from the parking lot were gone, and the only vehicles that remained were emergency workers left behind to secure the scene. It would be weeks before they reopened the gates, and that was only if they allowed crowds back in. More likely the only people who would come back inside would be the ones required to inspect each ride before they were disassembled and loaded onto tractor-trailers. It was anyone's guess if the county invited this company back next year to entertain their citizens.

"I know you never gave me a handbook, but I'm pretty sure there is a rule against interfering with people's lives." Riley surveyed the chaos his misadventure with the Ahemait caused. "Is there going to be a punishment from anyone for all of this?"

Primal-Death shook his head and answered, "No. It's not that we operate above the law, but our rules are unbreakable. I'm not saying there won't be repercussions for your actions. There is always a cause and effect as we move through the world. But I wouldn't worry about some benevolent being on a mountain raining down fiery judgment."

That was Riley's primary concern. He had severely screwed up his first solo job, and the idea of doing the same on his second attempt did not sit well with him. This did not, however, alleviate all his questions. "But what of the Strix? What did they say?"

"Oh, that. Yes, well, we don't want to upset them. I talked to Strix, and they believe that we restored the truce when the alpha allowed us to leave."

A weight lifted from Riley's shoulders as he feared a repeat of the destruction that spread out below them. "I'm hearing a long pause. What's the rest of what they said?"

"That was it. Though for your future clarification, the truce is not overly complicated. We don't kill them, and they don't murder mortals. I used to call what they did the other night hunting. Think of them on a normal night as scavengers, but if things get out of hand, they'll start hunting for their food."

Riley could clearly see that if those creatures were allowed to kill without restriction, the possible level of destruction would be unimaginable. "OK, yea, that's bad. Anything else I need to know?"

Azrael thought on it before saying, "You already know to leave them alone if there is no soul you can save. At the same time, they won't harass us for no reason. It's a lot of if we don't do $x$ to them, they won't do $y$ for us. The universe exists in a balance, with every force pulling in one direction. Something is pulling the other way. Even if you think it's for the greater good to yank hard on the rope, realize you could still tip the boat over."

The metaphor did not make complete sense, but Riley understood the message. "Got it."

Morning came with the rising sun, and Riley watched the light of dawn cresting over the horizon. Its blazing glory showed a radiance far behind anything he'd seen in life. He had caught a glimpse of this light when souls traveled to the Elysian fields, but he saw it in its glory at dawn.

Riley felt unsteady on his feet and reached out a hand to steady himself. It felt purchase on Azrael's, and the other angel steadied him so he would not fall. "Easy there. Sometimes best not to stare directly at the sun."

There was a joke in the voice, but truth to the words. Primal-Death continued to hold Riley so he would not fall. "I wasn't prepared. Is it always like that?" Riley asked.

"Every morning. You can catch a glimpse of Elysium," Azrael said this, but there was no love in his voice as he did. "It's the same view the new souls see that draws them home. But we will never be given a bridge. It's some great cosmic joke to abandon us and taunt us with what we'll never have."

Several minutes passed before the light steadied itself, and the dawn turned to day. With the light rising full into the sky, the brilliance of the promised land faded. Only then was Riley able to answer, "I don't think it's a joke. More like a reminder that things are not all as terrible as what we see every day. If all I had to go by each day was the death and destruction I saw, it could drive me insane."

Primal-Death understood this as well as anyone. He was the one who sought out a replacement because he could no longer fulfill the job's duties. Too many people died, and he witnessed too much suffering. "So what then?"

Tightening his fingers around Azrael's, Riley said, "I can live with everything those people went through tonight if someone can show me where they went."

Whatever response Azrael wanted to say did not match what he felt should be told, so he remained silent. This was an odd moment as his emotions collided against one another, as the solitary figure of death realized he was no longer going to be alone. "You are a strange man. You know that, don't you?"

Riley shrugged and let go of their hands. "I've had an interesting life. And from the sounds of things, it will only get stranger from there. Now, come on, you have a lot more to teach me before I can begin to feel comfortable doing this crazy job."

"I wouldn't worry about it. You'll pick up the ropes pretty quick. However, I wouldn't bother asking about a promotion. It is a bit of a dead-end job," Azrael said as he gave Riley a friendly shove. "But I never should have left you alone as I did."

"You did what you thought was best. I'm not going to say I agree with your decision. It was a bit of a jerk thing to do, but I'm sure you had your reasons." Riley searched around on the hill for anything to redirect the conversation but found nothing.

"It won't happen again. I'll stay here for the long haul as I promised."

"That's great," Riley said and tried to think of something else to talk about. "So what's next? I'm assuming there's more training that needs to be done."

Azrael hesitated before he withdrew the book and held it open. "Yes and no. There will always be things to learn. I don't know that you will ever stop learning, but there is something we still need to do."

The pages flipped until landing on one with the name Billy Green scrawled across the top line. From the date of death, Riley saw the individual was fated to die that day. At first, the name was not familiar to him. Riley could not recall knowing anyone named Billy, but then it dawned on him. "Dr. Green?"

There was no one else it could be. Why else would Primal-Death draw attention to someone with that name? Riley asked, "He's going to die today?"

"I'm sorry to inform you, but yes. Typically Strix would handle this one, but he's one of your fetters, so we felt it better if you were the one."

Riley still did not fully understand the fetters that Azrael continued to reference, but he knew Dr. Green was an important person to him. It would be good to say his final farewells to the man. "No, you're right. Thank you. I'm ready."

The two angels touched the name, and they were standing in Dr. Green's hospital room. He was not alone. Also in the room was a woman two decades younger than him and two adults who appeared to be her children. It was a place of peace and love as everyone said their goodbyes to the older man before taking him away for surgery.

Only Riley and Azrael followed him for two hours until his final death. Riley spoke first, "Dr. Green, Billy, come, let's step out of the room and leave the doctors to their business."

He hesitated at first but did not cast a look back at his body before following the two angels. "Do you want to see your family first," Riley asked. It was a delicate moment, and Riley did what he could to avoid shocking the man with his death. This was his first peaceful transition, and he wanted it to go well.

After considering the options, Billy shook his head, "No. We said our goodbyes." He then seemed to recognize Riley for the first time. "You used to work for me, didn't you?"

"Yes, sir. You were kind enough to give me a chance when no one else would. Thank you." As Riley said these simple words, a weight lifted from his shoulders, and he better understood why he was here. The need to finish business from before his death was vital if he were to complete his work as an angel.

Riley then guided Billy to the bridge, and the doctor left for Elysium. A tear stained Riley's cheek when he returned to Azrael. "It's easier to do when things are hectic. Without something to fight, there is too much room for sadness."

This was not something Azrael had considered before, but he nodded his agreement. "Yes, I suppose that's true. Then I'm thankful we do not often have to help those who transition peacefully. The Strix guide most of those souls. They must be built of stronger stuff than us. That or they have no love for the lives of people. I'm tending to guess it is the second."

"OK, let's get out of here. The longer I spend time in hospitals, the more I dislike them. They are not the places of healing I once thought. There is always a layer of sadness and suffering that everyone is trying to disguise."

Azrael nodded his agreement, "This is true, and likely why there are so many flowers."

Sheriff Wallace packed up his car and surveyed the carnival. How did everything get turned upside down so quickly? This was going to be another of those cases where they had more questions than answers. Thankfully, he only reported to the citizens of the county, and he could handle them through the media. Rarely did anyone want the truth. They only wanted a convenient answer that tied up loose ends and let them sleep at night.

Knowing the truth kept Wallace awake at night with a handgun and the lights on. One witness said they saw what looked like a large skinned wolf. No one paid any attention to that woman's statement. They brushed her to the side and treated her for shock. Wallace did his best not to show too much interest in her description as he took notes of the creature. He liked to be the one taking notes at large scenes. That way he could write what he felt was important rather than leave off details his deputies dismissed as crazy talk. This was the second sighting of the same monster in the county this month.

"Dispatch, this is Wallace. Show me ten forty-two," he said and released the button on his car's radio while tossing a notepad into the passenger seat.

"Ten-four. Try to get some sleep, Sheriff. We'll handle the day shift."

Wallace reached in and dropped the radio onto its hook, but when he stood back up, there was a new figure standing beside the car. The old sheriff did not so much as flinch at the apparition of the figure but took a step back to gain distance from him. "Wondered if you'd find your way back. All this your handiwork?"

Riley shook his head. "No, but it was my fault."

"Come on, get in the car. I'm headed to the house. You can bleed your heart over my front seat while we drive."

The two of them climbed into the late-model town car and together left the scene behind. "So, what's your sob story? And don't start with when you died, because I don't care. I just want to know about tonight. What happened to those kids?"

The tone forced Riley to close his mouth and reconsider his approach. It took him a minute, but then he started. "The creatures who caused the accident did it to get back at me. I did something wrong, and they were punishing me for it by hurting them."

When no interruptions came from the sheriff, Riley continued. "We could save most of the souls, but not all of them. I'm also pretty sure the treaty is back in effect, so they won't do anything like that again." He paused while trying to decide where to go from there and said, "I'm sorry."

"Really? You're sorry? That's all you've got? You screwed up and eight people died, not to mention how many went to the hospital and you're sorry. Well, so long as you're sorry, I guess that's all right then."

Riley had nothing to respond with. He had expected the encounter to be confrontational. So, he had to ask himself why he decided to speak with Wallace in the first place, other than his own need for confession. "I realize there is no way to really punish me for what happened, but I felt you deserved an answer."

Wallace snorted and pushed in the cigarette lighter while pulling out a pack of gum. "How many times have I heard that one? Look, I'm not your priest and these kinds of answers I can't use. Yea, they may be true, but they do me no good. How about you answer me a couple of questions?"

"Sure, anything. How can I help?"

"Other than by not getting a parade field of people killed?" He let that one sink in before he continued. "Are those dogs going to kill more people? Are they something I need to worry about? Can you do anything about them?"

It was more than one question, but Riley took them in stride. "I don't believe they will kill anyone again. That was uncharacteristic for them. Normally, they only go after those who are already dead."

"Good enough. You got anything else?"

Riley shifted uncomfortably in his seat and tried to decide how to word the next part. "There will be one more death, but it won't be from the Ahemait. I'm not asking permission. I just wanted to let you know."

"How gracious of you. So what do you want to tell me for? Actually, you know what? Here, do me a favor. Whoever it is, make sure when they die it makes sense. I don't need some phantom train hitting someone while swimming."

His request was straightforward, and Riley considered the implications of what would be required. "I'll see what I can do."

HIS NAME WAS ALBERTO BRISENO, though everyone knew him as Bob, and he made a stack of money collecting Clay's old debts. Only a few were left that needed to be called upon before he could comfortably disappear out west. But it was the offer of an older entry under the turncoat, Riley, that had him standing at the back door to Pancake House.

Bob rechecked the time. Whoever this person claimed to be, he was late, and Bob was only giving him another ten minutes before cutting out. For all he knew, this was another setup by the police. The entire situation continued to set off alarms the more he tried to put the pieces of it together. Riley's only friend was Glen, from what he knew, and he shot that little snot weeks ago.

The only sounds in the alley were from the Pancake House. People's voices blended together with cooks yelling orders and vehicles on the nearby highway. But that's not what caught Bob's attention; somewhere in the distance, a train screeched across rusted tracks.

What he could not see or hear were the two figures that watched him from the shadows of the penumbra. The first was an unassuming man in a grey hoodie. The hood remained pulled over his head but left room for a pair of eyes to stare out at the lone mortal. Besides the hooded man was a thin, feminine figure with her eyes bound in cloth. She asked, "And you will hold to our accord? Once the die is cast, there is no turning back the wheel."

Riley understood the risks, but this was worth it. "Agreed. No one should be allowed to exist who has caused as much suffering as that man." He said the words with venom and left his eyes locked on the target of his hatred.

Once they struck the deal, the Angel of Fate disappeared, and a policeman staggered out the back door. He appeared drunk though still wearing his uniform, complete with a belt and gun. How he came to be drunk at a restaurant that didn't serve alcohol was anyone's guess. The movement combined with Bob's irritation at the late hour, and he yelled at the figure, "About time you showed up, you turd knocker!"

If sober, the officer might have let the insult slide, but the words hurt his ego, and it didn't help that he recognized Bob from photos at the station. Alberto was wanted for a laundry list of offenses, and this drunk cop would be the one to take him in. He pulled his gun and aimed it generally towards the double outline of Bob.

Bob made a series of mistakes, which someone could sum up as seeing the gun before seeing the uniform. He then drew his pistol to defend himself before knowing the threat. When Bob realized his error, he tossed his weapon, and the fast motion caused the drunk officer to open fire.

Bob took three rounds to the chest and fell to the pavement as Riley watched with a sense of satisfaction. The sight of the man who caused his death by the police brought closure to his existence. But he was not finished. Riley did not move the body and soul as they lay on the pavement.

Time ticked by, and he continued to watch. Five minutes passed until a wave of heat announced the arrival of an Ahemait. The demon hound stepped into the alley and cast a furtive glance towards Riley, ready for the Angel of Death to strike.

No one moved. Riley stood still and watched as the Ahemait hesitated. Death's sworn duty was to defend souls from creatures such as this hound. Why would he not drive the demon away? Neither specter moved. The Ahemait took one step and then another, moving inches closer to the wayward soul. Riley did not move.

The demon lunged and grasped Bob by the leg, then dragged him away into the night. A wave of heat enveloped the two of them, and Riley was left alone with a drunk officer and a body. With the destruction of another fetter, Riley felt the weight of his former life lift from his shoulders.

Riley no longer stood in the alley between the seconds on a clock. Azrael put a comforting arm about the young angel. "I won't agree with what you did, but I understand why you did it. Now come, there is something we need to discuss before the next sunrise."

# ALSO BY MATTHEW SLEADD

## Ares Weapons Project

Atlanta: Zombie Queen

Zombies' Origin

## The Pantheon

Death Replaced

# ABOUT THE AUTHOR

 Mathew Sleadd's background is in criminal justice—and after years of service in the U.S. Army—he's hanging up his uniform to focus on his writing. Like millions of people around the globe—he battles daily mental health. Writing is a therapeutic way to creatively transfer his internal struggles onto paper. While none of his stories or events are based on real people—there are often elements of hidden truth in his writing.

When he's not writing, Mathew enjoys competitive shooting sports and fine cigars...but deep down he's a family man who loves everything Disney.

🏳️ Ally (he/him)